The Things
We Keep

Sally Hepworth has lived and travelled around the world, spending extended periods in Singapore, the UK and Canada. While on maternity leave, Sally finally fulfilled a lifelong dream to write. While pregnant with her second child, Sally wrote *The Secrets of Midwives*. *The Things We Keep* is her second novel. Sally lives in Melbourne, Australia, with her husband and two children.

Also by Sally Hepworth

The Secrets of Midwives

The Things We Keep

Sally Hepworth

PAN BOOKS

First published 2016 by St Martin's Press, New York

This edition published 2016 by Pan Books
an imprint of Pan Macmillan
20 New Wharf Road, London N1 9RR
Associated companies throughout the world
www.panmacmillan.com

ISBN 978-1-4472-8072-9

1 3 5 7 9 8 6 4 2

A CIP catalogue record for this book is available from the British Library.

Typeset in Electra LT Std by Palimpsest Book Production Ltd, Falkirk, Stirlingshire
Printed and bound by CPI Group (UK) Ltd, Croydon, CR0 4YY

Visit www.panmacmillan.com to read more about all our books
and to buy them. You will also find features, author interviews and
news of any author events, and you can sign up for e-newsletters
so that you're always first to hear about our new releases.

*For everyone touched by dementia,
especially for Pat Hanrahan,
who will never be forgotten*

Acknowledgments

As always, thank you to my editor, Jennifer Enderlin, for knowing how to take my words and ideas and shape them into something resembling a book. Thank you also to the talented and hardworking team at St Martin's Press who, I suspect, love books even more than I do (and that is saying something). To my publishers around the world, particularly Haylee Nash and Alex Lloyd at Pan Macmillan Australia, thank you for all that you do. As an aspiring author I used to dream about having a team of people who believed in my book, and now it's fair to say I have the 'dream team'.

To my agent and friend Rob Weisbach, thank you for tirelessly advocating for me and, more important, for showing me where to spot celebrities in LA. (Next time I'm not leaving until I meet Kevin Spacey.)

To those who helped with my research, especially Clare Dyer, for giving so generously of your time and resources – this book is so much richer for it. In particular, thank you for showing me the difference a good nurse can make, and how 'stepping into their reality' can mean the difference between joy and terror for a person with dementia. You must have brought a lot of joy to patients and their families over your career.

To Belinda Nixon at Alzheimer's Australia Vic, thank you for meeting with me on several occasions, and for reading this manuscript in its early form and providing feedback.

To the Hanrahan family, particularly Therese, for sharing your Alzheimer's experiences and always answering my questions. The way you keep your grace and humor through the seemingly endless challenges of life is truly extraordinary. I suspect you get this from your mother.

To Rosie Brennan, for sharing the true story that would become the heart and soul of this book – the story of 'Rodney' and 'Betty', the residents who held hands in the TV room of their nursing home every single day, not because they remembered to, but because they wanted to. Thank you also to Rosie for being my right (and left) hand when it comes to social media. If it weren't for you I'd still think LOL stood for 'Lots of Love'.

To my critique partners, Anna George and Meredith Jaeger, and my beta reader, Jacquelyn Sylvan – thank you for being the brilliant writers and astute readers that you are. Every piece of feedback is a gift, honestly. Also to my first readers, Geraldine Carrodus, Angela Langford, Dagmar Logan, Inna Spitskaia, and Jane Wharton, thank you for your insane positivity (something every insecure author needs).

To my friends Emily Makiv and Kena Roach, who

proofread for me in exchange for an early look at my books – the job is yours for life, if you want it.

To my great aunty Gwen, who wanted a mention in one of my books. Here it is. Go tell your friends.

To Mum, for making me love words, and Dad, who always taught me to never let the truth get in the way of a good story.

To Oscar and Eloise – I adored creating the character of Clementine, but no one could be weirder or more wonderful than the two of you.

Finally, to Christian for being my fiercest champion, and for being man enough to admit that this book made him cry.

The Things
We Keep

1
Anna

Fifteen months ago . . .

No one trusts anything I say. If I point out, for example, that the toast is burning or that it's time for the six o'clock news, people marvel. How about that? It *is* time for the six o'clock news. Well done, Anna. Maybe if I were eighty-eight instead of thirty-eight, I wouldn't care. Then again, maybe I would. As a new resident of Rosalind House, an assisted-living facility for senior citizens, I'm having a new appreciation for the hardships of the elderly.

'Anna, this is Bert,' someone says as a man slopes by on his walker. I've been introduced to half a dozen people who look more or less like Bert: old, ashen, hunched-over. We're on wicker lawn chairs in the streaming sunshine, and I know Jack brought me out here to make us both feel better. *Yes, you're checking into an old folks' home, but look, it has a garden!*

I wave to Bert, but my gaze is fixed across the lawn, where my five-year-old nephew, Ethan, is having coins pulled out of his ears by a man in a navy and red striped dressing gown. My mood lifts. Ethan always jokes that he's my favorite nephew, and even though I deny it in public, it's true. He's the youngest of Jack's boys, and definitely the best one.

Once, when he was four, I took him for a spin on my motorcycle. I didn't even bother asking Brayden or Hank; I knew they'd just say it was dangerous and then tattle to their mother. As far as I know, Ethan never tattled. Brayden and Hank know what's wrong with me – I can tell from the way they constantly glance at their mother when they talk to me. But Ethan either doesn't know or doesn't care. I really don't mind which one.

'And this is Clara.'

Clara wanders toward us with remarkable speed (compared to the others). She's probably in her eighties – but portly, more robust-looking than the rest. With a cloud of fluffy yellow-gray hair, she reminds me of a newborn chick.

'I've been looking forward to meetin' you,' she says, then gives me a whiskery kiss. A burst of fragrance fills my airspace. Normally I don't like to be kissed, yet from her, the gesture feels oddly natural. And these days, I make a point of respecting people who are natural around me. 'If you need anything at all, you let me know, honey,' she says, then wanders off toward a huge oak tree. When she gets there, she kisses the man in the navy and red striped dressing gown full on the mouth in a way that feels vaguely territorial, like she's staking her claim.

Beside me, Jack is talking to Eric, the center's manager – a paunchy, red-faced man with a thick Tom Selleck mustache and a titter of a laugh that, by rights, should belong to a female in her eighties. Every time I hear it (which is a lot, he seems to chortle at the end of every sentence), I jerk around, looking for a ladies' auxiliary group giggling over its knitting. He and Jack talk, and I listen without really hearing. 'We do a lot of activities . . . we'll keep her active . . . twenty-four-hour care and security . . . experience with dementia . . . the best possible place for her . . .'

Blah, blah, blah. Eric has a certain desperate-to-please manner about him that, a few years ago, Jack and I would have exchanged a look over, but today Jack is eating it up. He's happily oblivious to Eric's false laugh, his too-tight chinos, his gaze that wanders to the right (and vaguely near my chest), every few moments. Eric's only redeeming quality so far is that when we arrived, he asked my advice on an old knee injury that had been giving him some trouble (probably because he hoped I'd offer to give it a rub). He needed a doctor, not a paramedic, and I explained this, but I appreciated him asking. These days, the most interesting conversations I have are about my favorite color or type of food. I like it when people remember that I'm a *person*, not just a person with Alzheimer's.

Jack seems to have forgotten that. Ever since I went to live with him and Helen, he's stopped being my brother and started being my dad, which is beyond annoying. He thinks I don't hear when he and Helen whisper about me in the kitchen. That I don't notice them exchanging a look whenever I offer to walk the boys to school. That I don't see Helen trailing after me in the car, making sure I don't become disoriented on the way there.

Jack's been through this before – we both have – and I know he considers himself an expert. I have to keep reminding him that he's an attorney, not a neurologist. Anyway, the situations are different. Mom was in denial about her disease. She fought to hang on to her independence right up to the point when she burned down the family home. But I have no plans to fight the inevitable. It's why I've checked myself into residential care.

The upside of this place, if I'm choosing to be positive, is that not everyone is nuts. Jack and I looked at a few of those dementia-specific units, and they were like Zombie City, full of crazies and folks doing the seven-mile stare. This place, at least, is also for the general aging community – the ones who need their meals cooked and laundry done – kind of a hotel for the elderly (the wealthy elderly, judging by the zeros on the check Jack wrote this morning).

Still, I'm not exactly thrilled to be here. It was bad enough when Jack sent me to 'day care'. Seriously, that's what it's called. A day program for people *like me*. Also for people *not* like me, because with only 5 percent of Alzheimer's cases occurring in people under the age of sixty-five, there aren't a lot of people *like me*. That's what makes this situation all the more unusual. I'm not checking into just *any* residential care facility – no sirree. We've traveled all the way to Short Hills, New Jersey, from Philadelphia so I can live in a facility with someone *like me*. A guy, also with younger-onset dementia, someone Jack heard about through the Dementia Support Network. Since learning about the guy, Jack has been hell-bent on getting me into the very same care facility as him. It's like he thinks having two young people in a place filled with oldies makes it spring break instead of residential care.

'Would you like to meet Luke, Anna?' Eric asks, and Jack nods enthusiastically. Luke must be *the guy*. I wonder if he's going to rappel down from a tree or something. His entrance will have to be pretty impressive if they think it's going to make a difference to my mood.

'I just want to go to my room,' I say.

Jack and Eric glance at each other, and I feel the wind leave their sails.

'Sure,' Jack says. 'Do you want me to take you there?'

'Nope. I'm good.' I stand. I don't want to look at Jack, but he stands, too, gets right in my face so I can't look anywhere else. His eyes are full and wet, and I catch a glimpse of the soft-hearted man he used to be before his brushes with dementia and abandonment hardened him up.

'Anna,' he says, 'I know you're scared.'

'Scared?' I snort, but then my vision starts to blur. I *am* scared. One thing about being a twin is that you get used to having someone right by your side whenever you want them. But in a moment, Jack's going to leave. And I'm going to be alone.

'Get lost, would you?' I tell Jack finally. 'I have a pedicure booked in half an hour. This place has a health spa, right?'

Jack laughs a little, shooing a drop from his cheek. When we were younger Jack sported a golden tan, but now his skin is vaguely gray, almost as white as my own. I suspect this has something to do with me. 'Ethan! Come and say good-bye to Anna.'

Ethan thunders across the lawn to us and tosses himself into my arms. He strangles me in a hug. 'Bye, Anna Banana.'

When he pulls away, I take a long hard look at the large white bandage covering his left cheek and try to remember the angry red burns and welts underneath. I *need* to remember them. They're the reason I'm here.

The first time I knew something was wrong with me, I was at the mall. I was lugging my bags toward the exit when I realized I had no idea where I'd parked my car. The parking lot was seven stories high. In the elevator, I stared at the buttons. None seemed any more likely than the other.

Eventually I made my way to the security booth. The man behind the desk laughed and said it happened all the time. He picked up his walkie-talkie and asked for the license plate number. When I looked blank, he smiled. 'Make and model?'

It was such an easy question. But the more I tried to find the answer, the more it blacked out. Like a photograph with a question mark over the face, a criminal with his jacket over his head – something was there, but my brain wouldn't let me see.

The man's smile faded. 'The color?'

All I could do was shrug. I waited for him to say *this* happened all the time. He didn't.

I caught the bus home.

If I'd been tested for the mutated gene, as Jack was, I'd have known for sure it was coming. But finding out you're going to be struck down in your prime didn't fit into my life's plan.

After that, things started happening all the time. Usually, I could explain the incidents away. Sure, I forgot a lot of appointments, but I *was* a busy paramedic. Getting lost on the way home from work was a little stressful, but directions had never been my strong suit. Unfortunately, there were things that were harder to explain. Like the time I smashed my car window with a ski pole when I couldn't get the keys to open the door (and then found out the car belonged to the family across the road). And the time I showed up to work on my rostered day off (for the fourth time in a row).

It was the time I forgot the word 'twin' when introducing Jack to my buddy Tyrone, from work, that I really started to worry. It was a year after the parking lot incident. I remember staring at Jack, wondering if there was indeed a word for what we were. I searched the dark, dusty corners of my brain, but it was useless. Eventually I called him a person who my mother carried in her uterus at the same time as me. I know, I remember 'uterus' but not 'twin'. Tyrone laughed; he'd always thought I was nutty. But Jack didn't laugh. And I knew the jig was up.

I quit my job that day. If I couldn't remember the word 'twin', what would happen when I couldn't remember how to resuscitate someone or when I decided it was a good idea to move a patient with a possible neck injury? I had a feeling I'd already been off my game. And when I know something's going to happen, I don't see the point in dragging it out.

The same theory applies to life. Life's going slowly in one direction. I can stay in the slow lane, just keep rollin' on down that hill, gathering moss and cobwebs until finally, when I come to a stop, I'm so covered in crap, I'm unrecognizable. That's what Mom did. That's what most people do. But that's never been my style.

At Rosalind House, there are a lot of drugs. Enough that everyone has their own basket. Every morning and afternoon, the nurse rolls her table-on-wheels through the halls with the baskets, a veritable candy woman of pharmaceuticals. In my basket is Aricept, a round peach-colored tablet responsible for slowing the breakdown of a compound that transmits messages between the nerve cells. Also in the basket is vitamin E, clear and yellow, long and thin. Lastly there is Celexa, a powerful antidepressant responsible for making all of this feel like no big deal. That's the one I know *for sure* isn't working.

I don't get dressed until my second week at Rosalind House. When I do, I wonder why I bothered. All I do here is lie in bed, scribble in my journal, and stare out the window. Any visitors I might have had (Jack notwithstanding) have been told, at my request, that I'm at a facility on the other side of the country (Hey, I'm not likely to remember them anyway, and I need a 'pity visit' like I need a hole in the head). Eric, the manager guy, stops by continually, trying to cajole me into bingo. (Yeah. Like that's gonna happen.) Various nurses and staff have popped in.

But I've been out of my room only once, and when I did leave it, I got so twisted around that I couldn't find my way back. As far as blips went, this one wasn't so bad. At least I knew I was at Rosalind House. I knew I *had* a room. But the only thing my little trip out of my room taught me is that I'm in the right place. Residential care.

Today, outside my window, a handsome gardener prunes the boxwood. It's warm out, and he's stripped to a thin white T-shirt, which allows me to enjoy his ripped physique. A few years ago, I'd have leaned out and asked for a sprig of something, or even asked if he needed any help. (When I was a kid, Jack and I used to spend a lot of time in the garden with Mom, planting and weeding and mulching.) But now I can't even be bothered to return the gardener's smile. I'm too busy thinking about Ethan. About *the incident*.

It happened at night. I get restless at night, one of many joyous side effects of 'the disease'. I was in the living room, trying to figure out how to use the Xbox, when I heard his little footsteps behind me.

'Let's make fongoo.'

'Fongoo' was a loose derivative of fondue, and it was our word for melting candy bars on the stove and then dipping cookies, marshmallows, or whatever else we had handy into the melted goo. I said yes for several reasons: One, I love fongoo. Two, I'm not his mother – it is not my job to worry about his teeth or his lack of sleep. Three, my life is hurtling toward a point where I'm not going to know myself anymore, and while I do know myself, I sure as hell want to be making fongoo with my nephew.

We'd finished the fongoo and were playing Xbox when we smelled the burning. Ethan and I locked eyes.

'Shi–oot!' I said. 'The fongoo.'

I bolted for the kitchen, cursing. Burning the house down would do nothing to assure Jack I was a competent adult. I threw the door open, ready to reach for the fire extinguisher, but instead of finding it, I found the bathroom. I turned, opened another door. A cupboard filled with towels. I spun again. Where, in God's name, was the kitchen?

It wasn't the first time this had happened. I knew all I had to do was stay calm and wait for a few moments, and everything would come back to me. But the burning smell was getting stronger, and I couldn't see Ethan anywhere. And I couldn't even find my way out of the fucking *bathroom*!

That was when I heard Ethan scream.

According to Jack, after I ran in the opposite direction, Ethan tore into the kitchen and tried to take the saucepan off the stove. The handle was red-hot. He'd whipped his hand off so fast, he toppled the saucepan, splattering the burning chocolate onto his cheek. The worst part, except for hurting Ethan, was that it confirmed they were right about me. I can't be trusted with my nephew. I can't be left alone, even for a second.

'Knock knock.'

I roll my head toward the door, which is eternally open, thanks to the skinny helper lady, who has an unnatural obsession with fresh air. Every time I try to close it, she appears like a magical air fairy – *fresh air, fresh air, fresh air!* But this time when I look, Eric is there with a huge lion of a dog by his side. I feel my insides pull together to form an internal shield.

'Hey,' he says. 'How are you doing?'

'Fine.' I address the dog since I can't seem to look anywhere else.

'Everyone being nice to you?'

'Yep.'

It's a German Shepherd. Its teeth are yellow and shiny with saliva; its mouth is curved into that smile-snarl that dogs always wear to keep you on guard. *Am I happy? Am I angry? Come a little closer and find out.*

'Oh,' Eric says. 'Are you afraid of dogs?'

I try to put on a brave face, but I obviously fail, because Eric sends the dog out. On his way into my room he pauses at a watercolor of a leaf that Jack must have hung on my wall. It belonged to my mother.

'This is lovely,' he says.

'Keep it,' I say.

He frowns at me. 'You know you don't have to just sit in your room all day. There's a bus that goes into town twice a day. Some folks like to go to a shopping center or to a movie.'

I sit up. 'I'm allowed to do that?'

'Sure. Trish, one of our staff, is escorting the bus group today.'

I sink back into my bed.

'Or there are board games in the parlor,' he says. 'We try and encourage residents to congregate in there when

11

they're home. We find that people feel isolated when they spend all their time cooped up in their rooms.'

'I'm okay with being isolated.'

Eric perches on the edge of my bed, a frown bobbing on his forehead. My heart sinks. It must be time for the pep talk. I actually feel bad for Eric. He doesn't want to give it any more than I want to hear it. Deep down he probably knows that if he were a resident here, he'd stay in his room, too. But that's not the dish they're feeding us.

'Fine,' I say, cutting him off before he can start. (Mostly because I want him to get off my bed.) 'The parlor? That's the place to be? I'll go there today. Promise.'

Eric sighs. 'You don't have to go to the parlor. That wasn't my point. My point is that I want you to be happy here.'

'I know.' Everyone wants me to be happy here. If I'm happy, they don't have to feel guilty.

Eric rests his hand dangerously close to my thigh. 'Give us a chance, Anna. I won't pretend I know what it's like to be you. But I do know that your brother didn't put you in here to wither away and die in your room. There's still a lot of life to be lived, but you need to stay in the game.' He winks. 'Jack told me you were an adrenaline junkie. I have to admit, I was pretty excited when I heard that. The most adrenaline we get around here is on bingo night.'

He grins and I think I might actually vomit. 'You're right,' I say. 'You have no idea what it's like to be me.'

They say when you lose some of your senses, others get heightened. I think it's true. There was a time when I had

12

a razor tongue. If there was a joke at the offering, I was the first to snap it up (and then deliver it with more pizazz than anyone else). Now I'm not as quick as I used to be, but I'm more observant, especially when it comes to people's state of mind. So when a young woman with spiky blond hair bursts through my door, I know at a glance that she's not only lost, but that there's something on her mind.

'Oh, um,' she says. 'Which way is the visitors' bathroom?'

Obviously, I have no idea. When I was diagnosed, my neuropsychologist (Dr Brain, I called him) explained that memories tended to evaporate in reverse order. This meant my oldest memories would be the ones to hang around the longest, and new information, visitor's bathrooms included, were quick to disappear into the black hole of no return in my brain.

'I'm sorry, I don't know,' I tell the woman. Her face, I notice, is crumpled and red. Wet. 'Are you okay?'

She sighs, and I half expect her to turn and leave – continue on her search for the visitors' bathroom. But she stays.

'Yeah.' She sniffs. 'I mean no. It's my grandpa. He's . . . impossible.'

'Who's your grandpa?'

'Bert. Bert Dickens.'

'Oh,' I say, though I have no recollection of meeting Bert. 'Is he . . . okay?'

'He's fine, physically. Mentally, not so much. Sorry, I shouldn't have just barged in like this. Are you—?'

'I'm not busy.' It's the understatement of the century. 'What's going on with Bert?'

'Are you sure you want to hear this?'

'Sure I'm sure.'

'Okay.' She comes farther into the room. 'The thing is –' She extends a hand and wiggles her fingers. '– I'm getting married.'

I eyeball the diamond and smile like I'm supposed to, even though I've never seen what all the fuss was about when it came to those sparkly rocks. 'Congratulations.'

'Thanks.'

I glance at my own ring finger, naked for almost a year. The knuckle seems to protrude higher now, without its anchor weighing it down. 'Does Bert not like the guy?'

'No. I mean, yes. He likes him. But he doesn't want us to get married.'

'Why not?'

'He thinks our family is cursed. Yeah, and he's not senile either. He's always thought that. His wife, my grandma, died when my mom was a baby. And Mom died when I was four. He thinks if I get married, then the curse will continue.'

'I'm sorry about your mom.'

'Thanks.'

'Why does he think it's marriage causing the curse? Why not the baby?'

She gives me a strange look. This, I realize, is probably not helpful.

'Hey, I'm just pointing out that his theory isn't water-tight. Maybe you could convince him the baby part causes the curse?'

'But what happens when I have a baby?'

14

'You want a baby, too?'

She nods. Somewhere deep in my soul, I think she's being a little greedy.

'Well, do you believe the curse?' I ask.

'No. I mean, my family has had bad luck, but . . . No. I don't believe it. But I want Grandpa to come to the wedding, and he says he won't. He says he can't bear to watch me seal my fate.'

'Tell him if you don't get married, your fate will be worse than death.'

She watches me through narrowed eyes.

'Tell him if you go to your grave with him as your husband, you'll go a happy woman. Tell him that even if he's right, you'd rather have a year of true happiness than die without knowing what happiness is.' I think for a moment. 'If he says you're wrong, ask him if he wishes he'd never married his wife.'

'Wow,' she says. 'You're good.'

There's an expression that says this exactly, and I try to conjure it up. Slowly, it starts to come. 'A life lived in . . .' I try to continue, but the rest slips away. *Poof*. Gone.

'A life lived in fear is a life half-lived?'

'Right. Exactly.'

'You're right. He adored Myrna. There's no way he wishes he hadn't married her. Besides, if I listen to his silly superstitions, I'm reinforcing the idea that this curse could actually be true.' She sighs. 'Thanks for being the voice of reason. I'd better get back.' She cocks her head toward the closed bathroom door. 'Do you think she's okay in there?'

'Who?'

'Your . . . grandmother?' She squints at the silver name-thingy on the wall. 'Anna, is it?'

I often have trouble understanding things, so I don't worry too much that this goes over my head. I'm about to nod as if I understand completely – when suddenly, it dawns. She thinks I'm visiting an old person named Anna.

'Oh . . . yes. She's fine.' I smile at the girl whose name I didn't catch, if she told me at all. 'She'll be out of here really, really soon.'

2

There's something in my soup, floating between a chunk of carrot and a green bean. It's not a hair or a fly. It's white. It's about two inches long and curved around itself like a spiral. I reach into my bowl and give it a squeeze. It compresses between my fingers, then springs back like a piece of rubber. Before I even put it in my mouth, I know what it will taste like: bland, chewy, but appealing. I like this food. Why can't I remember what it's called?

'Tastes like an old boot, right?'

When I look over, the old lady next to me is watching me. I'm grateful it's her speaking because the alternative, on my other side, is an old bald man who keeps referring to the empty seat beside him as 'Myrna'. At one point, he even asked someone to pass Myrna the salt. So much for no crazies at Rosalind House.

'I'm sorry?'

'The pasta,' she says. 'It tastes like an old boot.'

Pasta! I feel a thrill akin to finding a missing, well, boot.

'Actually, the pasta's all right,' I say. 'It's the rest of it that's the problem.'

17

'I s'pose you're right,' she says, examining the spiral on her own spoon. 'Beans and celery and watery soup – the pasta's the savin' grace, really.'

The woman has a Southern accent, which cheers me a little. After all, how could you not like someone with a Southern accent? Then again, there's the rednecks and Ku Klux Klan, but this woman doesn't look like she's affiliated with either. She's younger than the rest of the residents, who remind me of mottled pieces of driftwood ready to sink to the ocean floor. This woman, on the other hand, while probably eighty, seems able-bodied – verging on spry.

'I seem to have forgotten your name,' she says.

I nearly laugh. 'It's Anna.'

'I'm so forgetful these days, aren't I, sweet thing?' Southern Lady looks at the old man next to her with such adoration that I feel something move in my stone-cold heart. Then she looks back at me. 'I'm Clara. This here's Laurie,' she says, pointing to the man next to her with a spoon, 'my husband.'

I observe Clara's face, looking for clues as to whether she actually forgot my name or if it was just a clever way of introducing herself. If it's the latter, I like her even more.

'I'm glad you came out for lunch today,' she says. 'I've been lookin' forward to having another young person to talk to.'

There's something nice about a woman in her eighties referring to herself as a 'young person'. I don't see any reason to tell her that I came out here only because Jack is visiting this weekend, and I know he'll ask me if I've ventured out of my room. If I can say yes, we'll have a nice visit, a relaxed visit. Maybe we'll even share a few jokes? In an ideal world, we'd also share a beer or two, but the world, of course, is not ideal.

'Have you met our Luke?' Clara asks, tipping her head toward the young guy opposite her. Somehow, I'd completely missed him. All at once, I realize Clara wasn't talking about herself when she mentioned another young person. She was talking about the other person *like me.*

'I don't think so,' I say, 'which means it's entirely possible.'

With his head down, he chuckles. I'm pleased to note he's not so far gone that he can't appreciate a little dementia humor. I give him the once-over. He has golden skin, straight white teeth, a dimple. His wavy hair is near black and long enough to tuck behind his ears, and his blue shirtsleeves are pushed up over his strong forearms. *Well.*

Clara lowers her voice, but not nearly enough. 'Sexy, right?'

'So you're my counterpart?' I say, ignoring Clara. 'Young person, old mind.'

He laughs again. 'I g-guess you could s-say that.'

My counterpart has a stutter, but otherwise he seems remarkably normal. He lifts his gaze. His eyes are the shade of weak black tea. The way I have it.

'How are you s-settling in?' he asks, and I shrug. 'Takes some getting used to, this place,' he says. 'The g-group meals, the activities, the showers . . .'

I wince, remembering the showers. Perhaps stupidly, it never occurred to me that I'd be assisted with those. But the laminated white square on my bathroom wall had other ideas. There, in erasable pen, I could find my scheduled daily wash time, and the moment the clock ticked over to that time, a helper lady barged in, ready to strong-arm me into the shower.

'*It's policy,*' she'd say when I explained that I did not require a chaperone. '*I'm not interested in peeking. I'll just wait by the door in case you need me.*'

Now I always consulted the laminated square and made sure to finish my shower by the time she showed up. When she asked me about it, I blamed the dementia. '*Oh, I was meant to wait for you? Silly me.*'

'I hate the showers,' I tell him.

'It's t-tough, the first few weeks,' he says. 'I remember.'

His dimple bobs on his cheek, and I can't help but smile. I suppose he does remember. My eyes drift down to his hands, which are resting lightly on the table – large, masculine, yet somehow elegant.

Clara's right. 'Sexy' is the word for this guy.

The room has become conspicuously silent. Under the table, something is brushing against my leg. Something . . . *hairy.* I whoosh backwards.

'It's . . . just Kayla,' Luke says. 'Eric's d-dog. She's h-harmless.'

I nod, eyes on the dog.

'You don't like dogs?' he asks.

'For someone with Alzheimer's, you're fairly perceptive.'

'Actually, I have fr-frontotemporal dementia.'

20

There's another beat of silence, and I peel my eyes from the dog to look at him.

'You lose memories,' he says, answering my unspoken question. 'I lose speech.'

I look back at the dog. Its tongue unrolls from its mouth, the most unwelcome welcome mat I've ever seen.

Luke's hand curls around its collar. 'You really don't like d-dogs?' he asks. I can tell by the way his toes curl under the dog's belly that he is a dog lover. 'Not even . . . puppies?'

Now I'm definitely aware of his speech. It's not only slow but also slightly slurred. And more than that, he seems to require an above-average amount of effort to project words from his throat. The disjointedness seems out of place, coming from such a young, healthy-looking man.

'Not even puppy embryos,' I say.

He gives the dog a pat, then guides her to the glass sliding door and lets her out. She pads outside, tail wagging.

'Was there an i-i-i-ncident?' he asks when he gets back. 'With a dog. To cause your d-dislike.'

I nod, pointing to the faint pink stripe slicing my right eyebrow in half. 'When I was three.'

'Family dog?'

'A neighbor's. You're clearly a dog fan.'

'Definitely. I used to –' He pauses, and his forehead creases like he's thinking hard. '– give my time to the animal shelter a few years back. I was in charge of p-puppy adoption.'

21

'Oh yeah?' An image of him snuggling a puppy against his chest flashes into my mind.

'Last call for the afternoon bus!' A man in a white shirt and trousers with a large name badge that says TREV stands in the doorway. 'Anyone need assistance?'

Luke turns to me. 'Plans this afternoon?'

'Yeah.' I laugh. 'My social calendar is packed.'

'Well, you heard the man. Last c . . . c-all for the afternoon bus.'

'Oooh!' Clara jumps up. 'I'd better grab my purse. The afternoon bus waits for no one.'

Clara hurries off, and Luke leans forward in his chair. 'She's wrong, you know. The afternoon bus waits for everyone.'

I laugh. And I feel a tickle low in my belly.

'You need anything?' Luke asks me. He makes a gesture that looks like he's hanging something invisible over his shoulder. 'Your thingy that you put stuff in?'

'Oh . . .' I know exactly what he's talking about, but in that instant, I can't think of what it is called either. 'Actually, I don't think I'll make it today.'

In high school, we always had a week of class after our exams were over. There was nothing left in the curriculum, because we'd completed – and been tested on – it all, but the idea was to give us a chance to 'finish off the school year *right*.' Whatever that meant. Most of the teachers played games with us. Some let us talk and hang out. One teacher, Mr Kaiser, continued with lessons as usual. The whole thing was beyond pointless, yet year after year, that's what we did. Heading to the mall with Luke now, ready to engage in getting-to-know-you conversation, feels just as pointless.

'So-socks to sort?'

'Yeah. Something like that.'

He nods and drops his head again. 'Looks like it's just us, Clara,' he says when she returns.

'Well, that's a right shame,' she says, looking at me. 'Are you sure we can't convince you to come, honey?'

There's a beat of silence as they wait, long enough to make me second-guess myself. Maybe I should be doing these things? One last trip to the mall? A last first conversation with a sexy man? But I shake off the doubts. I have enough to worry about without creating a heap of new 'lasts'.

'I'm sure,' I say. 'You two have fun.'

But as they drift away, I realize that if I was trying to avoid creating a new last, I'd failed. The whole exchange was, in fact, a 'last': It was the last time I'd say no to something I really wanted to do.

Dr Brain once told me that an Alzheimer's brain was like the snow on a mountain peak – slowly melting. There are days when the sun is bright and chunks drop off all over the place, and there are days when the sun stays tucked behind clouds and everything remains largely intact. Then there are days – spectacular days (his words) – when you stumble across a trail you thought had melted, and for a short while you have something back that you thought was gone forever.

I get the feeling that since the analogy involved the

words 'mountain peak' and 'spectacular', Dr Brain thought this news wouldn't be depressing to hear, when in fact, the opposite was true. I think I'd have felt better about my prognosis if he'd reworded a little. Something like, *The brain is like a filthy, stinking pile of crap. When the sun comes out, it stinks worse than you can imagine, and when it's cold or cloudy, you can barely smell it at all. Then there are the days that, if the wind is coming from a certain way, you might catch the cold scent of a spruce for a few hours and forget the crap is even there.* With that analogy, at least we'd have been calling a spade a spade. Because the truth is, if you have dementia, your brain *is* crap. And even if you can't smell it right this minute, it still stinks.

A little while after Luke and Clara leave, I'm still in my seat, but it feels lonelier. Everyone has left the eating-room, except me and the old bald man. And, I suppose, Myrna.

I'm about to head back to my room when the old bald man slams his spoon into his bowl. A shower of soup rains over his face. '*Hey!*' he cries. 'Who told you to take Myrna's lunch away?' He's staring at the cook-lady – a pretty Latina with dark hair and large hooped earrings. I've heard the other residents call her Gabriela.

She sighs. 'I'm sorry, Bert,' she says. 'I thought she was finished.'

'Well, she isn't. So you'd better march on into the kitchen and bring it back.'

'I've already dumped it out, and there isn't any left.' She doesn't say it unkindly, more wearily. 'How about I grab her a banana from the fruit bowl?'

Weird as it is, I kind of respect the fact that she's playing along about Myrna. But Bert doesn't seem charmed. 'Myrna don't like bananas.'

'A sandwich, then.'

'She don't like sandwiches.'

Gabriela puts a hand on her hip. Her eyes narrow. 'Well, what's she like, then?'

Bert raises his chin; a challenge. 'Soup.'

At this, I can't help but smile.

'Well, you've still got a bit of soup left,' she says, throwing a dish towel over her shoulder. 'You and Myrna will have to share.'

Bert mutters under his breath, and I feel a little sorry for him. He's a grumpy old thing, that's for sure, but I like his gumption. Standing up for his hungry (albeit fictional) woman like that? That's gallant, in my book.

'Don't you worry, love,' he says, pushing his own bowl toward the empty setting. 'You have mine. There's a good girl.'

Now Bert's face is transformed. His eyes are soft and admiring. His lips curve into a helpless smile. At first I think he's smiling at me, but the truth takes only a second to dawn. He's smiling at Myrna. On one level, I find this unimaginably sad. On another, it's the most romantic thing I've ever seen.

'Listen,' I say on impulse. 'I've barely touched my soup, and I'm not hungry. Perhaps Myrna would like to . . . finish it?'

I brace myself, aware that Bert might be insulted by the offer of leftovers for Myrna. He frowns at me, but after a quick assessment, gives a gruff nod. 'She'd like that very much. Thank you, young lady.'

I give Bert back his bowl and place mine in front of 'Myrna'. I start to leave, then hesitate by Bert's chair. 'Myrna's a lucky lady, you know that? I'd sure like to have someone to look out for me when I . . . I can't do things for myself.'

Bert continues to frown at me, but it's a little different now. Less irritated. More thoughtful. 'You never know, young lady,' he says. 'Maybe you will.'

3

Eve

Present day . . .

The man standing before me isn't what I expect. For starters, he's at least five years younger than me – thirty, tops – and he has a smudge of dirt on his left cheek. His eyes are deep-set, his skin is olive, and his hair is tawny. He's . . . gorgeous. But in green shorts, a thin white T-shirt, and sturdy boots, he's too disheveled to be the manager. I glance again at the small gold-plated sign next to the doorbell: ROSALIND HOUSE. GIVING THEM PEACE, GIVING YOU PEACE OF MIND. I'm definitely in the right place.

'I'm Eve Bennett,' I say. I have a brief flash of myself standing onstage, accepting the award for most promising graduate at the Institute of Culinary Education in New York, and another flash of Mother's face when I told her I was applying for a job at a residential care facility for the elderly. 'I have an interview at two o'clock. For the cook position.'

I wait for a greeting, a handshake, an *Oh yes. Please*

come in. But the man just stares. I see a glint of recognition in his eyes and my heart sinks.

My last job interview had been a tough one, too, but at least I'd got a hello. It was ten years ago, at Benu, the hot NYC Asian fusion restaurant (back when Asian fusion was the next big thing). Simply landing an interview for an apprenticeship at Benu was nothing short of a miracle. Word among my friends at the culinary school was that Min-Jun, the head chef, hired only blood relatives to work in his kitchen, for fear others would steal his famous brown sauce recipe. I met with Min-Jun in the kitchen, and rather than shaking my hand, he'd supplied me with a knife and a bag of carrots to julienne. In the hour I spent there, he barely said a word to me. Later, when he offered me the job (which I declined, stupidly), he told me it was the way I looked at the carrot, like I was in love with it, that got me over the line.

The disheveled man still hasn't spoken. I wait for him to curse me or slam the door in my face but instead he shuffles back and lets me inside. I step into a bright foyer with a sweeping staircase. Low polished timber side tables sit alongside well-stuffed pastel furniture. Though I haven't been inside many residential care facilities, I suspect this is a very nice one. A three-story shuttered colonial with a huge, rambling garden. It reminds me a lot of . . . well, my house.

'Are you Eric?' I ask.

The man turns, gesturing for me to follow. 'No.'

'Oh,' I say, relieved. 'So . . . uh . . . you are?'

'The gardener.'

He disappears around a corner and I have to run to keep up. I catch him at the end of the corridor, where he is already knocking on the door.

'Eric?' he says through the door. His gaze touches mine briefly. 'Eve Bennett is here to see you.'

The door swings open. The man standing there has a thick mustache and, unlike the gardner, is smiling.

'Hello,' he says brightly. 'You must be Eve. I'm Eric.'

The gardener makes himself scarce and I take Eric's extended hand. 'Good to meet you.'

'Well, don't just stand there. Come on in.' He ushers me inside. 'Is that a British accent I detect?'

'East London,' I say. 'But I've been in the United States nearly fifteen years.'

'Well, I won't welcome you to the country, then.' He laughs, an oddly feminine giggle. 'Only to my office. Please, have a seat.'

Eric pours a couple of glasses of water, and once we are sitting comfortably, picks up my résumé. 'I have to say we haven't had many applicants with your cooking credentials,' he says. 'Our current cook is self-taught, and while the residents are quite fond of her, I think they're getting a little sick of rice and beans and enchiladas for dinner every night. Gabriela's pregnant, and her last day is Friday, so we need someone pretty desperately.'

'I'm available immediately,' I say.

'Good,' he says. 'Then why don't you tell me why you are applying for this job. With your training, I imagine you could get a job at an upscale restaurant or café!'

Eric laughs again, and I feel a bolt of encouragement. Clearly, unlike the gardener, he has no idea who I am.

'This is close to home,' I say. 'And my daughter is at elementary school, so the day shifts suit better than regular hospitality hours.'

'Fair enough.' Eric's gaze darts to the right, and then down to my résumé. 'And why do you think you'd be a good candidate?'

He looks up expectantly, and I take a sip of water, buying some time. I don't think it's the moment to mention that this is my last-ditch attempt to get an address in Clementine's school zone. That without this address, she'll be zoned to the far less idyllic Buttwell Road Elementary, known to the locals, of course, as Butt Road.

'Cooking is my passion,' I say finally. 'I know what needs to be cooked fresh and what can be prepared in advance. I grow my own vegetables and try to use what's seasonal both for taste as well as keeping costs down—'

'Some of our residents have special dietary requirements,' Eric interrupts. 'High blood pressure, that kind of thing, so we need to keep our meals healthy and balanced, not to mention soft for those with dentures.'

I keep my wince on the inside. 'I know all about cooking for high blood pressure. And I love the challenge of making simple food taste great.'

Eric smiles, threading his fingers together behind his head. The buttons on his shirt strain against his doughy belly. 'And I don't suppose you've done much in the way of cleaning?'

I pause. 'I . . . er . . . thought this was a cook position.'

'Oh, it is. But our cleaner has just left us in the lurch, and I am hoping whoever takes this job can fill the void until I find someone.'

I swallow. 'I see.'

'Have you had any experience with cleaning?'

'Of course,' I manage, even though until six months ago, Valentina, our live-in maid, took care of all the housework at our place. Since Valentina left, I'd taken over, but the standard of cleanliness had taken rather a large dive.

'Wonderful . . . well, it's not a lot, really. The kitchen needs to be cleaned after meals, and the residents' rooms need to be made up each day. There's not much ironing, but some of the men like to wear a dress shirt on Sundays.'

I slump a little in my chair. I've ironed a couple of shirts before, but probably not more than a couple. When Richard and I were newly married, I'd made a great song and dance about being the one to iron his shirts. Once, I'd even done it naked. I thought there was something terribly romantic about ironing my lover's shirt before he set off for work in the morning. But after a while, I'd handed the ironing over to Valentina along with the rest of the household chores that didn't interest me.

'Shirts on Sundays,' I say, thinking of Butt Road. 'No problem.'

'What else?' he says, clicking his tongue. 'We have a fantastic nurse, Rosie, who does night shift, and we have caregivers here between eight and five. Trish is our personal care attendant, and Carole is her assistant. Angus, who let you in, is the gardener, and he also takes care of maintenance. As for the residents, we have twelve at the moment. One of our selling points is that we're intimate. A family, really. We have to make sure everyone is a good fit before they start.'

I nod, a false smile woven to my face. The one thing I'm convinced of is that I'm the opposite of a good fit. I'm a chef, specializing in fine dining . . . What do I know about being a cook and temporary cleaner at a residential home?

'We're a private facility,' Eric continues, 'one of several across the country owned by a group called Advanced Retirement Solutions. I am the administrator of this center. We are licensed and inspected annually by the New Jersey Department of Health and Senior Services.

'We are an assisted-living facility, not a nursing home, so our residents are all in good health – physically speaking. But we do have some residents with dementia. One of our older residents, Bert, is beginning to show some signs, and we also have two young residents suffering from the disease. Anna is thirty-nine. She has younger-onset Alzheimer's, the memory-related type of dementia that most people have heard of. Luke is forty-one. He has a variant of frontotemporal dementia, which affects speech and word production. He finds it physically difficult to speak as well as hard to find the words he needs. He's mostly nonverbal these days.'

'Wow.'

'Although you won't be responsible for caring for the residents, you'll be interacting with them daily. How do you feel about that? Do you have experience with the elderly or disabled? Grandparents?'

'I don't have any grandparents or any real experience with the elderly. But that's something I'd like to change.'

This part, at least, is true. I've become all too aware recently how tough life can be. And from the weight of Eric's nod, I determine I've convinced him, too.

'Well, you've come to the right place,' he says, and laughs again. 'Anyway, that's enough from me. Do you have any questions?'

'Just one,' I say. 'As I mentioned, I have a daughter at elementary school. Clementine will be at school for the bulk of the day, but she's with me in the early mornings and after school, so I'd have to bring her here. And I'll have to walk her there and back, but it's less than five minutes each way.'

I sit tall and try to look confident. Like this is one of twenty jobs I'm interviewing for, instead of my last hope.

'Actually, I think the residents would love having a child around,' Eric says. 'As long as it doesn't interfere with your work, of course.'

I let go the breath I was holding, and Eric rises to his feet.

'Well, then, how about a tour?'

I smile and haul myself upright, ready for a tour of my new life.

Four months ago, my life fell apart. Not slowly, like a terminal illness, but all at once, like a fatal car accident. At least, it was all at once for me and Clementine when

33

Richard told me what he'd done. And it was all at once for the thousands of investors who lost their money. But for Richard, it was more like lung cancer for a heavy smoker. He must have known that disaster was inevitable. But he chose to keep going, in the hopes he'd be that one in a million who came through it unscathed.

It was 3:15 P.M. on a Tuesday when his car pulled up. That should have been my first clue. I'd been married to Richard for ten years, and in all that time he'd never been home at three fifteen on a weekday. The funny thing was, I remember feeling pleased. I'd tried a new ingredient in my pumpkin shortbread, and it had just come out of the oven.

'Great timing,' I'd said when he let himself into the kitchen. 'You can be my first taste tester.'

He muttered something unintelligible as he landed on a barstool.

'Honey?' I said.

He bent forward, resting his forehead in his palm. He wasn't wearing a jacket, and his tie was loose.

'Aren't you feeling well?' I felt his head with the back of my hand. 'Ricky?' He hated it when I called him Ricky in public, but in private, it usually made him smile. '*Hello?* Anyone home?'

The house was full of tradespeople. We were getting the place ready for the summer. A man waved as he walked past the kitchen window, carrying a ladder. I waved back.

When Richard still didn't speak, I gave him a playful shove. His head tipped back, and that's when I saw his swollen, crying eyes.

34

'Richard! Oh my God.'

I'd never seen Richard cry. Not at his mother's or father's funerals. Not on our wedding day. Not at Clementine's birth. Richard was far more likely to punch a wall or drink one too many glasses of Scotch to blow off steam or emotion. 'What's wrong?'

His eyes met mine for only a second. 'I've fucked up, Eve.'

'You've . . .' I sat down beside him and swiveled his stool so he faced me. 'What do you mean? What have you fucked up?'

'My life. Your life. Clementine's life.' He twisted away, parking his elbows on the marble benchtop. 'I've lied about my investments, I've falsified paperwork. And I'm about to be caught.'

A quiet not-quite laugh came out of me. 'Is this a joke?'

'Do I look like I'm joking?'

It didn't make sense. Richard didn't need to lie about his investments or create false documents. Richard was brilliant at what he did. Still, I felt the pinpricks of uncertainty. His eyes were red rimmed, his collar loose. He'd been steadily losing weight for weeks now, drinking more. And a few days ago I'd found him in his study with a face that looked vaguely tear-stained. He blamed it on a head-cold and a lot of pressure at work. I hadn't thought to ask any more about it.

'But . . . falsifying documents?' I said, almost to myself. 'You mean like a—'

'—Ponzi scheme.'

A knot tied itself, slowly and painfully, in my gut.

'We're going to lose all our money,' he said. 'Our house. And I'll go to jail.'

I rose from my stool. 'Jail?'

'I thought it would be all right, as long as I reported modest returns. I thought . . . I thought it would be all right . . .' He began to sob, and that's when I knew this was real. When it came to business, Richard was always arrogant to a fault. I'd never seen him so defeated. With both hands, I formed a tent over my mouth and nose.

'I've tried to think of a way out of this,' he continued, 'but I can't.'

I began to pace. 'Holy . . . shit. Holy, holy, holy shit! This is crazy. How could you . . . ?' On the oven, I suddenly noticed the time. '*Shit!* I have to pick up Clem from school.'

I grabbed the keys and headed for the door. Then I stopped short. I had no idea of the protocol for this situation. Were the police about to turn up on our doorstep? Was he going to be hauled away in handcuffs in front of our daughter? And what then? Would we be marched out of our house?

'Richard—'

'It's all right,' he said, strangely eloquent now that he had shared the burden. 'We have time. Go and get Clem.'

I held his gaze silently for what felt like hours, but must have been only seconds. Then, with a stomach full of savage maggots, I turned and pressed through the swing doors.

My tour of Rosalind House is brief, and doesn't include an introduction to the residents, so much as a *viewing of* the residents. We pass a handful of people in the corridors and a few more in a high-ceilinged living room that Eric calls the parlor. Everyone else has been planted on the vast expanse of lawn that abuts the property, probably absorbing a year's worth of vitamin D from the brilliant, clear sky. The gardener, Angus, is standing on a short ladder, hacking at an overgrown bush.

'That's Bert,' Eric says, pointing at a balding man in his eighties. 'And over there, that's Clara. That was her husband in the parlor, Laurie. And that's Luke and Anna, under the tree.'

The young couple stand out, in a garden full of elderly folk. The man, Luke, sits on a garden bench. His head is down and his dark wavy hair spills over his face. The woman, Anna, sits a few paces away from him in a wheelchair, her hair a tangle of red-brown curls.

'They're so young,' I say. 'I can't believe they have dementia.'

'It *is* hard to believe,' Eric says. 'Some days are good and they just act like quiet, normal people. Other days are not so good.'

'Why is she in a wheelchair? Is that to do with the dementia?'

'Oh—' Eric scratches a sudden itch at his neck. 'Well, no—'

'She's dropped her scarf,' I say, stepping toward the lightweight linen dancing on the grass by Anna's feet. Its cheerful colors remind me of the painting Richard gave me for our first anniversary, the one the auctioneer showed great interest in last week when he came to peruse our possessions.

I snap up the scarf. 'You dropped this,' I say, resting it on Anna's lap. Up close, I can't resist taking a better look at her. She's not beautiful – at least not in these parts, where beautiful equals blond, slim, and symmetrical. But she is something – striking, perhaps? Her skin is alabaster and thickly spread with freckles, and her arms and legs are long and lithe. But what hits me the most is the color of her eyes: a pale, clear jade. Without the eyes, she might have been plain. But with the eyes? I can't seem to look away.

Before I can remove my hand, she cloaks it in her own and squeezes.

'Oh.' I pull back, but her fingers dig farther into mine. 'I didn't mean to alarm you. I just didn't want you to lose your lovely scarf.'

She's getting ready to speak, the cues are all there – the wetting of lips, the swallowing, the tensing of facial muscles. It takes only a fraction longer than, say, a thoughtful person would take, but I am hyperaware of her dementia and can't seem to think of anything else. 'Please,' she says finally. 'Help me.'

A prickle travels down the length of my spine. 'What did you say?'

I wait, but she doesn't speak again.

'Anna?' I persist, but already the comprehension in her face has fluttered away, replaced by a vacantness so at odds with her young, smooth skin. Her eyes film over, still beautiful but now empty. I stand straight.

'Eric,' I say, returning to him, 'she just said, "Help me."'

Eric blinks, the perfect picture of surprise. 'She did? Are you sure?'

'Yes. I mean . . . I think so.'

'What prompted it?' he asks. 'Did you say anything to her?'

I look back at her. 'Just that I didn't want her to lose her scarf.'

'I'll send Carole over,' he says, and a moment later, a staff member is scurrying in her direction. 'If there's something wrong, we'll get to the bottom of it.'

I nod and he gestures for us to return to the house. As he holds open the screen door for me, he says, 'The upside of dementia, of course, is if she does lose her scarf, she isn't going to miss it for long.'

4

As we drive through the gates of Rosalind House, Clementine's eyes widen. '*This* is our new house? Mom, are we rich again?'

In my surprise, I nearly lose my grip on the steering wheel. Clem had been utterly indifferent when I'd told her I was starting a new job. Utterly indifferent when I'd told her we were moving house. Utterly indifferent about everything since Richard disappeared from our lives. Because of this, when it came to my new work situation, I'd been sparing with details. Now I wonder if I'd been too sparing. 'What do you mean "again"?'

'You know. How Dad lost our money and stuff.'

For a moment, I'm punch-drunk, stupefied. Clem gives me a look that says *Seriously? Did you think I was stupid? Did I?*

I think of the house as we left it. Boxes lining the walls of the foyer, every room dismantled, packed away, and labeled with a yellow, pink, or green sticker – take, toss, sell. The 'sell' stickers were the most plentiful, labeled in green in the hopes it would correspond with the amount of green they'd bring in at auction. Was I a fool to think that Clem wouldn't have drawn her own conclusions? Particularly now, when everything we own fits nicely into one Samsonite suitcase and four garbage bags.

She stares at me, her brown eyes curved into inquisitive crescents, far too knowing for a seven-year-old.

'Clem—'

'My name's not Clem,' she says, rolling her eyes. 'It's Beatrice.'

I wipe at my brow with the heel of my hand. The name thing started a few months ago and is wildly inconsistent – sometimes she keeps a designated name all day; other days she changes it four, maybe five times. For now, it just seems easier to go with it. 'Okay, Beatrice, then—'

'How many bedrooms is it?' she asks.

And just like that, she is upbeat again. In the past few months, she's yo-yoed between euphoria (almost exclusively when she was in the company of her best friend, Allegra aka 'Legs') and a sullen, introspective demeanor befitting a teenager rather than a seven-year-old girl.

As she begins her involuntary bounce, the first part of what she'd said – *'This is our new house?'* – slips into my consciousness. I glance up at the beautiful house. *Of course* Clem assumes this is her new home. It looks a hell of a lot like her old home.

'Clem, wait,' I say as she reaches for the car door handle. *'Beatrice!'*

'Sorry.' I curse under my breath. 'Beatrice . . .'

But *Beatrice* has already swiped up the garbage bag containing her things and is leaping up the stairs. I charge

41

after her, and by the time I get there, like a déjà vu, the gardener is in the doorway.

'Oh, hello, again,' I say, flustered.

'Hello,' he says. His eyes drop to Clem. She stares at him, her mouth slightly open, then a little smile starts.

I can hardly blame her; he really is extraordinarily handsome. I'm suddenly aware of my jeans, my plain white-but-graying tee, my ponytail. My round face is bare of makeup and my hair hasn't seen a cut or highlight in months, leaving it well past my shoulders and a dirty dark blond. Worst of all, I'm wearing an ill-fitting bra that is digging into my shoulder blades and squashing my breasts into a strange, wavelike shape. I cross my arms.

'Hi,' Clem says, sliding behind my leg, her bouncy excitement replaced by shy awkwardness.

'May I take your bag?' Angus asks.

Clem's eyes widen. 'Are you the butler?'

Angus's eyes meet mine for the briefest of seconds.

'Oh no, Clem—'

'No,' he says. 'I'm the gardener.'

'Oh!' She nods and smiles as though now everything makes sense. 'Of course! You're the gardener. Well, you're doing a great job. The garden looks neat.'

'Thank you very much,' he says, taking her bag.

'Eric asked me to pop in tonight to meet the residents properly,' I explain to Angus. His responding shrug makes me feel foolish.

Clem darts inside and I chase after her into a high-ceilinged dining room. It is louder than I expected for a residential care facility – a cacophony of clangs, dings, and tremulous shouting. Residents and a few staff are parked in front of bowls of what looks like red beans and rice. Eric sits at the end of one table next to Anna.

'Well, hello there,' Eric says, rising from his chair. 'Glad you could make it.' He hushes the room with a wave of his hands. 'Everyone, can I have your attention, please? This is Eve Bennett. Eve is our new cook. She has studied at New York's Institute of Culinary Education, so you are in for a treat. Eve will also be doing some cleaning for us, until we hire someone permanent. I hope everyone is going to make her very welcome.'

Twelve heads swivel to me.

'Hello,' I say inadequately. 'I'm very pleased to meet you all. From what I understand, you are all fond of your current cook, so I know I have very big boots to fill.'

'You do realize Gabriela's not dead?' someone shouts.

'What did she say about boots?' says someone else.

'What I mean to say is . . .' I try again, 'this is going to be a steep learning curve for me, but if you'll help me, I'm sure we'll do fine. Please don't hesitate to let me know your favorite foods, and whether there are any foods you don't like. I look forward to getting to know you all.'

I end my speech with an awkward nod and an attempted smile. The residents continue to stare at me. I suddenly become aware of Clem, standing immediately to my right.

'My name is Clementine Harriet Bennett,' she says. 'Very pleased to meet you all.' The residents' faces, blank a moment earlier, start to upturn. 'I'm seven years old and I'm in the second grade. I'm also very good at Irish dancing, would you like me to show you?'

I pat her shoulder. 'Clem, we really better—'

'Is a frog's ass watertight?' says a gray-blond lady with a Southern accent. 'Go ahead, young lady.'

Clem shifts uncertainly – perhaps waiting for me to reprimand the lady for using the word 'ass' – but she recovers quickly. 'Okay, but I don't have my music here, so I need you to clap. Slowly at first, then faster and faster, got it?' A couple of residents nod, but most look puzzled. A man at the back adjusts his hearing aid.

'Okay, then,' Clem instructs. 'Start.'

As Clem kicks and hops around the room, a few residents clap. It's not a great clap – it's a little out of time and doesn't have much force behind it – but Clem manages to keep it together. I feel a little bit proud. She finishes up with a curtsy.

'Thank you very much. Tomorrow, I'll bring my recorder and play some songs. Would you like that?'

A few people nod, and I marvel at Clem's unbridled confidence. 'It'll have to be after school, Clemmy,' I say.

'Yes, yes,' she says, waving as though it were a packed audience at the Hippodrome. 'After school.'

Before we leave, I'm introduced to the night nurse, Rosie, a girl in her mid-twenties with a blond ponytail so high atop her head, it resembles an erupting volcano. We talk to Eric for a few more minutes, and then Angus walks us to the door.

'Which one is my room?' Clem asks.

'This isn't our house,' I say, as quickly and quietly as I can. 'We're just headed there now.'

'Oh!' Clem covers a giggle and looks at Angus. 'I guess I'd better take my bag, then!'

Angus hands her the garbage bag and opens the door. I hurry through it, but Clem pulls me back. 'Uh, Mom?'

'Yes, hon?'

'Aren't you forgetting something?'

For the life of me, I can't figure out what she is talking about. 'What?'

She pulls on my shirt cuff, dragging me down until my ear is level with her mouth. 'A tip!'

Any hope Angus might not have heard Clem's stage whisper is extinguished when I see his expression.

'Tell you what?' he says to Clem, throwing her a wink. 'This one's on the house.'

Clem giggles her thanks and scampers down the steps. But when Angus lifts his eyes to me, his expression isn't quite so warm.

It takes twenty minutes to drive to our apartment. Clem frowns as we press open the glass door set in a narrow gap between a pizza shop and a convenience store. The stairs are covered in worn carpet and curved like a row of sad smiles that sink and creak with each step. One patch of carpet is so sunken, I wonder if there's even a floorboard underneath. I make a mental note to avoid it in the future.

At the top of the stairs, I jiggle the key in the old lock and crack it open. Clem charges in first, does the circuit, then stands before me, all puzzled-looking.

'This is *it*?'

I bustle inside with the garbage bags. 'What do you think?'

I'd put off bringing Clem to the apartment for as long as I possibly could. Mother and I had been slowly moving the few pieces of furniture I had left into the place, hoping we could get it looking cheerful before Clem saw it. I'd lined up her toys on the windowsill and put out pictures in frames. But even the bunch of daises on the table and the *Frozen* poster on the wall weren't enough to brighten up the place.

'It smells like salami.'

CLEAN, FUNCTIONAL APARTMENT, the advertisement had said. Which meant a brown vinyl kitchen with electric hot plates, an open-plan living room with brown-flecked carpet tiles, and a shower room boasting a matching wooden toilet seat and vanity. And . . .

'There's only one bedroom,' Clem says.

I sit my purse on the counter, trying to find something that Clem will like about the place. But there's nothing. If Richard were here, he'd have made her laugh; he was the expert at that. But Richard wasn't here.

Clem's white-blond pigtails bob as she does another scan of the room. 'Well . . . where am I going to sleep?'

I glance over her shoulder at the double bed. All the parenting books I'd read when Clem was a baby had warned of the perils of letting a child sleep in your bed, and dutifully, I'd heeded their advice, choosing to spend evenings rocking her in a recliner, driving around the block with her in the car, even lying beside her crib on the floor rather than bringing her into the forbidden

46

marital bed. When I lamented to Mother, she'd practically spat her tea. *'For Heaven's sake, Evie! Wouldn't anyone prefer to sleep in warm, comforting arms rather than behind bars in a dark, scary room?'* Now, more than ever, I was inclined to agree.

'Where do you think?' I ask, then tackle her, tickling until we both crumple onto the bed.

5

Anna

Fourteen months ago . . .

My room at Rosalind House isn't an entirely unpleasant place to be, which is good, since I spend so much time in here. As much as I don't want to admit that the dementia is getting the better of me, I find myself more worn out than I used to be. Once, not so long ago, I would do a twelve-hour shift in the ambulance and still have an entire night ahead of me to dance, drink, and socialize. These days, I leave my room for a meal and upon my return, I am ready for a nap.

Now I drop into my chair and lean back, closing my eyes.

'Good girl. You decided to wait for me today.'

I open my eyes, sit up straight. The skinny lady – Trish, according to her name badge – is standing in front of me.

'Excuse me?' I say.

'Would you like to undress in here or in the bathroom?'

I blame the exhaustion for the fact that I haven't checked the laminated sheet for shower times. In truth, I'd actually forgotten the laminated sheet existed. Now it comes back to me like a fist in the gut. 'I'm fine,' I say. 'I don't need a shower.'

She sighs. 'Come on, Anna. Let's not make this difficult.'

Beyond the skinny lady, the door to my room is wide open. Someone trundles past the door on a walker. Does she actually think I'm going to strip naked right here? Is that what she wants me to do?

Clearly it is, because she comes at me, yanking me to my feet. She reaches for the bottom edge of my T-shirt, and I realize in alarm that she's going to undress me.

'Ahhh!' I yell. I know I sound crazy, but I'll take crazy over the humiliation of being showered by this woman against my will. 'Ahhh.'

I take a step back, but the wall is behind me, there's nowhere to go. Skinny Lady smiles. (I'll tell you something for nothing: The only thing worse than having someone undress you against your will is to have them do it *smiling*.)

I keep shouting, rhythmically and repeatedly. Skinny stands back. 'You've got visitors this afternoon, Anna. Don't you want to look nice for them?'

Another person passes my doorway, no walker this time. It's the young guy.

Skinny reaches for my waistband. 'How about we start by undoing your—?'

I open my mouth to start shouting again, but then I hear a noise – a smash.

Skinny's arms retract back to her sides. 'What on earth—?'

She darts out of the room. I drift after her as far as the doorway and see Young Guy, standing over broken glass.

'Oh, sweetie, what have you done?' Skinny is using a controlled, deliberate voice, but her irritation is only thinly veiled. 'Just stand back, I'm going to get something to clean it up. All right, Luke? Stay back.'

Skinny marches off, presumably in search of a broom. The moment she's disappeared around the corner, Young Guy – *Luke* – looks directly at me and realization dawns. It wasn't an accident.

I want to say something – do something – but my mouth just hangs open, intermittently filling and emptying with air, like a grocery bag in the wind. 'I'd . . . be quick if I were you,' he whispers. 'Whatshername, she's speedy . . . with that sweeper-thing.'

We stare at each other a moment and a strange, silent dialogue is transmitted between us. From some primal place inside, I feel a twinge.

There's a rustle as the broom closet opens and Skinny, presumably, rifles through it. I slip out of the doorway and into the bathroom, where I start the shower. And even though my short-term memories are supposed to be the first to go, a few minutes later, as the water pounds against my shoulders and back, I am still thinking about *him*.

The good thing, I guess, is that I've known love. At least, I think it was love, but how do you really ever know? I was twenty-eight when I met Aiden. I was stuck at a set of traffic lights in my beat-up old Ford when he pulled up beside my car on a Harley-Davidson. I still remember the ease of him, the way he leaned back slightly, like he had nowhere he had to be. His helmet covered only his head and ears, so I could see his chin, his stubbly jaw, his lips.

I wound down my window. 'I like your bike,' I said.

He regarded me curiously. 'Thanks. You ride?'

'Not a Harley.'

'But you ride?'

He was cute, this biker guy. I found myself wondering if there were full sleeves underneath his leather jacket. And what else might be under there.

'I've got a Honda 900 cc in my garage,' I said, 'just waiting for its momma to come home and take her for a spin.'

Now he leaned forward, assessing me. He seemed pleased with what he saw. 'How 'bout you give me your number, and we can go for a spin sometime?'

I found an old ticket on the dash just as the light changed to green and I steeled myself for the honking and cursing. But no one did honk as I scribbled down my phone number. Perhaps it was because Aiden rode a Harley that they didn't want to mess with him? Or perhaps it was because sometimes people were willing to wait for a glimpse of young romance?

I sped Aiden through the early relationship process, from first date to boyfriend without passing Go. We went camping at Yosemite. We hugged the curves of coastal roads on our bikes. We started our days with sex and, if Aiden hadn't been smoking pot, ended them with it, too. But afterwards, when we fell asleep, we were always sprawled out and separate – together in our desire to be alone. It wasn't the love from a romance movie, but it worked for us.

Getting married, I'll admit, was my idea, and at first, it wasn't very well received.

'You want to get *married*?'

I may as well have suggested we bungee jump without a cord. And I understood Aiden's surprise. I wasn't a 'white dress' kind of girl – this was out of left field. Yet there I was, close to thirty, and it had been on my mind.

'Well,' I said. 'Not if this is your reaction.'

It wasn't that I'd expected Aiden to drop to one knee and pull out a huge rock and get all choked up. God, if he had, I'd probably have said no. But I *had* started thinking that if we were going to do it, now would be a good time. Mom had been a year younger than me when she got married. By my age, she was pregnant.

'Okay, just forget it,' I said.

'Now, hang on a sec, let a man catch up.' Aiden's frown morphed into a grin, and he pointed at it. 'What if this is my reaction?'

He was sweet, Aiden, and if I'm honest with myself, easily led. He was happy to go along with my plan. But in the end, marriage wasn't enough.

'I want a baby.'

They say something happens to a woman when she reaches thirty-five and her fertility starts to ebb. Even the coldest, least maternal women start to feel the twinge. Maybe that's what it was? Kids weren't exactly something I'd always wanted, but all of a sudden, I started noticing pregnant women. I started looking in strollers and smiling at grubby faces.

Unfortunately, when it came to having a baby, Aiden was less easily led. 'Let's wait a few months,' he said. But a few months became a year. The clock was ticking, and not just the biological clock. I was forgetting things by then. There was no firm diagnosis, but the writing was on the wall.

'Jesus Christ, Anna!' it became, after a while. 'Will you let up about a fucking baby? Am I nothing more than a sperm donor to you?'

I wanted to be outraged. To ask how he could even ask me that. But by that stage, we both knew it was an accurate description for what he was. We rarely talked about anything meaningful anymore. The motorcycle trips were a thing of the past. We'd put our old camping equipment out on the sidewalk on garbage day. I may as well have put my ovaries there, too.

So I agreed with Aiden that a baby was a bad idea. And a few weeks later, when I was officially diagnosed with Alzheimer's, I left.

It's visitors' day at Rosalind House, and we're in the garden again – a practical decision, as with Jack and Helen and all the boys here, we couldn't all fit in my room. Apart from the sun, which is shining right in my eyes, I like it out here. It's Sunday, and most of the residents have visitors. Southern Lady sits opposite a woman who bears such an uncanny resemblance to her – from the floral dress to the puff of yellow hair – that she *has* to be her sister. Really

Old Lady has a visitor, a young man in gray sweatpants who, age-wise, is most likely a great-grandson, or even a great-great. Young Guy is flanked by an older woman who is either a mother or a grandmother and a younger woman, about my age. And Eric swans around the lot of us, like a King visiting his villagers.

'Can I have a ride in your wheelchair, please? I mean, if you're not using it.'

My nephew Hank beams at Really Old Lady. Clearly he's very proud of himself for saying please. He's definitely not expecting the pinch on the arm that he gets from Helen. 'Ow, Mom! What?'

Really Old Lady fiddles with her hearing aid. 'What did you say, young man?'

'Nothing,' Helen says hurriedly. 'Nothing at all.' She takes Hank by the arm and drags him away, toward the far end of the lawn, where Ethan and Brayden are playing.

Jack leans back on his garden chair and stretches his arms out. 'So? How's it been?'

I blink into the sun, wishing it would go behind the tree. 'Not bad. Actually, it's been better than I expected.'

'Seriously?'

'The fact that you look so surprised doesn't bode well for you, considering you were the one who tossed me in here like a piece of rotten fruit.'

Jack laughs. 'As I recall, you tossed *yourself* in. I just found the place.' He looks so happy, I'm worried he might cry. 'Hey, I think this place is great. I'm only surprised because I didn't expect you to . . . adjust to it . . . so soon.'

We both drop our eyes. By 'so soon', he means before

54

I started to really lose it. Before I forgot that he, or any of them, existed.

'Eric says you've started to get into the swing of things,' he tries again. 'That you've come out of your room a few times—'

'More than a few,' I tell him. 'I've even made some friends. That lady over there' – I nod at Southern Lady, who is surrounded by a cluster of little children and teen-agers – 'and him.' I point at Young Guy, whose eyes lift at that exact moment to meet mine. Quickly I point to another couple of residents that I've never seen before in my life. 'Her and him, too.' Since I don't remember anyone's names, I might as well include them all.

'Good!' Jack's enthusiasm is tragic. It reminds me of the way he used to cheer when Ethan finally went on the potty. 'That's . . . great.'

'Yep. There are lots of things to do. There's a bus that we can take to town, as long as we have a . . . a person that goes with us . . . and there's bingo on Friday nights.'

At this, Jack's enthusiasm is replaced by suspicion. 'Bingo?'

'I mean . . . I didn't play or anything, but they have it, so that's good.'

I need to backpedal, fast. I want Jack to think I'm happy, not crazy. But I get the feeling that, with bingo, I took it too far.

Helen and the boys run up, saving me at the eleventh hour. 'Anna, do you have one of those beds that goes up and down?' Hank asks.

'Bed goes up, bed goes down. Bed goes up, bed goes down,' Brayden and Ethan chant.

'Why don't you go have a look?' I suggest, because I have no idea if I have one of those beds. For all I know, I've been sleeping on a lump of clay since I arrived – beds have not been at the top of my mind.

They jog toward the house, trailed by Helen, and I watch them go. There's a floor-to-ceiling window, I notice, way at the top of the building, directly above the paved courtyard. I zero in on it.

Back when I was a paramedic, I'd once been the first to reach a woman who'd leapt in front of a train. Her right leg had landed over the track and had been sheared off at the knee. On the way to the hospital, she slipped into a coma.

Tyrone sat beside her, shaking his head. 'You gotta feel sorry for this one. This wasn't no cry for help. She wanted out.'

I nodded. 'I think you're right.'

'She needed height.'

'What?'

'Height,' he repeated. 'You fall from a certain height, you're dead. You don't need to be worryin' about the speed of the train or the amount of pills or the strength of the rope. You just need a bridge or a tall building. It's fool-proof.'

I stare at the window and think about what he told me. All of a sudden, I have my plan.

'*Anna?*' someone is shouting. 'Do you have any gum?'

I look away from the window at Ethan. 'What?'

'Gum,' he says. 'Do you have any?'

I blink. Gum? Do I have gum? The sun is still pounding down on me like an unrelenting beast, and I can't think. I close my eyes, but it just continues to beam, turning my eyelids red.

'Can someone turn off that *damn sun*?'

There's a silence. I feel my chair being dragged along the grass, and a second later, blissfully, the sun is gone. 'Well,' I say. 'Praise be to God.'

I open my eyes. Ethan is staring. '*What*? What are you staring at?'

'You're being weird,' Ethan says. 'Isn't she, Dad?'

Jack looks at Ethan and slowly back to me. Typical attorney – when you don't know what to say, say nothing.

'Is it because you're in this place?' Ethan asks. 'With these old people?'

Jack touches Ethan's shoulder. 'Buddy—'

'It's my fault, isn't it?' he says, ignoring Jack. 'Because I got burned?'

His eyes get shiny.

'Eath,' I say. 'Nothing is your fault.'

'Of course not,' Jack says, finding his tongue. 'Anyway, this place hasn't made Anna weird. Anna has always been weird.'

'He's right,' I say. 'In seventh grade, I was voted Weirdest in the Whole School.'

This isn't true, but I figure it doesn't matter. Ethan lowers his hands and sniffs. A tiny pathetic-excuse-for-a-smile appears on his face.

57

'How's this for weird?' I lean in toward him, bulging my eyes as wide as they go and waggling my eyebrows.

His smile swells. 'Pretty weird.'

'Told ya,' I say proudly. 'Your dad tried to beat me, but year after year, Anna Forster won for Weirdest. He's always been pretty sore about it, too.'

'Yeah, well, Dad's a sore loser. Sorry,' he says when Jack frowns at him, 'but you are.' He looks back at me. 'So you don't hate it here?'

'Nope. It's actually pretty nice. Don't you think?'

'I guess. I like the garden. And that's a good climbing tree.' He looks at me. 'Remember when we told Dad that we were stuck up that tree at the park, and we made him climb all the way up to rescue us even though we were fine?'

His face is so happy that I have to smile back. But it's a stretch. Because I have no recollection of what he's talking about. Not even the foggiest, haziest hint of a memory.

'Now, that,' I say, giving him a high five, 'was a fun day.'

I glance at the tree in this garden. Its long, thick arms are solid, forking out in different directions, many low enough even for Ethan to jump to from the ground. Once, I'd have noticed that tree immediately. I'd have been the one to suggest to Ethan that we climb it, all the way to the top, then throw acorns down on Hank and Brayden and Jack. Once, not so long ago.

When I look back at Ethan, he's already looking at me. His joker-smile is a question: *Are you game?*

I know what Jack will say: *It's not safe. Anna can't climb, her depth perception is off, she might fall. I'll climb with you Eath*, he'll say. So I don't look at Jack. Instead, I nod at Ethan infinitesimally. His smile widens. And together we sprint toward the low arms of the tree.

Now, *this* is the memory I want to leave my nephew with.

6

I sit in the parlor all afternoon. Southern Lady drifts off to sleep in the seat opposite me, and Young Guy stares out the window. It's nice, not having to talk, especially today. In the real world, people talk a lot. Conversations move quickly. By the time I've caught up enough to ask a question or make a point, everyone has already moved on. But at Rosalind House, things move slower. Everyone takes the time they need to digest what's been said. If I want to say something, I have time. And if I don't want to say anything, I don't.

Ethan and I had a good climb, and I managed to give Jack a hug without causing any suspicion (I think). It wasn't the good-bye I would have liked, and I don't think I had them utterly convinced that I was happy. But it will have to do. Because now I have a plan, tonight is the night.

'Visitors' day wears people out.'

I look up. Young Guy is watching me, stretched out, dwarfing the small armchair he is sitting in. 'No kidding,' I say. No one has said much all afternoon.

'You have a good visit?' he asks. He's wearing a faded

denim shirt with the sleeves rolled and jeans that are torn at the knees. It's a nice look on him, I decide. Scruffy-chic.

'Sure,' I say, though I'm not sure it's a good idea to be talking to him. At this point, the last thing I need is a distraction. And he – with his dimple and his scruffy-chic thing going on – is definitely a distraction.

'Who were they?' he asks. 'Your v-visitors.'

'My brother,' I say. 'And his family. Who were yours?'

Good one, Anna. So much for not talking to him.

'My mom.'

I picture the older woman, white-haired and stooped.

'Mom's old,' he says, answering my unspoken question. Then his face sort of tenses. It's virtually unnoticeable, just the slightest indication that speaking requires a little effort. 'She was . . . fifty when she adopted me.'

'And . . . the other woman?'

Once I would have felt too direct asking this. I would have spent time talking around the issue and tried to slip in questions naturally. But I've lost patience for that stuff. It's hard enough retaining new information without having to add in social graces. I can only hope he feels the same.

'Sarah,' he says, pushing his hair behind his ear. 'My brother.'

'You have a brother called Sarah?'

He frowns, and immediately I want to take it back, pretend I didn't notice. Then he shakes his head. 'Sister. I meant sister.'

I don't know much about Young Guy's specific form of dementia other than what he told me at breakfast the other day, but from his expression, I can tell his slip is dementia-related. Idly, I wonder how many slips I have without noticing. Less idly, I think about how I'd like people to respond when I do.

'My sister was here today, too,' I tell him. 'Jack.'

I watch as the joke connects with his brain and a smile wriggles onto his face.

'It looked intense,' I say. 'Whatever you were discussing.'

'Just . . . who is in ch-charge of my affairs when I can no longer hold a pen.' He grimaces, trying to come up with the word. 'You know the . . .'

'Power of attorney?' With an attorney as a brother, 'power of attorney' is probably the last expression I'll keep. After I was diagnosed, he bandied the word around more times than I could count, the one part of my disease that Jack could control.

'Yes!' Young Guy exclaims, and I feel a surprising thrill at being the one to provide him with the word.

'Mom has my p-power of attorney, but she's getting older. And she wants to g-give it to Sarah.'

'And you don't?'

'I'm just not sure she'll respect my wishes.'

'Which are?'

He looks at me. 'I want to live.'

'Ah,' I say, as though this makes everything clear. 'And your sister wants to kill you?'

He blinks, then laughs loudly.

'It's okay,' I say. 'I'm pretty sure my brother wants to kill me, too.'

Now we both laugh. It's one of those laughs that starts as a chuckle and winds up in a full-bellied guffaw. I get so lost in it that I startle when he suddenly leans forward in his seat, then falls onto his knees in front of me. My laughter vanishes. He's so close, I can feel the warmth of his skin on mine.

'Hey, you've g-got a . . .' He reaches for my face, and I forget to breathe. What is he doing? If I leaned forward an inch or two, my lips would touch his. I can't remember the last time I was this close to someone. Then again, I *wouldn't* remember.

'Eye-hair,' he says finally, swiping a hair from my cheek. He balances it on his fingertip for me to see. I get the feeling that 'eye-hair' is not the word to describe it, but I am too acutely aware of the proximity of his body to think of the right one. He blows the eye-hair away, then sits back. 'Sorry. What did we . . . what were we s-saying?'

I can't remember, and I suspect it has nothing to do with the Alzheimer's. I can still feel his warmth, the burn of his fingertip on my face.

'Uh, was it . . . your sister?' I ask.

'Oh. Yeah.' He shuffles, pulling his knees to his chest and wrapping his arms around them. 'Sarah's c-cash-rich, time-poor, and a believer in finding solutions.' His throat works with the effort of speaking. 'I just worry what she'll do down the road, when the next . . . "problem" p-presents itself.'

He doesn't need to explain what the next problem could be. I already know. Delusional episodes. Loss of bladder and bowel control. Feeding issues. Catastrophic reactions. DNRs.

'Sarah cares, b-but . . . I'm not sure that she'd make the

same decisions that I would, when it came to the crunch. I don't want . . . diapers . . . the first time I have an accident or to be f-furnished with a chalkboard when my speech deteriorates. I don't want to be . . . p-pushed in a chair with wheels when I can still walk.'

This little speech looks like it's taken an enormous amount of effort. And while I don't entirely share his convictions, there's something to be admired about his passion. It might be the fact that it's difficult for him to speak, or maybe just the pendulum of moods of Alzheimer's, but as I listen to him talk, my eyes fill.

'At some point, I'm going to have to start letting go of control,' he says. 'But I have n-no plans to do it without a fight. And Sarah, I can just see her – Luke's having trouble dressing himself, let's p-pay someone to do it for him. Luke's not doing enough . . . exercise; let's schedule some activities. Let's give him sleeping tablets to help him s-sleep, let's feed him. No. That's not what I want. I don't want to exist. I want to love.'

'Live,' I correct, but he doesn't seem to notice.

I have to admit, I think he's right to be wary of handing his affairs to his sister. It's one of the reasons I don't want my life to get to that point. As good as Jack's intentions are, I wouldn't want him pulling my puppet strings down the road.

'Brothers,' I say with an over-the-top sigh. It's funny, even though we've just been discussing dementia-related stuff, for the last few minutes, it didn't feel like either of us had dementia. It felt like we were just a guy and a girl, discussing life.

'Luke?'

We both glance at the doorway, where Eric is standing.

'Your doctor is here to see you,' Eric says.

'Oh. Sure.' Young Guy, *Luke*, rises to his feet.

'Would you like me to take you back to your room, Anna?' Eric asks.

Luke looks at me. He kicks his foot gently against mine – a benign enough gesture that somehow has me blushing. 'W-will you be here when I get b-back?'

I glance to where Eric is standing: red-faced, fat and smirking. Then I look back at Luke. 'Well,' I say quietly, 'I've had some pretty tempting offers, but yeah, what the hell, why not?'

To Eric I say, 'Thanks but I'm fine right here.'

Luke grins and wanders off toward Eric. In the doorway, he pauses, staring at the thin, shiny strip of metal edging on the carpet, separating the parlor from the hall. Then he lifts his foot to knee height, stepping over the strip as though it were a raised bar or stair. At first I don't know what he's doing. Then I do.

The first time I saw Mom do this was at my basketball championship. She'd been diagnosed with Alzheimer's six months earlier. She'd sat in the third row during the game, cheering and clapping when we got a three-pointer (and occasionally, when the other team did). After we won, everyone tramped onto the court, greeting us with hugs and high fives. As the shooter of the winning team, I was lifted onto my team's shoulders and tossed about. It was from there that I saw Mom. She was on the edge of the court, frowning at a line on the floor as though it were some sort of intricate puzzle she couldn't figure out. I tapped someone to let me down, but before I could get to her, she shimmied up her skirt and stepped over the line as if it were a waist-high fence. A few people looked, but most were distracted by the commotion on the court. Once over the line, she smiled at me, a little relieved, and gave me a hug. *'Congratulations, darling. Great game.'*

When I told Jack about it, he told me that for some people, depth perception is one of the first things the brain casts off when it starts to degenerate, making it difficult to tell the difference between flat and raised, high and low. That's the thing about dementia: You can forget for a moment, even an hour. But sooner or later, dementia reminds you – and everyone else – that it's there.

Before I had Alzheimer's, I used to listen to a radio competition called *Beat the Bomb*. Callers who dialed in had the opportunity to play for up to twenty-five thousand dollars. When the game began, the clock would start ticking, and every few seconds, an eerie, prerecorded voice would announce an amount of money. *'Five ... hundred ... dollars. One ... thousand ... dollars. Five ... thousand ... dollars.'* It kept going up. As soon as the contestant said stop, the money was theirs, but the longer they waited, the more they risked the bomb (buzzer) going off and getting nothing.

When I was sixteen, Jack and I came home one day to find Mom in the garage. The car was running, and she was in the passenger seat with the car windows open. Her head lolled against the open door. I ran to call 911 while

Jack dragged her from the car. By the time I got back to them, she was awake. Drowsy, making no sense, but awake.

'If I don't remember,' she muttered. 'Will I have been here at all?'

When the paramedics arrived, I listened as Jack explained that she had been diagnosed with Alzheimer's and that she was easily confused. She must have thought she was driving somewhere, he said. Or perhaps she thought it was her favorite chair and decided to have a sleep. I wondered if Jack really believed that. As he talked, I stared at Mom, trying to catch her eye. *Is that what happened?* I'd whispered. *Were you confused?* The fact that she wouldn't look at me told me all I needed to know.

After that, we never left her alone. She had a nurse that stayed with her all day. Dad had already left us, so Jack or I slept by her side at night. After a few months, she went into a nursing home. She'd gone downhill so fast that by that point, even if she'd still wanted to kill herself, she wouldn't have known how. The window had closed.

Most people who want to kill themselves can wake up and decide, *You know what? Today's not the day.* If I feel terrible tomorrow, I'll do it then. Or the day after. Maybe next year. But the thing about having Alzheimer's is that you're a ticking clock. You don't have the luxury of waiting. You have to beat the bomb.

I'm back in my spot by the window, sitting in my chair, looking into the dark night. I wonder if, after I'm gone, there will be an imprint left in this chair. A marker that

I was once here. I won't leave much else in the way of markers. No money. No friends. No children.

Something a lot of people don't understand about Alzheimer's is that while you won't find Alzheimer's listed as the cause of death on my death certificate, it will *kill* me. Trouble going to the bathroom will lead to bladder infections. Problems with swallowing may make it hard to eat. Less mobility will result in blood clots. And if I'm not eating and not moving while fighting infections and pneumonia, guess what? I'm on a one-way street to God's waiting room.

In front of me is a row of envelopes, clean and white, addressed with first names. Jack. Ethan. Hank. Brayden. Helen. (I didn't want her to feel left out.) Dad. I thought about that one awhile: Dad. What do you say to the man who left your mother right after she was diagnosed with Alzheimer's? On second thought, perhaps there was a lot to say to a man like that? I decided not to go with the torrent of abuse, tempting as it was, and instead wrote down memories. Of Mom's death-ceremony-thingy. My graduation. The birth of Jack's children. For some reason, it felt important to document them. Maybe it was my way of responding to the letters he'd sent me over the years, the ones I'd burned during my pyromaniac years, and simply thrown out after that. Or maybe I was trying to rub it in, to make him feel the sting of what he missed. Or maybe it was just the idea of having it all on paper, something tangible that would exist after I'd gone.

It feels a little strange leaving my room without a bag,

without keys. But it's not like I'm going to need them. The place is quiet. I'm ready.

I twist the doorknob quietly. It opens without a rasp, and I send a thank-you to the gods. But I speak too soon, because on my first step into the hallway, there's an almighty creak. I tuck myself back into my room, straining to hear something over my thundering heart. My favorite helper-person, the young one – Blondie, I call her – is on duty, and if she finds me, she'll probably offer to play cards or make me a cup of tea, and then I'll never be able to go through with it.

After a minute, when nothing happens, I step over the creaky board and pick my way along the corridor toward the stairs. I'm in my sleeping-clothes. I've thought this through. If someone finds me out here, I have a great excuse. *I have Alzheimer's. I'm lost. Confused. Take me back to my room. It may or may not happen again.* I am nearly at the stairs when I hear a click.

'I kn-know what you're doing.'

For a moment, I think about thrashing around, acting disoriented. Then I recognize the voice. Young Guy.

When I turn, he is standing there in a T-shirt and undershorts. His bare legs extend from his shorts, long and quite muscular. His left cheek is creased from the pillow, and his hair is mussed.

It takes me a moment to remember what he said. 'You know what I'm doing?' I ask when it returns to me. 'What?'

He takes a few silent steps toward me, and his eyes do a lap of my face. 'Doesn't take a . . . really s-smart person

69

to figure it out,' he says. 'Who wouldn't want to kill them-selves, d-diagnosed with dementia at your age?'

I blink. When he puts it like that, it does seem obvious. Yet Jack has never questioned me about suicide. Neither has Helen. Or Eric. The only one who asked me about it, as a matter of course, was Dr Brain. And only because it was a printed question on his list. Number seven. Or perhaps eight.

'*You* have dementia at my age,' I say. 'Do you want to kill yourself?'

'No.' He doesn't hesitate, even for a second.

'Well, then.' It's strange that I sound – even feel – triumphant. I've proved him wrong. Even though he's right.

'Why *not*?' I ask suddenly.

'I value life,' he says. 'As long as my heart keeps b-b-beating, I want to be here.'

'Even if you're stuck in a wheely-chair and you don't know your own name?' I ask.

'Who s-says I won't know it? Who says I won't be h-happy? Who says *you* won't be?'

I laugh blackly. 'I'll never save another life. I'll never run a marathon or ride a motorcycle. My best jokes are definitely behind me.'

A sudden, muffled snore punches into the silence, and I leap. Young Guy steadies me. I can smell the laundry soap on his T-shirt. It's unnerving, and also . . . exhilar-ating. His clothes are thin and so are mine, and for the second time in a day, I imagine leaning forward and pressing my lips against his mouth.

'Okay, so no m-marathons,' he whispers, letting me go. 'But w-what about the other stuff? Sitting in a garden. Eating eggs on toast. Spending time with loved ones. Doesn't that have value?'

'You should be a motivational speaker.'

'Thanks. But you . . . didn't answer my question.'

'No,' I whisper. 'I don't think that stuff has value. I don't think life is about eggs on toast. Life is about doing something *great*.'

'How do you know . . . something g-great . . . isn't still ahead?'

The question hangs in the air. I contemplate telling him the truth. On one hand, it seems unnecessarily cruel, on another, it might be the only thing that gets him off my back.

'My mom had Alzheimer's,' I say finally. 'And I promise you, there's nothing great ahead.'

As predicted, this silences his eternal optimism. I'm almost disappointed when he doesn't fire back immediately with a retort. He seemed so committed to life. I start toward the stairs.

'What was her name?' he calls after me.

'What?'

'Your m-mom. What was her name?'

The question stops me short. Since I've been diagnosed with Alzheimer's, lots of people have asked me if there is a family history. They're interested and sometimes saddened to hear about my mom. They express sympathy. Some say prayers for me.

Not *once* has anyone asked Mom's name.

71

I half turn back. 'It was . . . Valerie.'

'V-Valerie,' he repeats. As he says it, he nods like he's trying to commit it to memory. It does something to me. The room starts to move, and I realize I'm sinking to the floor.

'No . . .' I whisper when I feel his arms go around me, but the fight seems to have gone out of me. And when he guides me back to my room, I let him. Then I'm in bed and he's tucking blankets up around me and I'm crying, from a place deep within. I never had a good answer to Mom's question. *If I don't remember, will I have been here at all?* But maybe her question was flawed. Maybe it doesn't matter what you remember. Maybe if someone else remembers and speaks your name, you were here.

7

Eve

On our first morning in our new home, I wake early. Clem is beside me, sweaty and warm, and completely dead to the world. She's flat on her back with her arms outstretched ('the crucifix', Richard called it) while drool weeps slowly from her open mouth. Last night, once we'd got through the first twisty, turny hour, she'd been a delight to sleep with – a sweet-smelling deadweight to cocoon around. It was so welcome after four months of sleeping alone. So unbelievably welcome.

I decide to make poached fruit and muesli for breakfast, if only to mask the smell of salami. I gulp down some coffee, then peel my pears and apples, chop my rhubarb, get out my cinnamon and vanilla bean. *It's my first day of work.* Surprisingly, I find that slightly thrilling. During my study at the cookery school, I'd looked forward to this. Not working at a residential care facility, obviously, but cooking for a living. I'd visualized it – the fresh produce I'd procure from markets; the bustling nights in a hot, hectic kitchen; the new twists I'd invent on traditional recipes.

Mother didn't like it when I said things like 'new twists'. *'Why do you have to get all fancy all the time, Evie?'* she'd say. *'A bit of tradition never did anyone any harm!'*

I grew up on meat and three vegetables, but I'm not sure which three, because Mother always cooked them until they were so gray and mushy, they were unrecognizable. Everything was drowned in ketchup and swilled down with soda or, in Dad's case, a pint of Guinness. Condiments were used liberally, so were butter and cream. We lived by Dad's foolproof equation: Salt plus pepper equals flavor.

I still remember the day I tasted my first spice, on a date when I was seventeen. I don't remember the guy's name, but I do remember the warmth that shot into my belly when we wandered into that Brick Lane curry house in London. The scent of turmeric and cumin – so thick, I could taste it. The colors – yellows, reds, and greens – of the food on the table. The burst of fire when I chomped down on a surprise chili, the relief of the coconut rice against the roof of my mouth afterwards. That was the moment I knew cooking was in my future.

Six months later, I packed up and moved to New York to attend the Institute of Culinary Education. It was a lifetime ago now and so much had changed. Perhaps the one thing that hadn't changed was my love of cooking.

Once my fruit is poaching on the stove, I set out some bowls. I find the newspaper outside the door. The old tenants must have forgotten to cancel their subscription. I smile, thinking Clem will like it – a little like being at a hotel – until I see Richard's face on the front page. Actually, the paper is folded in half, so all I see is his chin – that sweet cleft Clem has inherited. The one I used to squash between my thumb and forefinger teasingly . . . I'd know it anywhere. And although after four months, I should be used to seeing Richard's face in the news, I feel the familiar flap of panic. What now?

I scoop up the paper and scan it quickly. I've probably got only another minute or so before Mother calls and tells me what it says anyway. And with the way Mother exaggerates, I'm better to read it direct.

RICHARD BENNETT'S ACCOUNTANT TO PLEAD GUILTY IN SCHEME

This was new. Ever since this whole thing blew up, Richard's longtime tax accountant, David Cohen, had denied knowledge of Richard's scheme. Most people were skeptical, but I'd given him the benefit of the doubt – after all, I'd shared a bed with Richard and had no idea what he was up to. Or did I? I'd been asking myself this lately. Is it possible that, on some level, I did know? Not the details, of course, but that *something* was up? Did I ask enough questions? Or had I been afraid that, if I did ask, I might uncover something I didn't want to know?

The funny thing is; I still haven't cried. I've started to – plenty of times – even set the stage for a proper weeping session, with wine and a warm bath and memories of good times. But the tears just don't come. And before I know it, I am thinking of the bad times, reminding myself of irritating habits, turbulent fights. The way he used to say yes to everything in the moment, and then come up with last-minute excuses when the time came. That, in particular, drove me crazy.

'If I had known you were going to work late,' I used to cry, 'I wouldn't have said we'd both be there! They've probably catered for you!'

'I'd *like* to be there,' he'd reply stiffly, 'but this is business.'

And business, of course, trumped everything.

I finish the article and the surrounding stories. Tales of people who lost money next to pictures of Richard boarding a private jet. Pictures of angry investors. Financial records. In one corner is a tiny studio shot of me. The media favors this photograph – young, doe-eyed, stupid – the kind of woman who doesn't notice that her fraudulent husband is running the biggest Ponzi scheme since Bernie Madoff.

On cue, my phone rings. I shove the newspaper into a drawer where Clem won't see it. 'Hello, Mother.'

I picture her at the hall table in her apartment, twisted around her phone, which, amazingly, still has a cord. 'Have you seen the newspaper?'

'Yes,' I say.

'Are you all right?'

I fall back into a squeaky armchair. 'I'm fine.'

Mother is quiet a moment. 'Good. And was your first night at the apartment . . . tolerable?'

I can tell Mother is thinking of the house Clem and I just vacated – its six bedrooms, its saltwater pool, its 1.5 acres of lush grounds.

'Perfectly tolerable,' I say.

There's a short silence; a sharp inhalation. I brace myself.

'Oh, Evie, it just makes me so angry! You and Clem stuck in that awful place when you two are *innocent* in all this! I swear if I could get my hands on that man I'd—'

I tune out. I can't bear to listen to it all again. While Richard did some terrible things, I still feel surprisingly uncomfortable hearing her slam him, particularly after she'd allowed Richard to move her and Dad over from England and set them up very nicely. I also feel uncomfortable since she spent a decade kissing his ass so wholeheartedly that even Richard felt awkward. (And Richard never felt awkward around adoring women.)

'Thanks, Mother, but we're fine. Really.'

'You're hardly fine, Evie. You've taken a job in a residential care facility! I must admit, I still don't understand why. Even if you didn't have the experience to become a head chef at a restaurant, surely you could . . . I don't know . . . open a little catering business or something?'

I don't bother to point out that in order to start any kind of business, I'd need *money*, something that was in desperately short supply for me right now. Instead I remind her that if we don't want Clem to be moved to Buttwell Elementary we need an address in the area. When I finish talking I notice Clem standing in the doorway of the bedroom, holding her tatty pink bunny by the ears.

'Clem's awake, Mother. I have to go.'

'Hold on a minute,' she says. 'Your father wants to speak to you.'

77

There's a shuffle, and then I hear Dad clear his throat. 'Saw the paper. You hang in there, baby. People will realize that you were dealt a rough card, too. The only one who should be suffering is your low-down scumbag of a husband . . .'

Clem climbs onto my lap, and I smile brightly. She watches me intently, her radar for knowing when people are talking about her father in perfect working order. 'Don't worry about me, Dad,' I say brightly. 'I'm fine.'

'You're a special girl, Evie,' he says softly. 'More special than you know.'

It's a sweet sentiment, but all the same, it makes me cringe. *'It takes a special kind of person to make someone else great,'* Mother said to me in the early days with Richard. *'To lift them up and help them achieve their dreams.'* I wonder what it says about me that the person I was supposed to be 'helping' and 'lifting up' is dead.

As Clem and I arrive at Rosalind House in the morning, Rosie, the night nurse, is scampering down the front steps. Even in an obvious hurry, she grins. 'Sorry,' she pants. 'Gotta flight to catch.'

'Where are you off to?' I ask as she skips past me.

'Jamaica for a week with the girls.' She turns and starts jogging backwards. 'Sorry I won't be around for your first week. Eric should be here any minute, so make yourself at home. Hey – cool dancing last night,' she says to Clem. 'You gotta show me your moves when I get back.'

Clem beams, and Rosie turns and jogs away before she can find out she has a friend for life.

78

Inside, a couple of residents mill about in the parlor, and Clem wastes no time launching into conversation with an old man named Laurie. She tells him about school; her best friend, Legs; the fairy princess party she had for her birthday. I sit beside them.

'Hey! Is someone going to help me out of bed, or am I going to spend the day in my jammies?'

The voice that fills the hallway is brittle and irritated. 'That's Bert,' Laurie explains. 'He needs a little push to get him on his feet. His walker is beside the bed. Trish or Carole usually do it, but I think they're helping other residents right now.'

I nod, trying not to let my uncertainty show. 'Well . . . I suppose I could do it.'

'Second door on the left,' he says helpfully.

I head in the direction the man pointed, and peek around the corner. Thankfully, Bert greets me with an expression much warmer than his voice. 'Oh, it's you. Just a little push, then, girlie. And don't go getting any ideas just because I'm a good-looking son of a gun. I'm a married man.'

He's either joking or senile, because Eric told me the only married couple at Rosalind House was the Southern couple, Clara and Laurie. Either way, I decide to leave the 'married' comment alone. 'You're safe with me,' I say, shoving him to his feet. 'I'm off men. Even good-looking ones.'

'Glad to hear it. Now, out with you. I have to get dressed.'

Out in the corridor, I hesitate. Are any other residents stuck in bed? Am I supposed to be tapping on all the doors, opening blinds, and wishing all a good morning? There's still no sign of Eric, so I have to improvise. The door next to Bert's is still closed, so I tap lightly. When there's no answer, I open the door. 'Good morning. It's Eve, the . . . cook. Do you need any—? Oh!'

I jump back when I see the Southern woman – Clara? – standing inside, in front of a mirror, naked from the waist up. I pull the door closed again, leaving it only slightly ajar. 'I'm so sorry,' I say into the crack, and at the same time, I hear keys rattling in the front door.

I race to the foyer.

'Sorry I'm late,' Eric says. 'How's it been going?'

'Actually,' I say, 'Bert needed help getting out of bed, and afterwards, I thought I'd check on the others. But then I walked in on one of the ladies half-dressed. I did knock, but I suppose she didn't hear.'

Eric chuckles. 'First of all, breathe. And try not to look so worried. You're probably more embarrassed than she is.' I wonder how Eric figures this, since I didn't mention which resident I walked in on. 'And it's my fault, really, for being late,' he continues, looking at his watch. 'Speaking of which, I don't mean to drop you in the deep end, but I only have about an hour until my first appointment. How about we get started?'

Eric and I go over mealtimes, appropriate food, and location of utensils, but that takes less than ten minutes. For the rest of the hour, Eric details the cleaning instructions. He has a nervous habit, I notice, of glancing around every few seconds, which has the unfortunate side effect of making him appear shifty. Worse, on a couple of occasions, I noticed his gaze lingering near my chest. I give him the benefit of the doubt and assume it's an accident.

He shows me my 'office', which is also the room where the mops and buckets are kept, and he reminds me to wear a mask and gloves while dealing with urine or feces. When he sees my face, he reminds me that the cleaning job will be just for a little while, but when I ask if he's had any applications yet, he's swift to move onto another topic. I'm introduced to twelve residents. Luke and Anna, the young ones. Clara and Laurie, the Southern couple. Bert who still talks to his wife, even though she is fifty years dead. May, ninety-nine years old. Gwen. A handful of others. I'm also introduced to the care manager, Trish, a brisk, forthright woman in her early forties who would be pretty if she weren't so alarmingly thin, and Carole, her assistant, a blond, thick-waisted woman in her fifties with a droning, adenoidal voice.

We do a lap of the grounds again, and when we're done, Eric glances at his watch and assures me that everything we haven't covered is outlined in the 150-page manual. Five minutes later, Eric is back in his office and I'm ready to cry. But the residents are hungry. So I have to do what I do best.

I put out cereal, fruit, and orange juice, then I scramble some eggs and smoked trout. I make a side of spinach and mushrooms, but when it comes time to garnish, I can't find a single herb. I make a mental note to talk to Angus about starting a vegetable and herb garden; then I head out to the dining room.

The room is surprisingly loud, and I'm pleased to see they're eating and, by the look of it, enjoying the meal. Even though she's already eaten, Clem is sitting at the head of the table like the lady of the house. I try to remove her, but when I do, the residents give me such dirty looks, I have no choice but to back away.

While they eat, I take a plate into Eric's office. 'Am I interrupting?'

'Not at all. What's up?' Eric swivels around, and his eyes widen in faux alarm. 'You're not quitting, are you?'

'No.' I laugh. 'I just brought you some breakfast.'

Eric's face is a blend of surprise and delight as I place it on the desk in front of him. 'For me?'

I smile. 'Usually I use fresh parsley, but I couldn't find any.'

'Smells great.' He waggles his eyebrows, which is vaguely disconcerting. 'Are you joining me?'

'I can't, I'm afraid. I have to get Clem to school.'

He pouts, picking up his knife and fork. 'Oh, but before you go, there's something I forgot to mention. Each night before bed, Luke's and Anna's doors need to be locked. Rosie usually does it, but she's on vacation this week. To-night there's an agency nurse on duty, so you'll need to let her know. It's all spelled out in the manual, but an extra reminder doesn't hurt. Usually I'm gone by the time they clock on, so that will be up to you.' Eric pushes a mound of eggs onto his fork and buries it in his mouth.

'Oh,' I say. 'Oh-kay.'

'They get night-restlessness,' he explains, his mouth still half-full. 'It's common for people with dementia to be wakeful at night and go wandering. It's not safe for them to be roaming the halls of this house. They could hurt themselves.'

'But . . . isn't it dangerous to lock them in? What if there's a fire?'

Eric loads up his fork again. 'Our fire safety plan includes evacuating Luke and Anna.'

'I see.'

We're silent for a moment or two, then Eric puts down his cutlery. 'The truth is, a few months back, Anna went to the top floor of the house and jumped off the roof.'

Without intending to, I gasp. 'You mean . . . a . . . ?'

'Suicide attempt.' Eric nods. 'Afterwards, I met with Anna's brother, and we agreed that locking the doors was the best way to keep her safe. And we didn't want to take any chances with Luke.'

I swallow, wetting my inexplicably dry throat. 'Is that why she's in a wheelchair? Because she . . . jumped off the roof?'

'Yes. It was a big fall. It's amazing she survived it.'

'Yes,' I say. 'Amazing.'

I'm trying to take this all in when I notice the time blinking at the bottom corner of Eric's computer. 'Shoot! I have to get Clem to school.'

'Go ahead,' he says. 'But it goes without saying that what we've discussed is confidential, Eve.'

'Yes,' I say. 'Of course.'

'And thanks for the eggs.' Just like that, his gormless smile is back. 'They really are delicious.'

'Sure,' I say. 'I've got a plate for Angus, too. Is he in the garden?'

'I think he's somewhere about.' Eric looks at his breakfast. 'Though . . . I'm not sure we need to be feeding the gardener breakfast! We're not running a soup kitchen, after all.'

I think of the mound of leftover eggs I have already cooked. 'Oh. Right. I won't bother, then.'

Back in the kitchen, I stack the dishwasher and wipe down the kitchen bench. Above the sink is a sash window with a view to the garden bed, where Angus kneels, weeding. I glance at the eggs.

'Clem?' I call down the hall. 'Can you come here for a sec?'

I pop a couple of slices of bread under the grill and flick on the stove to heat up the eggs.

Thirty seconds later, her head peeks around the corner. 'My name's not Clem, it's Sophie-Anne.'

'Sophie-Anne?' I lower my voice to a whisper. 'I'm making Angus a breakfast sandwich. Would you do me a favor and run it out to him?'

8

Clem is not only a wonderful dancer, but she also has a beautiful, silvery voice. As we walk to school in the perfect fall sunshine, she sings like a cardinal. Her tune begins with words from a pop song but quickly drifts to her own made-up lyrics. I hear the words 'first day' and 'homework' and 'best friend'. It's lovely, but as it's only a two-minute walk to school from Rosalind House, I need the time to fill her in on a few things.

'Clem?'

She pauses, mid-song. 'Yes?'

'I don't think I explained to you what I'm doing at Rosalind House.' Her frown reminds me of Richard's. Gentle, thoughtful, soft. If anything, it makes her more beautiful. 'You see . . . it's a residential care facility.'

She looks only faintly interested. 'What's a resi—?'

'A residential care facility? It's a place for people who need help looking after themselves.'

Clem blinks. 'Do *we* need help looking after ourselves?'

'No.' I chuckle. 'Not us. I'm going to help look after the people who live there. Cook their meals, do the laundry and clean up after them.'

The crease between Clem's eyebrows deepens – a ravine between two plump mounds of forehead. 'Like Valentina?'

'Well, yes. A bit like Valentina.' Clem continues to frown, and I run a finger over the ridges of her braid. 'What do you think about that?'

She keeps her eyes ahead. 'I don't know.'

'Do you want to ask me anything?'

She shrugs. 'Are we . . . poor?'

'No. We're definitely not poor.'

'Then—?'

'Clem! Clemmy Clemmy Bo-Bemmy Banana Fanna Bo-Banna!' Allegra comes bounding up to Clem.

'Legs!' Clem squeals. 'Allegra Egra Bo-Begra, Banana Fanna Bo-Banna.'

Contrary to what the name suggests, Legs is almost a full head shorter than Clem. Her hair is mousy and unremarkable, and her cheeks are chubby. But she has enormous hazel eyes and an earnestness that makes her impossible not to adore.

'First day,' Legs says. 'I hope we can sit next to each other.'

'If you *are* sitting next to each other, make sure you listen to the teacher and don't just talk the whole time,' Jazz says, appearing behind Legs.

I meet Jazz's eye, and she bumps her shoulder against mine in a friendly-ish way. It's not the best welcome I could have hoped for, but considering that most of the school moms I passed on the walk here completely blanked me, I'm grateful.

'How are you holding up?' Jazz asks dutifully. One thing

to be said for Jazz is that she fulfills her duties. She came to Richard's funeral but sat at the back. She left frozen meals from Houlihan's (the overpriced, organic deli – the only place for which I make an exception to the 'no frozen meals' policy) on my doorstep but didn't come inside. She'd invited Clem for a playdate a couple of times but declined when I'd asked if Legs wanted to come to our place.

'Not bad,' I say. 'Surviving.'

She appraises me discreetly from head to toe – my ponytail, ballet flats, and khakis – then gives me a strained smile. Unlike me, Jazz looks the part of a school mom with her highlighted hair, skinny jeans, and brown leather satchel, probably Prada or Ferragamo. Clem and Legs start toward the classroom, and we follow side by side. 'How is it,' she asks, 'working at the . . . ?'

'Residential care facility?'

'Yes,' she says. 'Yes, that's right.'

I shrug. 'Well, today's my first day, so . . .'

She smiles, and with that, conversation is exhausted. A few months ago, we'd have been tripping over our tongues to get a word in, then probably adjourning to the coffee shop afterwards to keep talking. Now, as we stare ahead at the children, I can't think of a single thing to say.

'My name's not Clem,' I hear Clem whisper to Legs. 'It's Sophie-Anne.'

Legs accepts this readily. 'Okay. And I'm Lucy.'

As we walk, Jazz's eyes dart around, probably scanning the playground to see who else is here. Most moms gather in blond clusters looking inward, apart from one or two outliers, who stand alone by their cars. It's funny to think that now *I'm* one of those outliers. Arguably the biggest one.

By the classroom door, I see the butter-blond head of Andrea Heathmont in the center of a knot of women. I'd recognize her back anywhere – her cream silk shirt, her wide bottom and low heels. The last time I saw Andrea, she was on my doorstep, hand-delivering a signed copy of the new Harry Walker cookbook. Now, as her head snaps around, her face is virtually unrecognizable. Her eyes are upturned crescents, her mouth a thin line. Her hands quiver as they are prone to do in the face of too much gossip and excitement. It's hard to believe that only last summer Richard and Andrea's husband, James, golfed together in the Hamptons.

'You must be Clementine's mother. I'm Miss Weber.' A smiling woman in an orange apron steps into my line of sight. 'I'm so sorry about your loss,' she says, lowering her voice.

'Thank you.' I tear my eyes away from Andrea and force a smile. 'That's very kind.'

'I'll be keeping a special eye on Clementine, and if there's anything you'd like to discuss at any time, please let me know.'

'Thank you,' I say.

'And you're Allegra's mother,' she says, moving on to Jazz. 'I did some substitute teaching in the first grade last year, so I met both Clem and Legs. Conjoined twins, I called them. I think we'll have a lot of fun this year.' She smiles over my shoulder to greet the next mother, pauses, then looks back at me. 'Oh, Mrs Bennett?'

'Please, call me Eve.'

'Eve. I believe you've recently moved. When you have a chance, could you fill out a change-of-address form for me and hand it in to the office? There are some forms in the green pocket on the door.'

'Yes,' I say. My voice echoes into the teeming hallway. 'Yes, of course.'

Jazz and I stand for a few minutes while Clem and Legs run around. Andrea actively avoids my gaze, as do most of the other moms.

'Can Legs come over after school, Mom?' Clem asks, crashing into my legs.

'Not today, Legs,' Jazz says quickly.

'Awww,' the girls say in unison.

I was going to say no, anyway, but the swiftness of Jazz's decline is a punch to the stomach.

Across the room, Andrea whispers something to Romy Fisher, and they both look over at me. I feel Jazz's eyes.

'What?' I ask.

'I just . . . I don't know how you can do this. It must be awful, everyone knowing your business. Have you thought about . . .' Her eyes point overhead as she tries to think. '. . . I don't know . . . leaving town or something?' A flush rises on Jazz's cheeks, and I know she feels like a traitor for suggesting it. 'I mean, I'd miss you, but . . . anything would have to be better than this. I don't know how you can do it, day after day.'

I suspect Jazz is actually wondering how *she* can do it; keep up the pretense of a friendship with a social pariah without becoming one herself. But I don't call her on it.

'People aren't falling over themselves to give Richard Bennett's widow a job, Jazz,' I say. 'Besides, Mother and Dad are around the corner, and I'm going to be relying on them a lot more now that I'm a . . .' I drift off, strangely unable to say 'single mother'. Instead I look at Clem and Legs, who have formed a human rope on the floor, hugging and laughing. 'Anyway, how could I break up the BFFs? It'd be the biggest split since Paris Hilton and Nicole Ritchie!'

Jazz smiles reluctantly. And a few seconds later, I feel her arm around my shoulder. It's brazen in a classroom full of cold stares. The small gesture sends tears rocketing to my eyes.

'You're very hard not to love, you know that, Evie?'

She says it gruffly, and I smile, because from Jazz, it's the sincerest compliment I could have asked for. Also, because I remember Richard saying something very similar to me once.

I was making guacamole when I met Richard. As part of our training at the culinary school, we were required to get some practical experience, and I'd managed to land a gig on James Mendoza's gourmet taco truck – The Mexican – on the corner of Wall and New Street. The taco truck was decent pay, and the upside was that unlike in a restaurant, we were outside, amid the bustle of the city. That day, the sky was a rich cobalt blue, and the air that blew in the serving window was warm and sweet. Full of promise.

'I'll . . . um, take a taco,' I heard a man say to Carlos. Carlos was a wonderful chef, but he should never have

90

been allowed in front of customers. If they didn't know exactly what they wanted, they didn't get served.

'Uh . . .' the man stammered when the silence continued. 'Just the taco, please.'

Carlos sighed loudly. He pointed to the board where the menu was listed then nodded at the next person in line. I wiped my hands on my apron. Part of my role, I'd quickly realized, was to smooth things over with Carlos's disgruntled customers. He needed my help fairly frequently.

'What kind of taco would you like?' I asked. 'There's beer-battered mahimahi, shrimp, lobster, turkey . . .'

I looked down at the man, who was our typical Wall Street guy – expensive suit, gold watch, shiny shoes. His hair was thick and black, his eyes chocolate brown. His adorably perplexed expression gave away the fact that he wasn't a regular at the food truck.

'My favorite is the mahimahi,' I said finally. 'We make it with fresh lime and cumin – it's a bestseller, I think you'll like it.' I arranged the fish on a flour tortilla and topped it with slaw and a dollop of Mexican *crema*. Then I rolled it up and handed it to him. 'Here you go.'

I'll never forget the way he looked at me – as though I were the most unexpected treasure, a nearly extinct animal he'd stumbled across in the wild. Beside me, oblivious or uninterested, Carlos grunted at the next person who dared not to know exactly what he wanted.

'Would you like to have dinner with me tonight?' he asked.

I laughed, surprised. Behind him, someone jostled him

and someone else yelled, 'Keep it moving, man!' But he didn't budge.

'I insist,' he said. 'A thank-you for this . . . this wonderful taco. I'm Richard, by the way.'

'Eve,' I said.

It wasn't the first time a customer had invited me to dinner. It was, however, the first time I'd been tempted to accept. Perhaps it was the fact that, unlike most of the Wall Street stockbrokers we served, he didn't seem entirely assured of my response? On the contrary, he seemed . . . nervous. It was endearing.

'Eve, I need guacamole,' Carlos yelled.

'I'll pick you up,' the man – Richard – said, moving in closer. His face, I noticed, was full of surprises, from his wide-set eyes to his cleft chin. He stood like a rock in a stream while customers flowed on either side of him. 'Around seven. Anywhere you want to go.'

Carlos thumped around, making his impatience known. '*Guacamole!*'

Richard's gaze pierced me, pinning me in place even as Carlos's thick arm reached around me for the guacamole. Then Richard closed his eyes, pressed his palms together in faux prayer.

'Yes,' I said, laughing. 'Yes, okay. Fine. Tonight.' I gave him my phone number and hurried back to the guacamole.

'Guess he's pretty convincing,' Carlos muttered when Richard was gone.

I wish I'd known how right Carlos was.

*

92

I am just inside the gates of Rosalind House when I hear the bushes rustle behind me.

'Hi,' I say, when Angus emerges.

'Hey.' He drops his secateurs into a bucket and dips to snatch up a larger pair of garden shears. 'Thanks for the sandwich,' he mutters, then turns his back and starts chopping.

'You're welcome,' I say. Angus's demeanor is barely civil, but I choose to be heartened by the fact he is talking to me. 'Actually, I'm glad I ran into you. I'd like to talk to you about starting a vegetable and herb garden.'

'A vegetable and herb garden.' He pauses, the shears still in hand. 'I guess we could do that.' He turns to look at me. 'How big do you need it?'

'Well, I'd like to plant carrots and potatoes. Plus herbs.'

I may be imagining it, but Angus seems slightly more upbeat. 'You'll want something with shade then.' He wipes his forehead with the back of his arm. 'There's a spot in the yard that might work, but you'd need a canopy. One that can be retracted—'

'You can buy those at Garden City,' I say, a little too enthusiastically. 'I used to have one above my vegetable garden at my old place.'

He gives me a long, cool look. 'I was going to say I'd build you one. I doubt Eric has money for a Garden City canopy in the budget.'

'No, of course not. I didn't think—'

Angus shakes his head. 'No. You wouldn't.'

'What does that mean?'

93

'Nothing.' He lifts the shears and starts hacking at the bush with sharp, aggressive strokes.

I stare at his back. 'Is there something you want to say to me, Angus?'

He turns around. 'You probably think you and your daughter got a rough deal, don't you? You lost your big house. Your money. You had to get a job in a residential care facility and have your canopies built instead of bought—'

I open my mouth.

'My sister and her husband lost everything because of your husband. Not just money but —' His throat works. '— they were in the middle of doing IVF. Kelly's forty-one. Now they can't afford to do it anymore, so she'll probably never have kids.'

I blink back tears at the unexpected outburst and Angus resumes hacking at the bush. I stay quiet. At least now I know why Angus has been so cold with me. His sister is one of thousands of people harmed by my husband. And, by extension, harmed by me. 'I'm sorry,' I say. 'But for the record, I don't think I got a rough deal. I got off lightly. I can live with losing my money and my house. I'll get used to being a social outcast, to working menial jobs and having no friends. I'd take all of it, and more, if it meant I could give my daughter back her father. So, say what you want about me, but don't lump my daughter into the same category. My daughter got one hell of a rough deal. And she is as innocent as your poor sister.'

With that, I spin on my heel and march toward the

house. As I walk, I think I hear Angus call my name, but I just keep walking.

I find a cart in the housekeeping closet and drive it down the corridor. I shouldn't have said that to Angus, but Clem is my Achilles heel. She seems like she's okay, but every now and then, I get a glimpse of her grief, and it worries me. Her father was her hero. But what will happen when she finds out he wasn't a hero at all?

Eric's instructions were that each room and bathroom be given a light 'going-over' each day. Empty, clean, and reline wastebaskets. Strip beds on Thursdays and make them on other days. Inner windows should be done weekly – Mondays are best because of grubby fingers from grandchildren on Sundays, when most residents have visitors. It's not exactly what I envisioned when I applied for a cook position, but if it keeps Clem out of Butt Road, I can do it for a while.

When I peek into Anna's room, I see Clara in the armchair by the window.

'Oh,' I say. 'I thought this was Anna's room.'

'It is,' Clara says, nodding toward the bed where Anna is lying. 'Anna, honey, Eve's just here to make the beds and clean up a bit.'

'Oh,' Anna says. 'Okay.'

I open the door wide and push my cart inside. The room is lovely, small but bright, furnished with just a bed, a couple of armchairs, and a dresser. It reminds me of a hotel room. What is *unlike* a hotel, though, is that everything is labeled – each drawer has a sign labeled UNDERWEAR, BRAS,

95

T-SHIRTS, PAJAMAS. The doors to the closet, the bathroom, and the hallway are labeled, too. It stuns me. Really? Does Anna really not know which door goes where?

'That . . . thin-jacket suits you,' Anna says to Clara. 'It's the exact blue of your eyes.'

'Thanks, honey,' Clara says. 'Blue's my favorite.'

I take a hand cloth and steal a glance at Clara. Her eyes *are* a striking blue, almost violet. The exact blue of her cardigan. I slide the cloth back and forth along the windowsill. It's already pretty clean, and all I'm doing is dragging the little dust that is there back and forth.

Behind me, pages of a notebook ruffle.

'Eve's the new cook,' Clara says to Anna. 'Started this morning.'

I look over my shoulder in time to see Anna visibly relax. '*That's* why you're not in my book.'

I glace at the spiral notebook in her lap. Three rows of Polaroid photos line the double page. I recognize Eric, and a bunch of the residents. A few of the people I don't recognize, perhaps family members? Underscoring each photo is a name in a thick black pen, as well as a one-word explanation – *Doctor. Resident. Friend.* Farther below are a few other notes, scrawled in blue biro.

Anna looks at me. 'But if you're the new cook, shouldn't you be cooking?'

'You would think so, wouldn't you?' I smile.

Anna smiles back and I get a strange feeling that somehow, she feels my pain. And for the first time, it occurs to me that perhaps I could just ask Anna what she meant when she said 'Help me' the other day. It's a long shot, of course, but worth a try.

'Anna, can I ask you something?' I say.

She looks surprised. 'Sure.'

I squat to rinse out my cloth in the bucket. 'The other day, when I was here for my interview, you asked me for help. We were out in the garden. Do you remember that?'

She frowns. 'No. I'm sorry.'

'I was handing you your scarf,' I persisted, 'and you grabbed my hands and said "Help me."'

There's a flicker on her face, and I allow myself to hope. 'Maybe I needed help registering for the New York marathon? I've been meaning to tick that off my bucket list.'

She holds my gaze for a moment, deadpan, then chuckles. A laugh bursts out of me. And something inside me, something that was tightly clenched, unspools. I don't know what I expected. That Anna would be incapable of humor? That she wouldn't be a real person? Yes, that's exactly what I'd thought. And after all the trouble I go to, to make sure Clem treats people with an open mind, I should have known better.

'Do we know each other?' Anna asks suddenly.

My smile fades away.

'You know, you do look familiar, honey,' Clara says.

I can't believe my bad luck. A person with Alzheimer's recognizes me.

'You probably recognize me from the newspaper,' I admit.

'The newspaper?' Clara asks. 'Are you famous, Eve?'

97

'Infamous, perhaps. My husband was Richard Bennett. You've probably heard of him.'

'Richard Bennett was your husband?' Clara gasps. 'Oh, you poor, poor dear.'

'Richard was running an illegal Ponzi scheme,' I explain to Anna. 'Because of him, lots of people lost a lot of money. And we, of course, lost our money. That's why I'm working here.'

'That sucks,' Anna says.

'Yes, it does, rather.' I laugh.

Anna's face becomes thoughtful. Her eyes are on her lap, her brow is gathered, and her lips work around silent words – like a child reading from a book.

Suddenly she looks up. 'Did I see you,' she says, 'in the . . . the garden?'

'Yes,' I say. 'That's when you asked me for help.'

'And . . . *he* . . . was there?'

A feeling of dread creeps in. 'Who?'

'*Him*,' she says. Her forehead creases. Her eyes dart back and forth, searching.

'Do you mean Luke, honey?' Clara asks.

I start to shake my head, but Anna's eyes go round like she's seen a ghost. 'Yes. Luke.'

This isn't what I expected.

Anna's gaze locks on mine. 'Please. You have to help me.'

'Is Luke doing something to you, Anna?' I ask.

'What?' She shakes her head. 'No!'

'But you said you needed help?'

'Just give her a minute,' Clara says gently. 'Too much talkin' makes it hard for her to think.'

So I wait, willing Anna to keep hold of whatever invisible thread was keeping her with us. Her hands shuffle in her lap, folding and unfolding. I try to imagine what it must be like, not being able to access the words and memories you need to say what you think. I wonder, just for a second, if that would make you want to kill yourself.

Finally Anna leans forward and tugs the sleeve of Clara's cardigan. 'I like that thin-jacket on you,' she says. 'It's the exact blue of your eyes.'

I finish wiping the mantelpiece, then move on to the bathroom. From what I've seen, there are still some lights on in Anna. As I finish making up her room, I can't help but wonder which lights are on, which are blinking, and which ones are completely out.

9

Clementine

Before Daddy died, my biggest wish was for a baby brother called Phil. He'd have chubby fingers and a toothy smile and legs that kicked when he was happy. I used to imagine the way my friends would gather around his stroller for a peek, and I would tell them importantly, *Move back! Phil is sleeping.* I would be the expert on Phil. When he cried, Mom would say to me, *Clem, can you tickle his toes for me?* and I would, and Phil would giggle. When we went to the mall, I would push his stroller so Mom could do the grocery shopping. And I would play *peekaboo!* with him when he got restless. I had it all worked out. I used to think about Phil all the time. I still do, sometimes. But he's not my biggest wish anymore. My biggest wish is that Daddy was still alive.

Miss Weber stands at the front of the classroom in a red dress with white spots and blue shoes with thick soles, called wedges. 'All right, class,' she says, 'I'd like everyone to sit in a circle on the mat. Now, since it's no one's birthday today . . . Clementine, would you like to sit in the birthday chair?'

The birthday chair is gold with red rubies all over it, like a throne for a princess. *Of course* I want to sit in it. Legs sits beside me on the floor and smiles because she is happy for me. Miranda doesn't smile. I think she wishes she was sitting on the birthday chair instead of me.

'Now, I want to hear a little about your summers,' Miss Weber says. 'Why don't we go around the circle and each of you can tell me what you got up to. Let's start with you, Harry,' she says. 'What did you do this summer?'

I like Harry. He has curly hair that is mostly brown but in the sunshine it turns gold and shiny like a coin. Usually he is really smiley, but today, he looks at his shoes. 'I visited my dad in Orlando,' he says.

'Wow, Florida.' Miss Weber smiles. 'Were you on vacation, Harry?'

'No,' he mutters. 'My dad lives there.'

Harry's daddy met a new mommy. They live in Florida and she has a baby in her belly and Harry says they kiss all the time and it's really gross. But Miranda must not know this, because she frowns and says, 'You mean . . . your mom and dad—'

'Did you go to Disney World, Harry?' I ask quickly, because Miranda can be a bit tricky sometimes. That's what Mom calls it, being 'tricky'. Being tricky is when you can make people feel bad without saying anything really mean. Miranda is good at being tricky.

Harry looks at me, and he smiles a little. 'Yep. All four parks. It was awesome.'

101

It's Miranda's turn next, and she tells the class that this summer she got a real-life pony called Farts. Everyone giggles, even Miss Weber. Then it's my turn.

'Would you like to tell us about your summer, Clementine?' Miss Weber pats me on the head, and her voice gets a little bit softer than before. 'If you don't want to—'

'I *do* want to,' I say. 'It was very busy. I moved to a new house and I went to five birthday parties and one was a princess party and I wore real high heels. Well, they were plastic, but still real. Also, my daddy went to Heaven. I wrote him a poem.' I unfold the paper from my pocket, then look at Miss Weber. 'Would you like me to read it for you?'

Miss Weber smiles, but it is a sad smile. 'We'd love to hear it, wouldn't we, class?'

'Okay,' I say, and put on my good reading voice:

Daddy, I miss you every day.
I miss the way we used to play.
You were the best dad in the world.
And I was such a lucky girl.
I miss how you always made me laugh,
When you did funny voices with my toy giraffe,
Now you're gone I want to cry.
And that is not even a lie.
Why did you have to die when I was seven?
I wish you could come back to me from Heaven.

When I look up, Miss Weber is wiping something from her eye. 'That was lovely, Clementine.'

102

I smile. 'Mom helped me with the rhyming parts.'

Freya puts up her hand. 'My gramma is in Heaven.'

'Mine, too,' says Harry.

'Heaven is in the clouds,' Miranda says.

'Actually,' I say, 'Heaven is in the ground. I know because I saw some men put Daddy there.'

Miranda doesn't say anything. I feel pleased that I told her something she didn't know.

'Heaven isn't like going to the Hamptons,' I continue. 'Because you can't come back after the weekend. It's a long way away, but people in Heaven can still see us and hear us.'

Everyone listens.

'In Heaven you never get sick. And you are never by yourself, because lots of people are there . . .'

I don't tell the class that I really don't understand Heaven. That it makes no sense because it would be really hard to hear and see someone from under the ground, even if you have really good ears and eyes. And that there might be a lot of people there, but not the ones you really love. I don't tell them this, because I just want to keep talking and feeling important. It's better than thinking about Daddy and feeling bad.

When Legs giggles, I giggle, too. I can't help it. As soon as I hear her giggle, even before I know why she is giggling, I'm just giggling back. Sometimes we giggle so much that by the time we stop and I ask her why she was giggling, she's forgotten. But when Miranda giggles, I don't giggle back. When Miranda giggles, I get a funny feeling in my belly.

Today Legs and I are skipping with ropes and Miranda is in a huddle in the playground with Freya and Audrey. They look over at us. 'Clemmy! Can you come here for a minute?'

I stop skipping, but Legs keeps jumping because she was trying to get to twenty without tripping.

'Come *on!*' Miranda giggles. 'We don't have all day!'

'Okay.' Legs finishes skipping and we walk over to Miranda's huddle. 'What?'

'Is Heaven *really* in the ground?' Miranda asks.

'Yes,' I say.

'But . . . worms are in the ground.' Miranda smiles. 'Does that mean that worms are eating your daddy?' She looks at Freya and they both snicker.

'No,' I say, but I hadn't thought of that. Worms *are* in the ground.

'Why not?' she says, all innocent. 'If worms are in the ground?'

'Because he's inside a box.' It only comes to me at that very moment, but as soon as I say it, I know I'm right.

Miranda looks at Freya. She's not smiling now. 'How did he die, anyway?'

Everyone looks at me, even Legs. I don't know what to say. Every time I ask someone, they tell me something different. Mom says it was an accident. Nana says Daddy had a sick head. The man who talked at Daddy's funeral said Jesus took him somewhere. I don't think anyone knows what happened to Daddy. Except that he went to Heaven, which is in the ground.

'He was old,' Legs says when I don't say anything. 'And sick.'

Sometimes I really love Legs.

And Miranda says, 'That's not what my mom said.'

I frown. 'What did your mom say?'

Everyone looks at Miranda. She takes a long time to answer. I want to grab her face and make her answer right away.

'She said he died because that bastard was too scared to face the music.'

Everyone goes really quiet. I don't know what that means, but I do know that 'bastard' isn't a nice word. Also, I know it's not true. Daddy wasn't even scared of going into the basement at night or of Maleficent when she turned into the giant snake in *Sleeping Beauty*. He would never be scared of music.

'What music?' Legs asks.

'Don't know,' Miranda admits. 'Probably some really scary music.'

The bell rings and Miss Weber tells us to line up in two straight lines. Miranda runs to the front and seems to forget all about the music and how Daddy died, but I keep thinking about worms and Heaven and what was so scary about that music.

10

When I get out of class, Mom is waiting. She's wearing a white shirt and jeans and flat shoes and she's standing by herself instead of with the other moms. I remember how, before, Mom used to wear earrings and a skirt and shoes like Miss Weber's. And she stood in the center of the group of moms.

I wave at her, and she pulls a gingerbread man out of her purse and puts it up to her face so it sounds like it can talk.

'Hello,' it says. 'I'm First-Day Fergus. Please don't eat me!'

'Of course I won't eat you, Fergus,' I say – then I bite his head off. Mom and I giggle.

Usually after school, I stay and play for a while so Mom can chat to Legs's mom, but today we leave right away. As we walk, I ask, 'Was Daddy scared of music?'

'No,' Mom says slowly. 'Why?'

'No reason,' I say, feeling relieved. Then I ask, 'Are the worms eating Daddy?'

Mom stops walking. 'What?'

'Miranda says if you're in the ground, worms eat you.'

Mom says something quietly that sounds like *cheeses*. Then she says, 'Daddy's in Heaven, remember?' She gives me a little sideways cuddle. 'I'm sure he's watching over us.'

I hate it when people say this. I don't want Daddy watching over me. I want Daddy *here*. So he can walk me to school tomorrow and do the funny voices of the witches when he reads *Witches Wear Britches* to me before bed.

'How did he die?' I ask.

Mom looks at me. 'We've talked about this, Clem. It was . . . an accident.'

'Was Daddy a . . . *bastard*?'

Mom doesn't say anything for a while. And then, 'Did Miranda say that, too?'

'Yes.'

Mom squats down. 'People might say things about Daddy, but they don't really know what they're talking about. Who knows Daddy the best in the world?'

'We do,' I say.

'That's right.' She smiles a little. 'Anyway, did Miranda even *meet* Daddy?'

'Once. At my fairy princess party.'

'Just that once?' Mom says. 'Well, what would she know?'

'Yeah,' I say, smiling. 'What would she know?'

Mom winks. Then she stands and we start walking and I don't worry anymore, because I know that Daddy wasn't scared of any music, and Miranda doesn't know what she's talking about.

*

107

I play outside for a while before Mom calls me for dinner. By the time I've washed my hands and got to the dining room, there's only one seat left, next to a bald man. I wriggle onto it.

'Hey!'

I look up. He's frowning.

'That's Myrna's seat.'

'Oh.' I slip off the seat quickly. The bald man is very cranky. 'Sorry.'

Another lady puts her arm around me. She's soft and has yellow hair and smells of flowers. 'Why don't you sit here, darlin', right by me?'

I like this lady. She has a nice smile and a funny voice, slow and long, like the people in the *The Princess and the Frog*. I sit beside her.

'Now, let me see,' she says. 'You must be about . . . six?'

'I'm seven,' I say. I do not look six.

'Ah, I apologize. I have a great-granddaughter who is six. Or' – she frowns – 'maybe she's seven? With twenty-seven great-grandchildren, it's hard to remember them all.'

I agree that does sound like a lot to remember.

'I'm Clara,' the lady says. 'This is my husband, Laurie.'

'I'm Clementine,' I say, forgetting to change it. Sometimes I like to pretend I have a different name. I don't know why, it just makes me feel good to pretend.

Mom serves fettuccini with bacon, cherry tomatoes, and spinach. When she comes to our table, I sink in my seat because I'm supposed to eat dinner in the kitchen, but Mom just winks at me. She must be feeling happy today.

'My daddy loved this pasta,' I tell Clara. 'It was his

108

favorite. We used to pretend it was Rapunzel's hair. Daddy would say "Rapunzel! Let down your hair." And I would hold the fork above his mouth and unwrap the pasta straight into his mouth.'

'It sounds like he was a good daddy,' Clara says.

'He was.'

'How was school?' she asks.

'Okay. I got to see Legs. My best friend. Allegra is her name, but everyone calls her Legs.'

'Well, these are my friends,' Clara says. She points her fork at some of the others at the table. 'May and Gwen and Bert.'

Bert is the bald one that kicked me out of his friend's seat. I notice that no one has sat in it yet.

'I'm not sure your friend is coming,' I tell him. 'I can ask my mom to keep something hot for her, if you like.'

The man looks straight ahead as if he didn't hear me. I know old people can't hear very well, so I say it again.

'Thank you very much, young lady,' he says, 'I heard you the first time.'

'Then why didn't you say so?' I ask.

Clara says: 'I hope you're going to do some more Irish dancing for us tonight, Clementine. We really enjoyed it, didn't we, everyone?'

Everyone nods and smiles and says yes, they enjoyed it. Not Bert. He just stares at the spot he saved for his friend. Like he can't believe she didn't show up.

'Maybe she's not feeling well?' I suggest.

Bert keeps looking at the chair. 'I don't think it's that.'

'Then why didn't she come to dinner?'

Bert looks at me for a long time without saying anything. Sometimes grown-ups just need a little longer than kids to speak. Their brains are a bit slower, I think. Finally, he says, 'She did.'

'She *did*?' I say, astonished. 'I didn't see her.'

'That doesn't mean she wasn't here.'

People are getting up now, ready to go to the front room. I get off my seat and climb onto the empty seat next to Bert. But he just stands up, too.

'Wait!'

Bert stops. He's frowning, but not like he's mad. More like he's tired. 'Yes?'

'Is your friend invisible?'

He smiles even though he looks like he doesn't want to. He looks different when he smiles. He looks nice.

'She's invisible to most people,' he says. 'But I can see her.'

'That is so cool.'

He smiles again. 'Yes, it is . . . *cool*, I suppose.'

Suddenly, I leap off my seat. 'Was I just sitting on her?'

Now he chuckles. He likes me, I can tell. Though, if I was sitting on her, his friend probably doesn't like me so much. 'No. You're all right.' Bert takes the handles of his walker and rattles it toward the door.

'Wait,' I say again.

He sighs. 'Yes?'

'Why can you see her and no one else can?'

Bert thinks about that for a minute. 'I can see her because I really, really want to.'

'You mean . . . if there's someone that I can't see . . . and I really, really want to . . . I can?'

'You can try.'

'And I'll be able to talk to them, too?'

He shrugs. 'Why not?'

'Even' – I lower my voice – 'if he's *dead*?'

Bert frowns. I guess that was silly of me. Of *course* you can't see or talk to someone who is dead! But Bert bangs his walker toward me and bends until he is around my height. It looks like hard work, the bending. I hope he doesn't get stuck like that. 'If I were dead,' he says, 'and a pretty young lady like you wanted to talk to me . . . I sure as heck'd be coming back for visits.'

I'm so happy that my eyes fill up with tears and I throw my arms around his neck and almost knock him to the ground.

11
Eve

The day passes like a mile-long train. I change sheets with suspicious-looking stains. I almost throw out a set of false teeth with a half-filled glass of water. Now I wipe the last of the crumbs from the kitchen bench, then rinse out the cloth and hang it over the faucet. My back aches. I'd always fancied myself as being fairly fit, but housework is something else. I feel withered, broken, in pain.

Clem is in the front room, watching TV, waiting to be taken home. Emerson, the agency nurse, is in the parlor, reading a novel. The residents are in their rooms, readying themselves for bed, and I can't wait to do the same. I wash my hands, pick up my manual, then head up the hall to say good night to the nurse.

'I'm off for the night, then.'

Emerson looks up from her book. 'Okay. Shall I pop in and see the residents before bed, or are they best left alone?'

I have no idea. On one hand, I'm reluctant to disturb

them, given the way I walked in on Clara this morning. On the other hand, after my conversation with Anna this afternoon, I'd like to check in on her again. Maybe she'll remember what she meant when she said 'Help me'.

'I'll check on them before I go,' I say.

I come to Luke's door first, which is ajar, and suddenly Eric's words jump into my mind. *'Luke's and Anna's doors need to be locked.'* I make a mental note to remind Emerson and knock loudly. 'Luke? It's Eve. Just checking you're okay.'

I wait, peering through the crack, but there's no response and no movement.

'Luke?' I nudge the door. 'Are you in here?'

When he still doesn't answer, I open the door completely. *Dear God, may he not be naked. Or worse, naked and disoriented.* I slowly advance inside. His bed is made. Empty. 'Shit!'

'Everything okay?'

I spin around. Emerson is in the doorway. 'Luke's not here,' I say.

My anxiety is mirrored in Emerson's eyes. This isn't good.

Emerson gets it together first. 'The front doors are locked, so he must be inside. I'll check the building. You check with the other residents.'

'Yes.' I nod maniacally. 'The other residents.'

Amidst my alarm, I find myself wishing I were checking the building while Emerson woke up the confused, sleepy old people, admitting that we'd lost a resident.

I step out into the hallway and look at the closed doors.

113

Light shines out the bottom of Anna's and Bert's doors; the other rooms are in darkness. I move toward Anna's door. Pretty unlikely, I reason, that Luke would be visiting a grumpy old man at this time of night.

I tap lightly. 'Anna, it's Eve. Are you there?'

I wait a moment, my panic rising. Still there's no response. Is Anna missing, too? Not waiting another second, I swing open the door. In my mind's eye, I can already see it: Another made bed. Another missing resident. This whole thing spiraling out of control.

At the sight of Anna's feet, I go limp with relief. Thank God! I continue into the room until the whole bed comes into view; then I gasp and quickly retreat.

'I've checked the building,' Emerson says, appearing beside me. 'No sign of Luke.'

'It's okay,' I tell her, even though I'm fairly certain that it's not. 'I've found him.'

12

Anna

Thirteen months ago . . .

You know what I don't miss? The doctors' appointments. A year ago, when I was diagnosed, there were a lot of them. The geriatricians (I know, right?), the neurologists, the neuropsychologists. The memory clinics, the PET scans. An interesting fact about Alzheimer's is that a definitive diagnosis can be made only through autopsy. For this reason, Dr Brain diagnosed me as having 'probable Alzheimer's'. The 'probable' part always made me laugh. It might be a bit macabre, but the idea that after you're dead they might slice open your head and say, *Well, looky here. She didn't have it after all*, struck me as funny.

It's been six weeks since Young Guy accosted me in the hallway . . . and I'm still not dead. It's unexpected, but life has been pretty good at throwing me curveballs lately. I haven't forgotten about what I was planning to do that night, nor have I decided that I'll never go ahead and do it. I guess, like a lot of callers on *Beat the Bomb*, I've simply decided that I am willing to take my chances hanging on a little longer.

Today, it's pet therapy day. Not my favorite day of the week, given my dog phobia, but I'm inside and all the dogs are outside, so I can't complain. Young Guy, the dog lover, loves this day. Usually he spends the entire time outside with the dogs. He opted to stay inside today, but I can tell he'd rather be outside because his eyes are glued to the window, where a hairy fluff ball sits on Southern Lady's lap, licking her face. I shudder.

'Myrna don't like dogs neither.'

I look up, uncertain who has spoken. I notice the old guy, whom I've nicknamed Baldy, is looking at me. 'What?' I ask.

'Dogs. Myrna don't like 'em.'

Old folks can be so random. Baldy's voice is gruff and irritated, like I am an inconvenience, even though he's the one who started talking to me.

'Oh.' I sit back as a lady – Liesel, according to her name badge – arranges the world's fattest rabbit in my lap. I call it Sumo Bunny. 'Myrna and I have something in common, then.'

Young Guy grins. He's been my right-hand man these last few weeks – where I go, he goes. I'm not sure if it's because he's worried I'm going to try to kill myself or if he just enjoys my company, but the result is the same – we're always together. It's actually pretty convenient. A couple of times when I've been disoriented, he's been able to help me find my way. And one time, when we were both a little disoriented, we decided there was safety in numbers and just stayed where we were until someone came to find us.

I watch him now. He's looking at the animal in his lap, his eyelashes dark against his pale face. The top two buttons of his shirt are casually undone and the sleeves are rolled up. I stare at his chest but when he notices me looking, I quickly look back at Sumo Bunny.

Young Guy generally doesn't say a lot, and I don't know if that's because of his type of dementia or if he's always been a man of few words. Either way, there's something nice about the lack of chatter. When he *does* talk, he asks me questions. It's funny the things he wants to know – my favorite films, the music I listen to. My answers are boring and predictable, but he listens with absolute attention, like there's nowhere else he'd rather be. I ask about his favorite things, too, and he tells me a few, but I can tell speaking makes him tired. After a while, he starts to look frustrated, so I let conversation drift back to me.

'Can you turn that damn TV off?' Baldy shouts suddenly. Grumpy old bastard. He points to the arm of my chair, where the remote control is resting. I pick it up.

Just so you know, there are about a million buttons on a remote control. Some are green. Some are red. Some are gray. The writing below each button is all gobbledygook – INPUT, AUDIO, AV. I try a gray one. The room fills with loud static noise.

'Are you trying to burst my eardrums?' Baldy yells.

I quickly press another button, a green one. The noise

117

remains, but the picture on the screen changes, then changes again.

I wish Ethan were here. Or Brayden or the other nephew. Kids are so good with electronics.

'What are you *doing*?' he asks.

'I'm trying,' I say, because I really am. I press a red button, but it just gets louder. I look at Young Guy desperately.

He grabs my hand. 'Quick,' he says, standing. The animal on his lap jumps off and scampers away. He grabs my hand, and even through the noise, I feel a rush of energy at his touch. Sumo Bunny slides off my lap as he pulls me to my feet. 'Let's . . . go . . . out of h-here,' he says.

'Hey!' Baldy cries. 'Where are you two going?'

We turn a corner, then another, and finally we stop next to a small table and a mirror and a vase of flowers. My eyes roll over his strong jaw, his dimple, his tea-colored eyes. A warm tingly feeling rises through my body. I'm so transported; I don't even break his gaze when a woman in a green T-shirt enters the room. Her name badge says LIESEL.

'There you are, Luke!' she says. 'We're just feeding the dogs. If you want to see them, you'll have to come outside now.'

'Not . . . t-today,' he says.

'You should go,' I tell him. 'You love those damn dogs.'

He shakes his head firmly, definitively. And despite my protests, my heart begins to sing. 'No,' he says again. 'I'm h-h-happy right where I am.'

*

There's a knocking sound, somewhere in my room. It sounds like a woodpecker. *Knock, knock, knock.* I glance at the window at the same time as the door opens.

Suddenly the manager guy is in front of me. 'Anna? You have a phone call.'

'A phone call?'

I feel strangely untethered today, on edge, like I'm waiting for someone to sneak up on me, but they never do. I know I'm in my room, at Rosalind House, but when I look for the familiar, I don't find it. It's like I'm straddling the line between dementia and reality, and I can't tell which is which.

'Yes,' he says, 'a phone call. Follow me.'

I haven't had a phone call since I arrived. Not that I'd remember, I guess. I don't have a phone in my room – too distracting for people with dementia, they say. I'm okay with this. I find it hard, talking on the phone: no facial expressions to rely on, no rising eyebrows or conspiratorial glances. Still, it's a little excitement, I suppose. A phone call.

As I weave my way to the manager's office, it occurs to me that it could be bad news. A death? An accident? One of the nephews? By the time Eric hands me the talking end of the phone, I'm fluttery in the chest. I hold it next to my ear, but it takes me a few seconds to remember to say something. 'Um . . . hello?'

There's a deep throaty-noise, and then . . . 'Anna?'

'Dad?'

There's a pause. 'Anna, it's Jack.'

I feel a flash of humiliation. 'I know. That's what I said.'

119

I fight the urge to slap myself in the head. *Dad? Seriously?* Did I think after a twenty-year absence, he'd just call up and say hi?

'How you doing?' he asks.

'What is it, Jack?' I sound snappy, I know, but after my embarrassing slip, I just want to get off the phone. 'Did something happen?'

'No, it's about tomorrow. I have to take Brayden to Little League, so Helen is going to pick you up. Okay?'

I have no idea what he's talking about, but the pause goes on and on, so I figure he's waiting for me to say something. So I say, 'Okay.'

'I'm really looking forward to seeing you.'

'Yep,' I say. 'Me, too.'

I glance at the doorway. The manager is waiting there. I want to tell him he doesn't have to wait, that I'll be able to find my way back to my room, but I'm not so sure I will. Probably best that he waits right where he is.

I stand for a moment longer, and then I realize the phone is beeping into my ear. Jack must have hung up. The manager is still in the doorway, and I don't want him to know that Jack hung up on me, so I say loudly, 'All right – bye, Jack.' Then I put the talking end of the phone on its cradle and follow Eric back to my room.

At Rosalind House, people fall asleep a lot, but never in their beds. During the day, while sitting in armchairs, they drop like flies. One minute they're chatting away, and the next, *zzzzzz*. Dreamland. But at night, when a comfy bed is at the offering, *wham*. Wide awake. In this, as with so many things these days, I sympathize with the oldies. I'm tired a lot, and all day I look forward to a nice, restful sleep. But the moment I slip between the sheets, my lids are on stalks.

Tonight when I can't sleep, I get out of bed and walk into the hallway. Blondie is there.

'You okay?' I ask her. There's a room at the end of the corridor designated for the nurse on night shift, and usually by this time of night, she is in it.

She laughs. 'I was about to ask you the same thing. Couldn't sleep?' Blondie sounds happy and cheery, as usual.

'Thought I'd walk around a bit,' I say. 'That okay?'

'Fine by me.' She holds up her thick-cup by the handle. 'Want a hot chocolate? I'm making one for myself.'

I tell her no thanks and she heads for the kitchen. I go in the opposite direction. Rosalind House is a beautiful building, but by the light of only a couple of floor lamps, anything can look creepy, especially when you are alone. In the dark, I feel agitated. What am I supposed to do? Turning on the TV isn't an option, as the residents are light sleepers and I'd rather be captured by gremlins than wake up Baldy. He's grumpy enough on eight hours' sleep. So my choices are to stand here in the dark . . . or to walk.

My legs feel tingly, so I walk. A few times up and down the staircase. I vaguely remember Dr Brain telling me exercise was good for Alzheimer's. For some reason, this makes me laugh. What a diligent student I am!

After a minute or so, I stop walking. I'm tired now. It often happens this way – wide awake one minute, and the next, weariness hits like a train. I turn to head back to my room, then pause. Am I upstairs or downstairs? I glance around. I'm on a flat area of carpet. Right ahead is a corridor with doors leading off it on either side. I must be downstairs.

I turn to face the stairs, but instead of rising up before me, they fall away, like a hole. I look around again. Corridor, doors, giant hole. I must be at the . . . Nope. I can't work it out.

I pace a little, staying well clear of the hole. I'm sleepy and I just want to go to bed. It's like I'm in a box. A fucking box. Like that spooky room in *Willy Wonka & the Chocolate Factory*, the one with only one door that no one can find. What if *I* can't find it? What if I'm stuck in this box forever?

'Damn.' I kick the wall. 'Stupid. Fucking. Stairs.'

I hear footsteps. *Blondie!* She'll save me. I turn and, before I can stop myself, gasp. There's someone at the bottom of the hole, and it's not Blondie. I feel a twinge of fear or excitement or something.

'What are you d . . . doing?' Young Guy asks.

'Just walking,' I say. For some reason, I'm too proud to tell him I'm lost. 'I've got a dead leg.'

'Wanna see s-s-omething?' He points beyond me. 'Up there.'

Before I can answer, he's dropped to his hands and knees and is crawling up the stairs. Must be to do with the depth perception – ten points for creativity. At the top, he rises to his feet and grins at me.

I try to grin back, but it sticks halfway.

He's wearing a white V-neck and thin, navy-blue sweat-pants – so thin, I can make out the shape of his legs (muscular) underneath. He makes sweatpants look pretty good. He gives me a one-eye blink and walks past me toward the front of the house.

'Come on,' he says. 'Walk copy me.'

I'm getting used to his funny use of words, even starting to find it charming. He doesn't seem embarrassed by any of it: the crawling, the stuttering, the muddled language. The way he owns it; it's inspiring. And dead sexy.

He takes me to another set of stairs and crawls up. I follow on two feet. Then, at the end of the corridor, he opens a door. My heart is thundering. *What are we doing? Where is he taking me?*

'A-a-after you,' he says.

'No thanks.' My voice trembles a little. 'After you.'

He goes in and touches a thing on the wall, and the room lights up. It's a big room, like the parlor, but empty, apart from a few irregular-shaped mounds covered in white sheets. At one end of the room is a huge floor-to-ceiling window.

'Wow,' I say. 'How did you know this was here?'

'When it's n-nighttime and there's no one around, you . . . find all many . . . things.'

Young Guy does a lap of the room, past a lamp and a fireplace that is covered with newspaper. He stops just inches in front of me. My breath catches. Considering I've known Young Guy only a short time, I've been up close to him quite a lot. Enough that the slope of his cheeks and the faint smatter of stubble on his face are comforting.

Comforting yet, at the same time, terrifying.

I become aware that the silence has gone on awhile, so I open my mouth to fill it. But he shakes his head.

'Just . . .' he says, 'don't talk . . .'

His arms find my waist and pull me closer. And he presses his mouth to mine.

His lips are soft and warm. And suddenly, it feels like I'm floating. Young Guy tastes like peppermint; smells like it. I breathe him in. And then, as fast as it started, the kiss is over.

'Wow,' I say.

He smiles shyly, then drifts over to one sheet-covered mound and flicks off the sheet. Underneath is an old-fashioned record player.

'You like Nat King Cole?' he asks.

'Sure,' I say, but my voice is hoarse. Did that just happen?

'G-good. Because that's a-a-all there is.'

He slides the record out of the cover, parks it on the dial, and lowers the pointy bit. In the next breath, Nat King Cole's rich baritone notes fill the room. Young Guy and I stare at each other, expressionless.

'This is a joke, right?' I say as the swell of tension gives way to laughter. '"Unforgettable"?'

'No,' he says, even though he's laughing now, too. 'I've listened to this record before, but I don't remember hearing this song.'

124

'You . . . don't' – A wave of hysteria hits. Now I'm laughing so hard, I can barely get the word out – *'remember?'*

That sets him off, which sets me off again. Which sets him off again. And for the next few minutes, he and I are just two young people. Laughing. Kissing. And listening to Nat King Cole.

13

When Jack and I were in third grade, he brought me for show and tell. (Well, he didn't *bring* me, because I was already there, but he did tug me out of my seat and drag me to the front of the room.)

'This is my sister, Anna,' he told the class, which of course, they already knew. He hadn't done me the courtesy of forewarning me of this sideshow, and judging by the way Mrs Ramsey's eyes shrank into her head, he hadn't done her the honor either. Anyone else but Jack – the teacher's pet – might have gotten into trouble for not preparing, but Jack, even at nine, was smooth as a silk tie. 'And for show and tell today, I'd like to tell you about her.'

It was, when I think of it now, classic Jack. I was the tough one; he was the sensitive one – the perfect yin to my yang.

'Anna can write her name in Chinese,' he started.

He looked so comfortable, standing at the front of the room. The only time I'd stood at the front was when I was getting in trouble. This was different. Thirty pairs of eyes watched me as Jack offered me a piece of chalk and stood there, grinning, until I wrote my name on the blackboard in Chinese.

'Anna has broken three bones,' he said when I was finished. 'She didn't even cry when she broke her wrist, so Mom didn't take her to the doctor for three days!'

The class oohed at this, and I grinned and said, 'Yes, it's true,' and 'No, it didn't hurt so bad.'

'Anna ran into the haunted house on Nicholson Street and knocked on the door when no one else was brave enough.'

Mrs Ramsey's eyes almost disappeared. I shrugged noncommittally.

'Anna can ride a bike without holding the handles.'

This wasn't actually that hard, but Jack had always been easily impressed.

'Anna can do lots of things that I can't do,' he finished up. 'I'm really lucky to have such a cool twin.'

Jack shifted to put his arm around me, which was weird, but I allowed it. He could be such a cornball sometimes.

'Jack's brought up an important point, class,' Mrs Ramsey said. 'We're all special in our own unique ways. Even Jack and Anna, who are twins, have lots of differences. Anna, why don't you tell us something special about Jack? Something he can do that you can't?'

Jack was still right beside me, holding me like I was some kind of trophy. At nine, the idea of 'uncoolness' was already starting to hover around the edges of my consciousness, but Jack just looked so proud, I thought he might cry.

Mrs Ramsey was looking at me, waiting for an answer,

so I said: 'Jack is really good at math,' and we took our seats again. But later, when I thought about it, I wished I'd said something different. I wished I'd said, *Jack knows how to make you feel like the most important person in the room.*

After I've lived in the big house with all the old people for two months, I'm allowed a 'home visit'. Everyone talks about the home visit in *tra-la-la* voices, as though it's some kind of prize – a conjugal visit for a prisoner who's been behaving himself. It makes me think of *The Bachelor*. Toward the end of each series, the final four girls are invited to take the Bachelor back to their homes to meet their families, let him see them in their home environment. When the girls find out they've made the final four, they squeal and cheer. *We're getting a home visit! Woop-Woop!* To me, it always seemed shortsighted. After all, odds are there won't be a second visit. Three of the girls are about to be booted off the show. The fairy-tale ending is unlikely at best. And for me, it's even less likely.

I'm in the parlor when the woman comes in, tossing her bouncy hair. She's wearing jeans and a pink cardigan and large hoop earrings, and she's smiling at me. I'm starting to wonder if she's simple when it dawns on me: It's Helen. After a long night of kissing and dancing (nothing else) in the upstairs room with Young Guy, my brain isn't all here.

'Anna!'

Helen and I don't normally hug (as I recall), but as she comes at me with open arms, I feel it would be rude to point that out. I also decide it'd be rude to ask why the hell Jack – the blood relative, the family member – isn't here to pick me up. But I ask anyway.

'Jack and the boys are at Brayden's Little League game.' Helen pulls back slowly and frowns, like she's suddenly noticed I've grown a third nostril. 'Remember? Jack called yesterday to tell you. They'll be home when we get there.'

'Oh, right,' I say. No need to point out that Jack had forgotten.

When we arrive, as promised, they're there. They've even erected a banner: WELCOME HOME ANNA. My first thought is . . . but I'm not home. I'm here for my 'home visit'.

The worst thing about my home visit is that no one stops talking. Everyone gathers around me, catapulting questions so fast, I can barely figure out who said what. By the time I *do* figure it out, and look at the person so I can respond, either they've moved on or they're giving each other what I now call the 'third-nostril look'. Like I'm the one who is nuts.

I'm much happier when we progress to the 'watching' stage of the visit: 'Watch me bounce on the trampoline, Anna.' 'Watch me sit on Hank's face and fart, Anna.' 'Watch how far I can kick this ball . . . all the way into the neighbor's yard!' This part, I like. I can just sit on my deck chair, clapping and waving. And I can hear myself think again.

After a few minutes of this, Helen arrives with a cup of tea, a tray of brown eating-things in little wrappers, and her own deck chair. Jack is on the grass, watching the kids

129

and being quiet, which is fine with me. I wish Helen would follow his lead, but unfortunately, she didn't get the memo.

'It's great to have you here, Anna,' she says, dispensing a cup of tea with no milk. It smells funny. 'I got your favorite. Peppermint tea.'

I frown into my mug. Peppermint is my favorite?

'Jack drank some by accident the other day and then spat it out all over the kitchen counter.' Helen covers her hand with her mouth and chuckles. 'The boys thought it was hilarious.'

Jack mutters something unintelligible. I take a sip of my tea. It's actually pretty good.

'Anna, watch this!' Ethan calls.

'No! Anna's watching me,' says Hank.

'*Me*, Anna,' says the other one. 'Watch *me*!'

I turn back to Helen. 'What did you say?'

Helen's smile fades. 'Oh . . . just that Jack tried your tea and—'

'*Anna!*' Ethan is swinging from the tree by one arm, like the hairy animal that eats bananas. With his dangling hand, he tickles his opposite armpit. 'Oo-oo-ee-ee! I'm a monkey.'

A *monkey*. Right.

Beside me, to my right, Helen is still talking.

'You're not a monkey,' says the boy in the red T-shirt. 'You're an ape!'

The boys all break into laughter, except for the little one, who begins to cry. He lets go of the branch and finds the ground.

'Would you like a muffin?' Helen says. 'Baked fresh this morning. Anna?' She holds up the tray of brown things.

I rise to my feet. Someone is talking. I don't know who. My head hurts.

'Anna, are you all right?' someone says.

The littlest boy is standing in front of me, arms outstretched. His face is red and wet, and he's muttering something about the other boys being mean. I step toward him, and he wraps his arms around my waist.

'Eath, give Anna some space,' Jack says.

The little boy protests that he doesn't want to, and then the other little boys start screaming something. The woman talks louder, over the top of them. I close my eyes. I can't hear individual words, just . . . noise. Loud, continuous noise.

'*Shut up!*' I scream, and it actually feels good. For a second, the sound of my voice is all I can hear. That also feels good.

But the moment I stop screaming, the woman starts talking again. 'Anna, why don't you just—?'

My brain is going to explode. 'I said *shut up*. You!' I jab my finger at the little boy, the crying one, who has let go of my waist and stepped back a few paces. 'And *you!*' This time I point at the other boys, the ones in red and green, standing before me. 'And *you!*' The woman. She's the most annoying of all. 'All of you, *shut up!*'

Jack gets up off the grass and starts toward me. I don't want him to touch me. I don't want anyone to touch me. I pick up the tray of brown things and hurl it as hard as I can into the garden. He stops. Finally, the chatter, the whining, the talking, stops, drowned out by one continuous, high-pitched roar. My roar.

'She's degenerated really fast . . .'
'. . . spoken to her doctor . . .'
'. . . what did Eric say?'

I know Jack and Helen are talking about me. If I really wanted to, I could tune in, but why bother? It would take up too much of my brain space, and I don't have much to spare. So I just continue eating my dinner. Whatever it is. For someone who spends so much time in the kitchen, Helen isn't a very good cook.

'Anna?'

They're looking at me. Terrific. Now I'm probably going to have to listen.

Jack drags his chair a little closer to mine. 'Do you want to talk about what happened today?'

'No.' I take a mouthful of whatever it is Helen has cooked. It's so hot, it takes the skin off my mouth, and it tastes like tomato paste. Even Latina Cook-Lady's rice and beans is better than this.

'Anna,' he tries again, 'did we do something to upset you?'

'No.'

'Are you sure?' Apparently, he's not letting this go. I wish he'd shut up and let me eat my tomato paste.

'I'm sure,' I say. 'It's just that I don't like it here. Too . . . noisy.'

Jack and Helen's faces shift in unison, as if moved by the same puppeteer. The long blink. The jaw drop. The

132

swift glance at the other. I shovel in another mouthful. *Ow.* Crap! Hot.

'Anna—'

'If it's all right with you, I'd like to go home now,' I say before the questions start again. And when I say the word 'home', I'm surprised to realize that I'm talking about the big house with all the old people.

14
Eve

'I probably should have explained something yesterday –' Eric perches on the edge of my desk and lets out a long, world-weary sigh. '– about Anna and Luke. What you saw the other night? It isn't the first time.'

'I beg your pardon?' I hear him fine, but I want to hear him say it again.

'It's a sensitive topic, and I didn't know how much to say earlier. But I've spoken to Anna's brother, and he agrees that I should fill you in. The truth is, Anna and Luke were friends.' He pauses, shakes his head. 'They *are* friends. But shortly after they arrived, they developed quite an attachment. A romance, you might say. It was a great thing for both of them; it gave them a lift and possibly even extended their mental dexterity a little. We were going to let it run its course and we figured eventually it would take care of itself, that they'd forget their friendship. Usually that's how these things play out.'

'These things?' I ask. 'You mean . . . there have been other—?'

'—romances? Oh, yes,' Eric says, grinning. 'There's more lust at a residential care facility than in high school. Didn't you know?'

There's something about Eric's obvious enjoyment of this that I find a little off-putting.

'It's especially common with dementia patients,' he continues. 'Human beings are programmed to form attachments in order to survive. So it makes sense that when you have dementia, new attachments are formed to replace those that are lost. It's a good thing, it can reduce loneliness and depression. But in this case, it was a little more complicated.'

'Why?'

'We became aware that Luke and Anna were intimate. Which in itself is complicated, but for them, it opened up a host of other issues. For example, is Anna – or Luke, for that matter – of sound mind to consent to this?'

'But . . . you said they'd developed a relationship. Surely that implies consent?'

'Actually, it doesn't. Among other things, as dementia develops, an individual's inhibitions can become lowered, causing them to act uncharacteristically promiscuous or flirtatious. Even if they are saying yes, we can't be sure they would be saying yes if their judgment wasn't impaired. Then, of course, there was the other incident – Anna's suicide attempt. After that, we had no choice but to start locking the doors. We didn't come to that decision lightly. But all things considered, it made sense.'

'Are Anna and Luke okay with it?' I ask.

'As okay as you can expect, really. Sometimes they

become upset at night, but again, that's normal for people with dementia. Most likely, Anna's distress is simply the night-restlessness and she doesn't remember Luke at all. It's possible Luke does remember, but even if he does, we can't allow him free access to Anna's room at night. They can spend time together during the day, but the staff try to keep them busy and redirect them if they try to go off privately together. I'll ask you to do the same,' he says, 'if you happen to see them together.'

I think of Anna asking for help. Of her asking if *he* was there, then saying she was talking about Luke.

'All right, Eve?' Eric repeats.

'Yes,' I say. 'Okay.'

But my facial expression must give away my true feelings because Eric continues. 'The important thing is that we abide by the families' wishes, for everyone's sake.'

'Of course,' I say, though I can't help but wonder if abiding by the families' wishes is really for everyone's sake. Or just for everyone *else's* sake.

Clem aka Alice is quiet on the way to school. I try to engage her by asking her if she wants a special dinner, but she just shrugs. Even seeing Legs on the way into the classroom isn't enough to pep her up.

I have a quick word with Miss Weber, who says she'll keep a special eye on her. She also asks for my change-of-address form, which I supply with a stomach full of knots. If she suspects anything, I can't tell.

Then I have to run off to work. It strikes me that this is a cruel irony. Before, when I had the most well-adjusted, happiest little girl in the world, I had nothing but time to spend with her. Now, when she could really use her mother around, I have to work.

Back at Rosalind House, the parlor is full. Laurie is reading a newspaper, Bert is chatting quietly to himself. Gwen dozes. Luke and Anna are perched at opposite windows. As I wipe down the mantel, I can't help stealing a look at them. They seem content enough, staring into the garden, but who knows? Do they wish they were side by side?

'That's lovely,' Bert says, startling me. At first I'm not sure what he's referring to; then I realize I've been humming.

'Oh,' I say. 'Well . . . thank you.'

'That tune?' he says. 'What is it?'

'It's . . . Pachelbel's Canon.' Why had I chosen to hum my wedding song? 'Do you know it?'

'Of course. I like it.' He frowns. 'Why did you stop?'

I smile and continue to hum. There's something warm about Bert, gruff as he is.

'Are you all right, my love?'

I look around. This time it's Laurie talking, and not to me.

Clara has drifted into the room, carrying a Maeve Binchy novel. 'Fit as a fiddle,' she says, kissing him on the mouth. Her eyes close, and for a heartbeat, she looks completely blissed out. 'Don't you go worryin' yourself.'

'You should tell the doctor when she gets here,' Laurie says.

'You think she's interested in my headache?'

137

'Dr Walker is interested in everything,' Laurie says. 'At our age, anything is a symptom.'

Clara *pffts*, but with a smile. 'At our age, a headache is still a headache.'

I give the coffee table a spritz. Spraying, I realize, is surprisingly pleasant – the *shush* sound it makes, the way the products mist out evenly over the surface, ready to make something clean. It's impossible to be bad at spraying. Wiping, on the other hand, is loathsome. It makes no sound. It takes a lot of effort, and if you're not any good at it, it shows you up as the amateur you are.

'Tell the doctor,' Laurie orders.

'You're not the boss of me.'

'I am,' he replies. 'I'm your husband.'

I continue to hum, soothed by the pleasant squabble of a couple who've been married sixty years.

'Ah, I nearly forgot,' Laurie says. 'Enid called.'

The silence that follows is long enough for me to look up.

'When?' Clara asks.

Laurie shrugs. 'Before.'

'Before *when*?'

'I'm an old man.' He waves his hands about as if that emphasizes his point. 'Keeping track of time is too depressing.'

He winks at me, and I hum louder – proof that I'm not eavesdropping.

'What did my sister have to say for herself?' Clara asks.

'Just that she's coming to visit.'

'From Charlotte?' Clara's voice rises like a Chinese sky lantern. '*Why?*'

The coffee table is nice and shiny, and I really should move on to the kitchen. But I get out my bottle and give it another spray. I've missed my daily gossip sessions with Jazz. Hearing about who has had Botox, who is leaving her husband for the personal trainer. While this conversation isn't anywhere near so scandalous, I feel myself getting sucked into it. I'd have expected someone like Clara to talk to her sister every day, to send cards and gifts and exchange photos of respective grandchildren. But by the way she's acting, you'd have thought Laurie had said Satan himself was coming to visit.

'Enid comes every year,' Laurie says slowly. 'Why not this year?'

Clara shrugs. 'It's a long way for her to travel, is all.'

'As you point out every time. Now, are you going to get all worked up as usual, planning activities for every solitary second of her trip, or are you going to let her have a nice visit this time?'

Clara narrows her eyes. 'Since when are you so worried about my sister getting a nice visit?'

'Staying out of it,' Laurie says.

'You do that.'

Clara thumps down her book and heaves herself out of her chair.

'Where are you going?' Laurie asks.

'Where do you think? I'm going to call Enid. Get this visit planned and over with.'

Clara disappears and the room falls silent again, apart

from my humming. Laurie starts whistling, so comfortable as to his place in Clara's life, he doesn't need to waste his time worrying. I'd always thought that one day, Richard and I would be old and comfortable in our ways, after a lifetime of marriage. We *would* have been. But Richard ruined it.

I finish dusting some books on the coffee table, then tuck my cloth into my apron. That's when I notice Anna.

'Anna?' I say cautiously, edging toward her. 'Are you . . . all right?'

Her face is slick with tears. She's staring right at me, but unseeing, so I squat down in front of her and take her hands. 'Anna?'

Finally she sees me. Her eyes go round, panicked. 'They're having us followed.'

'Who is having you followed?'

She tips her head toward the doorway. 'Them.'

I look at the doorway, which is empty. I shake my head. 'No one is having you followed, Anna.'

'They *are*,' she says. Her hands are fists, pounding against her knees. Her face becomes twisted with frustration. 'And soon, I'm going to forget him.'

She isn't making any sense. I glance around, looking for Carole or Trish or Eric, but they're nowhere to be seen.

'Anna, I promise you no one is—'

'They *are*!' In a sudden movement, she throws her hands up, and I lose my balance and tumble backwards onto the rug. I'm just getting up again as Carole and Eric come jogging in.

'See?' Anna says, pointing at them. Her face is almost victorious. 'I told you! They're following us. Where's Jack?' she asks Eric snippily. 'Where's your partner in crime?'

Eric runs over to me. 'Are you all right?'

I stand upright. 'I'm fine.'

'It's all right, sweetie,' Carole says to Anna. She approaches her quickly, getting right up in her face. 'Everything is all right.'

'No, it's not!'

Unlike my push, which I think was unintentional, this time Anna gives Carole an almighty shove. Carole hits the floor with a thud, landing awkwardly on her elbow.

'We need to restrain her,' Eric says. 'Trish?' he calls out.

'Oh no,' I say, 'I don't think—'

But Trish is already jogging into the room.

'Anna is getting agitated,' Eric says. 'She's just pushed Eve and Carole.'

'She didn't mean to push me,' I say. 'It was an accident—'

'Do you need a tranquilizer?' Trish asks.

'No!' I say at the same time as Eric says, 'Probably best to be safe.'

I can't believe this is happening. Anna still seems agitated, but she's not exactly wielding a knife. She's just in her chair, looking at her lap, muttering quietly. I hear what she's saying, but it doesn't make any sense. It sounds like 'beat the bomb, beat the bomb'.

Before I know what's happening, Trish is back with a syringe. She approaches Anna from the side, so she doesn't

141

see it coming. When she drives the needle into her arm, Anna lets out a high-pitched, pained wail.

My hands find my mouth. I want to look away, but for some reason, perhaps out of solidarity with Anna, I can't. *Help me. They are following us. Beat the bomb.* I search her words for a common thread, a clue to what she's trying to tell me. But they just sound like the words of someone at a disconnect with reality. Someone with Alzheimer's.

'There you go, sweetie,' Trish says as Anna sinks back into her chair. Anna continues to stare at me for a few seconds with something like pleading in her eyes. But as the tranquilizer works its way into her system, her expression dulls away to nothing.

15

One of the best things about cooking is that, by and large, you can control it. If something is too spicy, you can counteract it with cream or yogurt. If something is too sour, add sugar. Dealing with real life is nowhere near so simple. Since Richard died, some days I get the feeling I'm falling down a hole with nothing to grasp on to. On those days, I grasp on to food. That's why, the afternoon after Anna is sedated, I go to the grocery store.

I don't know what it is about squeezing an avocado that fills my heart with song. My basket is full of sweet corn, butternut squash, Dutch carrots, and free-range eggs. At intervals, I raise my basket to my nose simply to inhale. It feels so good to be back at Houlihan's, my old grocery store. I've missed the organic produce, the high-end brands. In here, it's easy to forget the reality of my life as a widowed housekeeper – even for an hour.

It takes me a while to realize that I'm not shopping for two anymore and my basket isn't going to cut it. I'm on my way to the front to retrieve a shopping cart when a crisp iceberg lettuce catches my eye – perfect for a cold wedge salad starter. If I throw in some flat-leaf parsley, tomatoes, cucumber, and a couple of hard-boiled eggs, it will be lovely for this evening. Olive oil and cider vinaigrette for dressing. Even the residents with dentures could cope with that.

I reach for the top lettuce, the biggest one, still beaded with water from the mister. But before I can touch it, I feel a weight on my shoulder and I'm whipped around so fast, I drop my basket. There's a crunchy sound: eggs breaking. Before I can steady myself, a hand shoots out and *thwacks* against my cheek.

'You!'

I step back, away from the finger that is now thrust in my face, and grasp the cool metal rail behind me. What on earth? I don't recognize the woman standing before me. She's older than me, perhaps forty, with a neat brown haircut.

'Well?' she cries. 'What do you have to say for yourself?'

The part of my cheek where the slap connected begins to throb. My ear is ringing in a long endless line, like a hospital beeper after someone has died.

'My parents invested their entire life's savings in your husband's scheme! They weren't those big-time investors who had money to burn, they were a hardworking couple who wanted to secure their future. Now their home is in foreclosure and they are broke.'

My mouth goes dry. Shoppers have hushed; people look up from their baskets, exchange glances by the potatoes. I can actually feel their eyes on me. *That's Eve Bennett. So much for her getting her comeuppance. She's a fraud. Just like her husband.*

144

In the dead quiet, there's a sharp intake of breath. I see Andrea Heathmont peering around the end of the aisle. Another blond is beside her, Romy Fisher maybe. My heart sinks further.

'Because of you,' the lady continues, 'my parents have shopped at Bent and Dent these last few months! And you're shopping for organic produce at the most expensive food store around? Where's the justice?'

My eyes drop to my basket. 'Oh! No. This isn't for me.'

'And why should I believe you? You're probably a liar and a swindler just like your husband. That man did the world a favor when he—'

'That's enough.'

From nowhere, Angus appears. He steals around me, positioning himself between me and the woman. The woman looks startled, but only for a moment. She starts to walk around Angus, but he blocks her way.

'Actually, it's not nearly enough, after what she's done!' she yells over his shoulder. 'Do you know who this is?' she asks Angus.

I glance at Andrea, who is still watching. She whispers something to the other woman and I curse myself for coming to Houlihan's. What was I thinking?

'Yes, I know who she is,' Angus says quietly. 'She's a woman, trying to get on with her job, cooking for the elderly. You've just assaulted her, which is a crime, and you've damaged this produce, which will cost the store money, unless you pay for it.'

'*I'm* not going to pay for it,' the woman says, but some of the heat has gone from her voice. Tears build in her eyes. 'The only person who should have to pay is this bitch.' The woman stabs her finger in my direction, but that appears to be all she has left. She abandons her cart and scurries out of the store via a side door.

Immediately the bustle of the store resumes: a hushed voice, the roll of shopping cart wheels on linoleum. Andrea watches for another moment, then disappears, too.

I look at my upturned basket. A single egg rolls free, and by the look of the yellow spray around the edge of the carton, it's the sole survivor. I squat, bundling it all back into the basket. My cheek radiates with heat, like a nasty sunburn. The ringing continues in my ear.

Angus squats beside me. 'My truck is out front.' He tucks a set of keys into my palm. 'Go. I'll take care of this.'

I shake my head, blinking against tears. 'I . . . I have to finish the shopping.'

'I'll finish it.'

'But . . . I don't have a list.'

I used to pride myself on never having a list. I found them creatively stifling, I'd tell people. *What if I planned to make French onion soup but then saw some impossibly delightful-looking artichokes?* Now the thought seems as frivolous as it does ridiculous.

Angus is looking at me. His face is a stark contrast to mine. Calm. In control. 'I'll finish it,' he says again.

This time I don't protest. I can feed the residents hot dogs and frozen peas for a week, if that's what it comes to.

With his keys in my hand, I leave via the front door. Angus's truck, blessedly, *is* right out front. I recognize it

146

from outside Rosalind House. I let myself in the passenger door and slide onto the vinyl, locking the door behind me.

I don't remember driving to pick up Clem from school the day Richard told me he was going to jail. I don't remember parking the car or walking through the gates or greeting any of the other mothers. But I *do* remember Clem's smile when she saw me. And I remember thinking: *I wonder when I will see Clem smile like that again.*

The drive home had been filled with her usual random, fluttery chatter. I answered the odd question, made the odd *ooh* or *ahh* but my mind was miles away. I didn't have any intention of telling her what Richard had done. Richard would have to do that. The twenty or so minutes I'd taken to pick up Clem solidified my shock into something cold and hard. Richard hadn't just betrayed his investors; he'd betrayed us as well.

A truck was blocking the driveway when we got home. I'd ordered some plants for my new garden bed and some ornamental stones. *Ornamental stones!* How ridiculous it seemed to have ordered ornamental stones. The trades-people who swarmed the house probably wouldn't get paid for the work they were doing. The ornamental stones would have to go back. The decent thing to do, I realized, would be to go around tapping them on the shoulder right now, telling them to stop work and go be with their families, but my cowardice, it turned out, was stronger than my righteousness.

Inside, I went straight to the kitchen and was surprised

to find Richard wasn't there. After what he'd told me, the idea that he could get up and move around freely seemed preposterous somehow. But his barstool was empty, swiveled to the left as though he'd got off in a hurry. I put some shortbread and cut-up fruit on a plate for Clem and then went looking for him.

'Richard!' I called. I wandered back through the house, across the parquetry floor Richard had insisted we have, past the paintings he'd ostentatiously bought at auction. '*Richard?*' I knocked on the door to his study. Somehow the fact that he went in there, into that place where he'd caused all this trouble, felt like more of a betrayal. 'Are you in there?'

There was no answer, so I barged inside, angry now. *How dare he ignore me after the bombshell he just dropped!* I took two steps into the room, and that's when I stopped. Dead.

Angus's truck is remarkably clean. It has one of those little plastic bags hanging from the glove compartment for rubbish. Like so many things about Angus, it isn't what I expected.

It's a short but uncomfortable drive home. Though it's warm, rainclouds curl in the gray sky, threatening but not delivering. Part of me yearns for the rain to start streaming down, a gray blanket to disappear into. The shopping bags, filled with Lord-knows-what, are in the back. Once he loaded them in, Angus got into the truck without so much as a word, and started driving.

About halfway home, I feel the need to say something. 'I appreciate you stepping in like that, Angus.'

Angus shrugs, keeping his eyes on the road. If Mother was here, she'd say it was impolite not to respond when someone spoke to you, but in this case, she'd be wrong. A quiet shrug, *no big deal*, was the nicest response he could possibly give.

I try for a laugh. 'I guess I'll have to start shopping at Bent and Dent.'

His eyebrows shoot up and his glance touches mine for a heartbeat. 'Why? Because one woman who didn't have her facts straight assaulted you while you were trying to do your job?'

'Because,' I say to my lap, 'I'm not strong enough to go through that every week.'

We crunch onto the driveway of Rosalind House. Angus shuts off the engine but doesn't get out. 'I'm sorry about what I said the other day,' he says. 'Of course your daughter has lost more than her home and her money. Obviously you have, too.'

Now I'm the one to shrug. Mostly because I don't trust myself to speak.

Angus lifts his hand, and for a second I think he's going to touch my cheek, but he stops a few inches short. 'How's the face?'

'Fine,' I say, though it's starting to throb again. I glance in the mirror. There's a fairly distinct hand mark. 'Nothing that won't heal.'

'Are you all right to go inside? I can take the groceries in if you'd rather hang out here for a while.'

'No,' I say. 'Let's just go in.'

Angus insists on carrying the bags, and I follow him toward the house.

'What were you doing at Houlihan's, anyway?' I ask.

He raises his eyebrows. 'You don't think a gardener could be interested in organic food?'

It is, I realize, exactly what I'd thought. Angus rolls his eyes but with a smile.

We arrive in the kitchen, and Angus sets the shopping bags on the counter.

'I needed saffron,' he says. 'That's why I was at Houlihan's. I'm entertaining tonight, and I'm making paella.'

'*Seafood* paella?' I try to keep the surprise out of my voice, but I think I fail.

Angus looks a mixture of irritated and amused. 'Is there any other kind?'

Actually, there are other kinds. Paella Valenciana. Paella mixta. But I don't point that out. Instead I start unloading the groceries. Pak choy. Roma tomatoes. Risoni. Mushrooms. No sign of the hot dogs or frozen peas I'd feared. 'If you're making paella, just make sure you don't skimp on the—'

'Sofrito?' he says. 'Don't worry, I know.'

We lock eyes. As I look at him, I get the feeling that, although I've seen Angus many times before, I've never actually *seen* him.

'I'm cooking for my sister,' he says. 'She knows her paella. And she'd never let me skimp on the sofrito.'

Keeping my head down, I nod. His *sister*. The sister who would never have babies because of Richard.

150

'Well,' he says. 'I'd better . . . get back to the garden.'

'Do you know Anna and Luke very well?' I ask as he wanders toward the door, and it has only a little to do with the fact that I want him to stay a bit longer.

'I've known them as long as they've been at Rosalind House,' he says.

'What were they like? When they first arrived, I mean.'

He thinks for a minute. 'They were a lot more lucid. Almost like regular people, if you didn't press them too hard to do anything complicated. Luke's speech wasn't great, even back then, but mentally, he seemed pretty sharp. They both did.'

'Eric tells me that . . . they were friends?'

Angus nods. 'More than friends, I think. I'm not sure if they were *together*, but they were certainly always together, if you know what I mean.' Angus smiles and his eyes go faraway. 'You know what was sweet? I don't know if Eric told you, but Anna is terrified of dogs. She was bitten, I think, when she was a kid. But Luke, he loved dogs. During pet therapy, he always had a dog on his lap or at his feet. But after Anna came to Rosalind House, Luke started staying inside with Anna, away from the dogs.'

'Pet therapy?'

'It's a volunteer group; they come every other week with dogs and rabbits and kittens for the residents to pet.'

'And Luke stopped going outside with the dogs so he could stay inside with Anna?'

Angus nods. 'Sweet, right?'

I exhale. 'Yeah.'

'It's been a while since I've seen that, though,' he says.

151

'They've degenerated a lot. Mostly they just sit around, staring off into space.'

'If I had dementia,' I say, 'or any kind of disease, I'd want the person I loved within arm's reach as much as possible.'

Angus gives me a quizzical look. 'I didn't say they were in love.'

'But it's possible, isn't it?'

'I guess. But even if they loved each other once, they can't really love each other now, can they? How can you love someone you don't remember?'

I shrug, because I have no idea.

Angus smiles. 'Pretty heavy, huh, for a Tuesday afternoon?'

I smile back. 'Yep.'

'Well,' he says, 'I'd better—' He jabs his thumb over his shoulder.

'Okay. Thanks again for your . . . help today, Angus.'

'No problem.'

He starts toward the door and I turn my back, tying on my apron and then grabbing a canister of flour from a high shelf. As I lift the lid, a tiny cloud of white powder puffs out and scatters, absorbed into the air.

'Oh, Eve?'

I nearly launch right out of my skin. When I turn, Angus is still there. 'Yes?'

'I do my grocery shopping every Tuesday afternoon. If you ever want some company – or a bodyguard! – just let me know.'

And then, without waiting for a response, Angus strides

away. And whatever it was that had been on my mind just a moment ago floats up into the air and vanishes, just like the flour.

That afternoon, while I'm attempting to iron one of Bert's shirts, Mother calls.

'I'm picking Clem up from school today,' she says in her no-nonsense voice. 'And I'll keep her overnight so you can go to Book Club.'

I laugh-cough. 'Book Club?'

'It's tonight, isn't it? The third Wednesday of the month?'

Wow. She's right. Her memory can be crazy good when it suits her.

'Uh, yes, but . . .' It's hard to find words to describe why I shouldn't go to Book Club, mostly because it's so plainly obvious. For one thing, I haven't been to Book Club in four months. For another, I suspect the members of the book club – Andrea Heathmont, Romy Fisher, Jazz, and a bunch of other mothers from school – would sooner eat the selected book than discuss it with me over red wine and soft cheese.

'I don't know what book they're discussing,' I say weakly.

Mother laughs. 'As if anyone reads the book! Isn't it just an excuse for a midweek glass of wine with the girls? Who knows, you might end up going into town and having a dance?'

'Mother, I really think—'

'I'm picking Clemmy up, anyway, so suit yourself. But I think you should reach out to your friends. They may have their grievances with you, but if you don't stick with them, how can you expect them to stick by you? Like your grandmother used to tell me, the best cure for melancholy is your girlfriends. Go. What have you got to lose?'

That night, I lie on the couch in my pajamas with Mother's words on auto-play in my head. *What have you got to lose?* Maybe she's right? The truth is, I don't have a whole lot left to lose, and who knows, perhaps the ladies would understand it wasn't my fault?

I look at the clock. It's 8:01 P.M. If I leave now, I'd be late, but I'd still make it.

Ten minutes later, I'm out in the evening air. I still have my reservations, but I feel surprisingly free. Maybe I *can* do this? I am, after all, one of the founding members of Book Club. When it started, the members had been just Jazz, Andrea, and me. We used to meet in our living rooms, but when the girls started kindergarten, we invited a few other moms to join and moved the location to the back room at Emilio's Wine Bar. Now we have about fifteen members, though generally only seven or eight come to any particular meeting.

Emilio's is quiet up front, but from the entrance, I can hear shrieks of laughter out of the back room, and I get a boost of confidence. It feels like forever since I've gone to Book Club. And how long has it been since I *laughed* like that?

As I round the corner, I count about twelve heads around the table – a good turnout. Romy is talking to Madeleine, a glass of wine hovering at her lips. Andrea digs a piece of flat bread into spinach dip, laughing at something Carmen is saying. Clearly the group discussion has finished (if there even was one), and now the women clump in twos and threes, gossiping. This is the good part of Book Club. I made the right decision to come.

'Eve!' Jazz is the first to notice me. Her face is the image of shock – open mouth, wide eyes, pink cheeks. It takes a few seconds because of the music, but one by one, heads turn.

'Hello,' I say, forcing a smile. 'Room for one more?'

'Sure,' Jazz says eventually. 'Yeah. Take a seat.'

A couple of women shuffle over, and I sit next to a kindergarten mom I know vaguely. Someone pushes an empty wineglass toward me. I look around eagerly but everyone remains silent.

'So,' I say. 'What's the book?'

'*Gone Girl*,' someone says. 'Have you read it?'

'Yes,' I say. 'Yes, I enjoyed it.'

I sound a bit formal, a bit nervous. There's an open bottle of red on the table and I pull it toward me and pour the remaining few inches into my glass.

'So . . . how *are* you, Eve?' Carmen asks, leaning forward on her elbows. 'You must be having an awful time.'

'Oh, no,' I say. 'I'm fine.'

'And your . . . little one? Clementine? How is she?'

Carmen is talking loudly and Jazz and a couple of other mothers look over, casually interested. A few others resume chatting among themselves.

'Clem's fine,' I say, wondering if this is true. 'She's grieving, of course, but she's a tough little thing. She'll get through it.'

'Good.' Carmen pulls on her gold necklace and smiles

155

a little too brightly, the same smile as the woman next to her, and the woman next to *her*. 'Good.'

I smile back. It's bizarre, but it's bound to be like this for a while; I know that. Soon people will lose interest. There's always something or someone new to talk about.

'So where are you living, Eve?' someone asks, and my throat closes up. At a loss, I take another swig of my wine, draining the glass. 'Shall I order another bottle?' I ask.

Nobody speaks. A few heads turn; a few silent conversations are had. The song that was playing ends, and there are a few moments of dead air before the next one starts up.

Finally a chair screeches back. 'Actually, I'm going to head off,' Andrea says, standing. Her gaze touches mine for a second. 'Busy day tomorrow.'

'Yes – me, too,' Romy says. 'I have an early start.'

There's a general hum of agreement. People look at their watches. It's late. They're tired. One by one, chairs scrape backwards.

'Nice to see you, Eve.'

'You take care.'

'Might see you around sometime.'

Ten minutes later, it's just Jazz and me. The room looks sad now, full of the evening's remains. A half-eaten dip platter, empty glasses, used napkins. But what does it matter? With a good bottle of wine, we won't even notice.

'What do you say, Jazz?' I say. 'One more bottle? Or just a glass?'

I'm tempted to say *for old times' sake*, but I hold it in, hoping our friendship is still current enough not to require that particular enticement. But Jazz just glances nervously around, as though she's forgotten there's no one left to save her.

'Better not, Evie,' she says finally. 'It really *is* getting late.'

I nod and tell her, 'Yes, it's fine, we probably should get an early night.' But as we reach for our purses, I glance at my watch. It's 8:30 P.M.

16

Clementine

'All right, class!' Miss Weber says, 'Good news. The second grade Family Dance Night is *next week*!'

It's after recess and we are sitting in home circle. I'd been zoning out, staring out the window, but suddenly, I'm listening.

Miranda puts up her hand. 'What's Family Dance Night?'

'We do it every year,' Miss Weber says. 'It happens after school, in the gymnasium. There'll be food and drinks and dancing. All the second graders are invited to bring a friend or family member with them. It could be a grandparent, a friend, or you could bring your mom or dad—'

'Oh!' Miranda says. She says it in a long and drawn-out way, like this *finally* makes sense. 'The Daddy Daughter, Mommy Son Dance, you mean?'

I see a twig on the floor in front of me and I pick it up and I dig it into a groove in the carpet. Last year I went to the dance with Daddy. He'd called it *a date*. I remember him arriving at school in his work clothes with a bunch of flowers. Red and pink and yellow and purple. No one else's dad brought flowers, not even Miranda's. He opened the doors for me and took off my coat, like he did for Mom. And when the dancing started, he let me stand on his feet and we swished around the room like a King and Queen.

'That's what we called it last year, yes.' Miss Weber's cheeks turn pink. 'But this year, we thought it would be more fun to let people bring whomever they wanted—'

'In case they don't have moms or dads?' Miranda asks.

'Or in case they'd rather bring someone else,' Miss Weber says.

Miranda puts up her hand again, but Miss Weber looks over her head and keeps talking. 'Anyway, we have lots to do. We need to get our decorations ready – streamers, banners, balloons. So, I'd like everyone to find a partner.'

Miranda grabs Legs's knee. 'Partners?'

It's the third time Miranda has done that this week. It's like, all of sudden, Miranda is *in love* with Legs or something.

Legs looks at me.

'You don't mind, do you, Clem?' Miranda says. Her voice is all singy, like she's trying to be nice, but she's just being *tricky*. 'You could be partners with . . . hmmm, let's see—' She looks around, tapping her bottom lip with her finger.

'I'll be your partner, Clem.'

It's Harry who says it. He smiles and pushes his hair out of his eyes.

I'd rather be partners with Legs, but Harry is nice, too. I tell him, 'Sure, we can be partners.'

'*Yes!*' Miranda says. 'Harry and Clem *should* be partners. Neither of them have daddies.'

'Miranda!' Miss Weber says.

'What?' Miranda says. 'It's true!'

Miranda still has one hand on Legs's knee. I look at it, and my face starts to get hot. I'm sick of her being so tricky all the time. I'm *sick* of her saying things about my daddy. I put my twig between two fingers and flick it. It flies up and stabs her in the eye.

'*Ow!*'

'Sorry,' I say. Her eye is all red and watery and it makes me feel much better. 'It was an accident.'

I look at Harry and we both smile. Sometimes I can be tricky, too.

'What are you staring at, young lady?' Bert asks.

It's after school and I'm at Rosalind House. Mom is in the kitchen making dinner and I am in the parlor, staring at Bert. 'Your eyes,' I say. 'They're yellow.'

He coughs. 'They're not.'

Gwen is sitting beside Bert, smiling. Gwen always smiles at Bert.

'They're yellow, aren't they, Gwen?' I ask her.

'Well, uh . . . I don't have my glasses on.'

I look at his eyes again. You don't need glasses to see that they're yellow. 'Do you want me to get you a mirror?' I ask Bert.

160

He looks at me like he wishes I'd go away. 'At my age, you don't like to look in the mirror too much.'

'Why not?'

'You ask a lot of questions,' he says.

I shrug. 'You asked the first one. About what I was staring at.'

He looks annoyed that I am right. Then he says: 'Is there something I can do for you, young lady?'

Bert says 'young lady' a lot. I think it's because he doesn't remember my name. 'Yes,' I say. 'I'd like to talk about Myrna.'

'Why do you want to talk about Myrna?'

'Ummm . . . because she's invisible?' *Der.*

'Oh.'

'So, if I want to talk to someone invisible . . . is there anything I need to do? Touch my nose? Blink twice?'

'Touch your nose?' he says, then waves his hand. 'No. No.'

'Okay,' I say. 'What then?'

'Well, I suppose I think about how Myrna looks. The way she used to curl up her hair. The kind of rouge she wore on her cheeks. Once I do that for a while, I guess, I can see her.'

I nod, my chin cupped in my hand. 'Okay.'

'I think about what she would have said. Would she have laughed, screamed, cried . . . that sort of thing. And then, well, then I can hear her.'

I repeat it all in my head, so I don't forget. *Think about how they look. Think about what they would have said.* I notice that Gwen is still smiling at Bert.

161

'Have you ever thought about any other ladies?' I ask. 'Ones that aren't invisible?'

Bert coughs again. 'The sun will shine out of my nether regions before that happens, young lady.'

I frown, curling my mouth around the words. *The sun will shine out of my nether . . .*

'Oh,' I say eventually. I think it means no.

'Daddy?'

I'm in the garden, by the tree. A few old people are across the yard, but I don't look at them. I really don't know what is supposed to happen, but I close my eyes and concentrate really hard. In my mind, I can see him, holding a bunch of flowers out to me. But when I open my eyes, *poof.* He's gone.

'Daddy?' I try again. 'Are you there?'

I try to remember what Bert said about Myrna. *'I see her because I really, really want to see her.'*

'The Family Dance Night is next week,' I tell him because even though I can't see him, he might be listening. 'Remember we went last year? That was fun, right? Remember you brought me flowers?'

Legs had really liked my flowers, so I asked Daddy if we could give her one and he said yes. Daddy liked Legs. *'Any friend of yours is a friend of mine,'* he said.

'Mom is going to take me this year,' I say. 'But I wish *you* could take me.'

I squeeze my eyes closed and I remember last year. After I'd danced around the room on his feet, Daddy had watched Legs and me do Irish dancing while he clapped and clapped. He said that was his favorite part.

'Show me your dancing.'

My eyes fly open again. I don't see him. I don't even hear him, exactly. It's weird, but I kind of *feel* the words. I feel them from the tips of my toes all the way up to the hairs on my head.

'Please,' he says. 'Show me?'

'Okay,' I say, nodding. 'Are you watching?'

I step into position and give myself a little shake. *Come on, Clem. He's watching.* I put my arms by my sides, then start my routine. Three skips, two point-hop-backs, two side-sevens. Repeat. It's the same dance I did for Daddy at the dance last year. At the other end of the garden, I see Clara and May and Laurie clapping.

'Bravo,' Daddy says in my mind. 'Bravo, my sweet Clementine.'

'Take a bow!' Laurie shouts when I stop spinning. And I do. But the bow isn't for him. It's for Daddy.

17

Anna

Twelve months ago . . .

My mother used to say, '*If you give up too many things, you don't live longer, it just feels like you do.*' I think she's right. Since I've been at Rosalind House, I haven't denied myself anything. Cake. Red alcohol. (I was pleasantly surprised to find that they serve it with dinner.) Online shopping. (Jack still allows me one low-limit credit card, which I use to buy politically incorrect toys for the nephews – what's the point in having a mentally ill aunt if she can't buy you a Nerf Super Soaker Electrostorm Blaster?) I've downloaded countless books to my online-book-thingy even though I'm more of a TV watcher lately. (Novels seem to favor complex plots, and my mind can't keep up.)

Also, I haven't denied myself kissing.

Young Guy and I are in the upstairs room again, lying side by side on the floor. His lips are on mine, and my hands are on his face. Sometimes we just do this for hours. Sometimes I forget who we are and why we are here.

'I'm g-glad you're . . . here,' he says, kissing my hair. I'm lying in the crook of his arm and I've just finished telling him about the time I punched Jack's friend Greg for trying to kiss me in third grade. Old memories come to me the easiest these days, and I enjoy sharing them. And Young Guy, judging by his comment, enjoys hearing them.

'Well, I had a lot of other offers,' I tell him, 'but I thought you'd be lonely, so . . .'

Young Guy twists to look at my face. He smiles. 'No, I m-mean. I'm g-glad you *didn't* . . .'

With a sinking heart, I realize what he means. 'You should know,' I say, 'that I haven't made any final decisions about that.'

He disentangles from me a little. 'But—'

'I'm sorry if you thought different. But the truth is, I have only a short window of time when I'll be able to do this, and that window is closing fast. And I haven't decided to slam it shut just yet. That's all.'

He pales so much, I think he might be sick. And there's no more kissing after that. After that we lie there in silence, and all I can think is, *This is my future with Young Guy.* Silence.

The strangest part is, it doesn't seem so terrible.

In the big house with all the old people, it's the little things that make people happy. Roast night. The day those animal-people come. Bingo. Tonight it's movie night and they're showing *Romeo and Juliet.* For the most part, the residents are excited, but Baldy has been whining all day. Apparently, we're watching a modern version of the film,

165

and Baldy doesn't *do* modern. As for me, I wouldn't say I'm excited but I am glad that, for once, people won't be going to bed at 8:15 sharp. And Young Guy and I will have some company for the evening.

Young Guy picks me up at my door for the movie, which is pretty sweet. It is probably the closest thing to a date I'll ever have again. But when he stares at me just a moment too long, I start to regret wearing makeup. Even before Alzheimer's, I wasn't much good at it, but now, it's like a puzzle. All the compacts and tubes for the different parts of the face. Tonight, I opened a few compacts, smeared them on, and put it all away again but now I wonder if I should have taken a little more care.

'What?' I ask.

'Nothing. You just . . . look pr-pr-pr . . .'

'Pretty?'

Normally I don't try to finish his sentences, but tonight he doesn't seem to mind. He nods. I'm wearing black jeans and a stripy top. No heels or anything, though I am, I suppose, wearing shoes. And, yes, the makeup. But the way he is looking at me, you'd think I was in full war paint.

He holds my hand on the way to the parlor. Usually he and I sit in matching seats by the window, but tonight the room has been reconfigured so all the chairs face the white wall, where the film is being projected.

Young Guy and I sit in the back row. The love seat.

I'm just getting comfortable when Skinny glances over at me once, then quickly again. Her face tells me something is very wrong.

166

My stomach does a flip. 'What?'

'Nothing, sweetie,' she says, but she beelines for me, pulling a scrunched-up white thing from her pocket and wiping it across her tongue. 'You've just made a bit of a mess of yourself. Don't worry. I'll get you cleaned up.'

She rubs the white thing over my face and when she pulls it away, it's covered in black and brown goo. Then she does the same again. All the oldies are staring right ahead as though they don't notice, but how could they not? I look at Young Guy and he shrugs. *Whatever,* his shrug says. After that, I don't worry anymore.

After three cloths have come away, stained, from my face, Skinny smiles and says, 'There now. Much better.'

Then the film starts.

'What in God's name!' Baldy exclaims, a few minutes in. 'Since when did Romeo and Juliet have *guns?*'

'It's a remake,' Skinny says hastily. She sounds nervous. 'The story's the same. Well, you know, basically.'

'It's a load of rubbish,' he says. 'I'm leaving.'

But Baldy makes no move to leave. In fact, his eyes are glued to the screen. It's probably the most excitement he's had in years.

I try to concentrate on the movie, but it's too quick. Too loud. After a while, there's too much noise, so I just lean back, close my eyes, and let the music wash over me. I feel Young Guy take my hand, intertwine it with his. It's enough to drown out the yelling, the noise of the guns, the music, all of it.

In high school science, my teacher once told us that the brain was responsible for these kinds of lustful

167

feelings. Apparently, during moments of intimacy, the brain sends messages to the heart to pump more blood and to the stomach to contract. If that's true, then I'm grateful to have a faulty brain. Because if the burst of happiness that explodes inside me were any greater, I'd almost certainly need medical attention.

When the names of the actors start to roll, the room lights up again and we untangle our hands. Most of the residents, I notice, have nodded off. But Baldy's still awake. Southern Lady. Really Old Lady. Young Guy and me.

'So?' Skinny says. Judging by her red eyes, she's been crying. 'What did you think?'

'I think,' says Really Old Lady, 'that Romeo was a playboy. One minute he was in love with Rosaline, and the next he'd run off with Juliet!'

'Which one was Rosaline?' someone that I can't see says.

'The one Romeo loved at the start of the film, before he met Juliet,' Southern Lady explains. 'But surely you don't hold that against Romeo, May? He met his true love. All's fair in love and war.'

Really Old Lady folds her arms, decided. 'If he'd stuck with Rosaline, became a one-man woman, he'd have been better off. Perhaps he even would have stayed alive.'

Baldy makes a noise, like a *phwar*. 'You're not suggesting Romeo should have forfeited his true love and settled for second-best in order to add a few more years to his clock? Time is important only if you've found the right person to spend it with. Romeo was better off having the love of his life for a few days than fifty years with the wrong gal.'

The conversation has a lot of participants, and it is moving pretty fast. But, using tremendous concentration, I manage to follow. And I find myself nodding to Baldy's comment. The day I left Aiden was the day my diagnosis was confirmed. With time being cut so suddenly short, another day in the wrong relationship was simply too much.

'I hate to say it,' I say, 'but I agree with him.'

Young Guy's hand continues to stroke mine, and I realize he's been silent. Southern Lady must notice, too, because she asks, 'What do you think, Luke?'

Luke! I say it in my head three times. *Luke. Luke. Luke.*

Luke is typically thoughtful, taking a moment and shifting in his seat before he speaks. 'I th-think,' he says, looking directly at me, 'that it all became pointless when they decided to kill themselves.'

18

Tonight, when Young Guy walks me to my door, I feel distracted.

'Are . . . you . . . ?' he asks at my door.

'I'm okay,' I say. I don't need to ask what he means anymore; usually I just know. His comment plays in my mind on repeat. *'It all became pointless when Romeo and Juliet decided to kill themselves.'* I wonder if that's true. I wonder if the fact that they died changed what they shared when they lived.

A few months ago, presented with the knowledge that life wasn't going to be what I'd planned, I wanted to check out, close the book. But now, it's like suddenly I've found a few more pages. And it feels like, against all likelihood, the last chapter might be the best one of all. The last chapter, in fact, might be something *great*.

'U-upstairs?' he says.

I reach for Luke's hand and it slides into mine: a perfect fit. 'I have a better idea,' I say, and pull him into my room.

The last time I had sex was the night I left my husband. I packed my bags while he was at work and loaded most of them into the car. The furniture, the mementos, everything except my clothes was his to keep – where I was going, I wouldn't need them. Then I waited in the hallway, sitting on a suitcase.

Aiden arrived home at the usual time. The door jammed on my suitcase as he flicked on the light. 'Hey,' he said, 'what are you doing?'

'Leaving you,' I said.

Aiden continued hooking his coat on the hall tree. 'Oh yeah?'

'Mmm-hmm,' I said. 'You seem to be taking it well.'

He turned, taking in my suitcase and somber expression. 'You're . . . serious?'

I'd never threatened to leave him before, but we had a certain way of talking, a light way, that made everything seem like a joke. As I held his gaze and nodded, realization dawned.

'Shit, Anna.' He raked his hands through his hair. 'I know we have problems but—'

'I have Alzheimer's.'

There I went again, dropping a bombshell. Somehow it helped me feel in control of this conversation and I wanted to be in control of *something*.

'Seriously?' Aiden sank to his knees. 'Oh God. I'm . . . I'm so sorry.'

We'd talked briefly about the possibility early in our relationship, but never since. Aiden was like me – if there was something unpleasant to be thought about, he found something else to do.

'But . . . you're leaving? Now?'

Admittedly, it didn't make much sense. Many people would have stuck in a failing relationship upon the diagnosis of a terminal illness, but I was not most people. The only way I knew to deal with this was to leave. And though he never said so, I suspected Aiden was relieved.

I drove straight to the bar. A cliché thing to do, but I was too thirsty to care about cliché. And, as it turned out, I only had to pay for one drink.

I don't remember the guy's name, though I blame the Jack Daniel's rather than the Alzheimer's. I do remember the scramble of hands and clothes – the fevered desperation to be free of my clothing. I remember the gravel in the parking lot rolling under his feet as he pinned me against the cold brick wall. I remember the bliss and agony of being ridden by a stranger who didn't care a thing about me. I remember the awkward aftermath of rising zippers and buttoning shirts.

Afterwards, the bartender called me a cab.

'Where to?' the cabdriver asked, hanging his arm over the back of the bench seat. I rattled off my address and dozed on the way home, drunk and spent and sore. When I got home, Aiden looked up from the sofa and stared at me as though I were a ghost.

'What are you doing here?' he asked.

'What do you mean?' I'd said, headed for the fridge. 'I live here.'

Aiden made me a bed on the sofa that night. And the next day, I had to leave all over again.

*

172

When Luke enters me, we knock heads – my chin into his nose. It's amazing how something can feel awkward and wonderful all at once. There's laughter, and a shudder. And then we're off.

Luke holds my hands beside my ears as he rocks against me. *Yes.* I look at his face. A face so new, yet so familiar. A face soon to be unfamiliar, but for now, I don't care. Not about anything that's happened, or anything that's going to happen. Why should I, when all either of us has is right now?

His breath becomes rough and raw, and a deep noise rolls from his throat. Here, nothing about him stutters or stammers. I don't feel disoriented or confused. I'm not worried about what I might say or do wrong. I feel like I might die from the loveliness of it.

I might not remember this. But I'm glad I got to live it.

19

Eve

It takes a few weeks, but I get to know each of the residents. I even have a few favorites. Clara, of course, is easy to love, with her Southern accent and her penchant for calling everyone 'honey'. Her husband, Laurie, is equally delightful, if only for the way he adores his wife. There's May, quiet and so old, I often find myself checking her breathing when she falls asleep in her chair. There's Gwen, stout and cheerful, and always knitting. Then there's the perpetually grumpy Bert, who somehow is still a favorite. Perhaps it's the fact that Clem has taken a shine to him? Or maybe it's that he's still head over heels for the wife he lost fifty years ago? Whatever it is, I get the feeling he's a favorite of Gwen's, too, if the way she looks at him is anything to go by.

I've been at Rosalind House about a month now, and there's no denying that the place is starting to look shabby. The mirrors have little specks of God-knows-what all over them, and the carpets are covered in hair and dirt. And, as Eric has yet to hire a cleaner, it is *my* responsibility to do something about it. Still, I continue to find excuses to cook rather than clean. If the ladies notice, they don't say anything. Bert, however, is a different story.

'You realize my bathroom's not self-cleaning, right, girlie?' he says one afternoon within earshot of Eric. After that, I know I can't dillydally any longer. And that's where Eric finds me: on my knees, scrubbing Bert's toilet.

'What's that cooking in the kitchen?' he asks, hanging around the bathroom door. 'It smells incredible.'

'Ground beef and spinach parcels,' I say. 'There's plenty if you're interested . . .'

'Better not.' Eric pats his stomach, which is hanging proudly over the top of his belt buckle. 'Actually I just wanted a quick chat. I understand you've been doing the grocery shopping at Houlihan's.'

I sit back on my haunches, cringing. He must have heard about the slap.

'The thing is,' he says, 'the last bill was nearly twice our weekly food budget.'

This is not what I was expecting. 'Oh. I'm sorry.'

'It's not your fault,' Eric says. 'I should have specified where we go to buy groceries. I just . . . didn't expect you to go to Houlihan's!'

He lets out a short laugh and I feel a pulse of shame. Clearly being married to Richard had left me out of touch. But twice the weekly food budget? Was that possible?

'You mean . . . your previous cook managed to feed everyone for a week on half that amount? All twelve residents, three meals a day, seven days a week?'

'She did.'

'Wow.'

'Going to a regular or discount grocery store extends the budget quite a bit,' he says pointedly. 'And buying seasonal items, items on special.'

'Okay well . . . where shall I go? Houlihan's is . . . the only one I know in the area.'

'You could try Food Basics or Aldi,' he says. 'Or Bent and Dent . . .'

I laugh, assuming Bent and Dent is a joke. But Eric nods and smiles like it's a done deal.

'Oh and I nearly forgot!' he says, handing me a letter bearing Clem's school emblem. His frown, when it appears, bears a trace of curiosity. 'This came for you yesterday. Sent to this address—'

'Oh!' I take it and drive it deep into my own pocket. 'Sorry, I didn't have a fixed address when I enrolled Clem, but this, uh . . . this is great.'

I smile. Eric continues to stand there. I start to sweat.

'Was there anything else, Eric?'

'Actually there is one other thing. It's May's birthday tomorrow – one hundred years old. Her family is planning a party for the weekend, but I'd like to do something with the residents tomorrow. Just some balloons and maybe' – he looks coy – 'a cake?'

'I'm sure I can throw something together,' I say.

'Carrot cake is her favorite,' he says. 'And I'd like it to be a surprise, if possible.'

'No problem,' I say. 'But I'll need to go to the store again for ingredients. Bent and Dent,' I add quickly. 'I can come back tonight and bake it here.'

'I'd owe you one,' he says. His eyes rest on mine long enough to make me uncomfortable. 'In fact, how would you like to check out one of the local wine bars, say Friday night? We can share a good bottle of red? My treat.'

I blink.

'Just two single people, hanging out,' he says, smiling. 'No big deal.'

I imagine myself at Emilio's with Eric. The redness of his cheeks, his teeth stained black, his belly peeking out between buttons. I'd almost certainly run into someone I knew. Andrea or Romy would be overjoyed. *Karma*, they'd whisper to each other, *it's a bitch*.

Eric watches me, eyebrows raised. He thinks he's a shoo-in. There's a cockiness about him, I realize. He thinks that whatever he wants, he can take.

'I'm busy Friday,' I say. 'Perhaps some other time.'

That afternoon, it's time to work on the vegetable patch. It's warm and still, and the sky is pale blue, mottled with cloud. A perfect planting day.

'Okay,' I say to the residents. 'Who's ready?'

Gwen and Clara stand before me in wide-brimmed hats and floral gardening gloves. Clara was an avid gardener, she tells me, with a thriving vegetable garden in her yard that used to win her plenty of prizes at the community fair. Gwen isn't quite so experienced, but her enthusiasm makes up for it. Anna and Luke have also joined us, and while I haven't been able to assess their level of enthusiasm, they certainly didn't put up a fight.

Our patch is in a lovely sunny part of the garden. Angus

has already loosened the soil and worked through the compost and limestone, not to mention built a retractable canopy that's every bit as good as the ones in the stores. Now he's in an adjacent garden bed, weeding and mulching and watering. Angus and I have made some headway since that fateful day at Houlihan's. We're not best friends, but the long cold stares, at least, are a thing of the past. He even gives me the odd wave if he sees me through the kitchen window, and the other day he showed me how to make a special nonchemical spray to keep the bugs off my vegetables.

'Clara,' I say, 'since you are the expert, why don't you take this quadrant of the bed and transfer the started plants. You can show Gwen what to do. Anna and Luke, we can take this section and scatter the seed.'

I've given this a lot of thought. Luke and Anna can follow simple instructions, so scattering seeds and watering will be perfect for them, and easy for Anna to do from her wheelchair. While Clara and Gwen get to work, I get out my packets of seed.

'Okay – Luke, Anna. We're going to plant arugula seeds. The earth is all ready, all we need to do is open the packet like this . . . and then scatter it.'

I sprinkle a few seeds, then check to see if Anna and Luke are following. But Anna's eyes are on Clara and Gwen, who are digging holes for the transferred plants. Luke is watching Anna. After a moment, they both look back at me.

'Try to spread them thinly and evenly,' I say, turning back to the garden. 'Now, who wants to try?'

When I look back, Anna has wheeled herself over to Clara and Gwen.

'You need to go deeper or the roots won't take,' she tells them, gesturing at them to dig. They do as she says. 'There,' she says, nodding. 'Like that.'

'She's right,' Clara says to Gwen, 'we were being lazy.'

'I didn't know you could garden, Anna,' I say.

'Did you know I was a champion boxer?' she says, not looking up.

'No.'

'That's because I'm not,' she says, and everyone bursts into laughter.

Anna tells us her mother was a gardening enthusiast and she had spent many summers with a trowel in her hand. As she talks, I notice she is so much more than her Alzheimer's. She's funny. Witty. Warm. And something else. A leader? Whatever it is, as we all move and shift and clamber around the garden bed, she always remains in the center of the group.

After a while, I pick up my packets of seeds. 'Well,' I say, 'how about I scatter these seeds?'

Anna looks up at me and gives me the biggest grin. 'Go on, then,' she says. 'Get busy.'

When everything has been planted, I head inside to make a jug of lemonade. I return a few minutes later and pour everyone a glass, then take one over to Angus. He's wiping his forehead with the hem of his T-shirt, exposing a tanned, muscular stomach.

A flash of Richard, shirtless in Hawaii on our

honeymoon, comes to mind. Richard's body was nothing on Angus's, but it was broad and taut. I remember watching him brush his teeth one morning, a crisp white towel at his waist. I thought to myself that one day, that body would be old and wrinkled and sagging at the elbows. I remember that the thought had made me smile.

'For me?' Angus says when he lets the T-shirt fall.

I shrug. 'It's warm out here.'

'That it is.' He drops his trowel, grabs the lemonade, and takes a sip, then wipes his mouth with the back of his hand. 'It's good.'

I know it's good. My homemade lemonade is famous in these parts. Last year, the school practically begged me to run a stall at the fund-raiser, and I was told it was the most lucrative stall of the day.

This year Romy and Andrea were running an orange-juice stand.

'It's a favorite recipe of mine,' I say.

Angus takes another sip. 'So who taught you about cooking, then?'

'I was self-taught before the cookery school,' I say. 'I became interested in flavors in high school, I guess. Were you always interested in plants?'

I wait as he drains his glass. 'Nope. I wanted to be a professional football player.'

'You did?'

'Didn't every guy?' He laughs. 'Unfortunately, I wasn't any good at football.'

Now *I* laugh.

'Eh, a guy's gotta dream,' he says. 'My grandmother

loved gardening, though. I practically grew up in her garden. When I realized the football thing wasn't going to work out, I thought . . . there are worse things than spending your life in the garden. As Grandma says, now I'll never stop smelling the roses.'

Automatically, I glance over at the roses. They are pink and white, climbing up a trellis on one side of the house. 'Except in winter,' I point out. 'You won't smell them then.'

Angus gives me a searching look.

'I just mean,' I say, 'that nothing lasts forever.'

He holds his glass out to me. 'Some things last forever, don't they?'

I look over at Anna and Luke. 'Honestly?' I say. 'I have no idea.'

That night, after I've cleaned up dinner, I head to the store to pick up ingredients for May's birthday cake. By the time I make it back to Rosalind House, most of the residents are in their rooms and the place is low-lit and quiet.

It's strange being at Rosalind House at night. Usually, the place is bustling and *alive*. Now, apart from the bubble and swoosh of the dishwasher, it's dead silent, which is vaguely unnerving.

Mother is watching Clem at our apartment and I call to say goodnight around 8 P.M. An hour later I'm grating lemon rind into my cream cheese frosting when a woman's scream pierces the silent air. I drop my spatula and follow the noise to Anna's door.

181

'Eve?'

Rosie appears beside me and I am flooded with relief. 'I . . . I heard the screaming,' I say.

'Pretty hard not to.' She smiles, resigned. 'I'll look after her, don't worry.'

As Rosie reaches for the lock, I'm struck by how unruffled she is. Unsurprised. Then I remember Eric's words. *'Sometimes they become upset at night.'* I'd pictured sleeplessness. Nightmares, perhaps. Not this.

Rosie steps into the room, and instinctively, I shadow her. We find Anna sitting up in bed. Her blankets are kicked off and hair is wild around her face.

'What's going on, Anna?' Rosie asks. 'You sound upset. Can I help?'

'I want to go *home*!' Anna's voice is a razor, intended to hurt. 'Take me home.'

'Why don't I turn on this light?' Rosie advances slowly but confidently. 'Help you see a bit better.'

'No!' Anna shouts. 'Where is he?'

A tingle runs down my spine.

'Is there someone we can help you find?' Rosie asks.

Anna nods. 'Yes. Him.' Then her face starts to crumple. 'I . . . want to go home.'

'All right,' Rosie says cheerfully. 'I'll take you home. But it's pretty late for driving right now. How about a cup of tea first? Then, when it's light, you and me will hop in the car? Sound good?'

Anna watches Rosie carefully. 'Is Jack at home? And Mom?'

'Everyone's there,' Rosie says. 'But it's nighttime; they're probably fast asleep. We don't want to wake them.'

'Okay,' Anna says, a little suspicious. 'But in the morning, you'll take me home?'

'Absolutely.'

Rosie's voice is so soothing that *I* almost believe her. Except for the fact that Eric told me Anna's mom was dead.

'Would you mind making us some tea, Eve?' Rosie says. 'Anna likes peppermint and I'll have chamomile. And would you mind checking that the other residents are still asleep? I'm going to stay here with Anna for a bit.' She produces a tissue and discreetly wipes Anna's nose.

I nod. 'Yes. I'll do it now.'

I listen at the doors of the other residents, and miraculously, all I hear is snoring. They've all slept through it. Something to be said for poor hearing. The place is quiet, peaceful. All except for Anna.

'Everyone's sleeping,' I say when I return with the tea. Rosie is sitting next to Anna on her bed, giving her a hand massage. I set the tray on the table.

'Thanks,' Rosie says. 'Anna and I are going to hang out for a while. I love watching the late-night infomercials, and now I'll have company.'

'Would you—?' I start, then wonder if it's going to sound strange or presumptuous. 'Would you like some more company? My cake is just out of the oven and it needs to cool a little before I ice it.'

Rosie shrugs. 'What do you think, Anna? Would you mind if Eve stayed to watch TV with us?'

183

Anna's eyes, narrowed and searching, settle on me. 'Okay,' she says. 'That's okay.'

Rosie throws me a pillow and I wedge myself onto the bed. Anna is in the middle, leaning back against the pillows with Rosie and me, her bookends. She seems calmer now, but she jitters a little, whispering under her breath. 'Where is he? *Where is he?*'

She's talking about Luke; of that, I'm now certain. And after tonight, one thing's for sure. If this is what her life is like – being locked up in her room, alive but not living – I understand why she jumped off the roof. If I were kept locked up, away from the ones I loved, I'd want to kill myself, too.

After Anna falls asleep, Rosie and I slip out of her room. We convene in the hallway, in a puddle of moonlight.

'I get the feeling that's not the first time this has happened?' I say.

Rosie yawns. 'Sadly not. Night-restlessness is common. It happens to Luke, too, from time to time.'

'That's who she meant, isn't it? When she said "Where is he?"'

'Probably,' Rosie admits.

'So why couldn't we just take her to him?'

'The families have decided they don't want them to be together, so there's no point in entertaining it,' she says. 'It's better to just change the subject.'

'But they were . . . friends, weren't they? Why wouldn't the families want them to visit?'

Rosie says nothing.

'Do you think they—?' I start.

'Still have a connection?' she says.

I nod, relieved that Rosie has already considered this. 'It's a tough one,' she says. 'No one really knows for sure what people with dementia are capable of.'

'But . . . ?'

'But,' she says, 'my guess is that they are capable of a lot more than people think. At the last place I worked, there were two residents with Alzheimer's, Rodney and Betty. Every afternoon they sat together and watched soap operas and held hands. Their diseases were fairly progressed, and there was no way they could remember that they did this every day, so for them, every time was the first time. Rodney always made the first move, letting their hands touch a little, as if it were an accident. Then, when Betty smiled, he went all in, linking fingers and stroking the back of her hand with his thumb. It was *exactly* the same every day. On the odd occasion that one of them had visitors or an appointment at that time, they still watched the soap operas with the other residents, but they always seemed a little agitated. And neither of them ever held anyone else's hand.' She smiles. 'Dementia steals things – memories, speech, other abilities. But I don't think it changes who you are, or who you love.'

'If that's what you think . . . how do you feel about the door-locking?' I ask.

'Well, Anna *did* jump off the roof,' she says. I notice that Rosie is not meeting my eye anymore.

'Rosie,' I say. 'What is it?'

She waves a hand at me. 'Look, in an ideal world, of

course the doors would be unlocked. There'd also be plenty of staff who could stay up with them all night, and they'd have a well-lit area where they could do activities. But even private facilities like Rosalind House don't have the funding to staff twenty-four-hour activities. I do what I can. But Eric has told me in no uncertain terms that Anna and Luke need to stay in their rooms and that I am to lock the doors. I know it seems cruel. But instead of focusing on that, I try to focus on the things I *can* do to make life better for them. Every shift I have here, I have the power to make life a little better for them. That *is* my goal.'

'So why did you tell Anna you were going to take her home?' I ask. 'And that her mom would be there? You know her mom is dead, right?'

'Yes,' she says. 'But Anna thought she was alive. Did you want me to break it to her that not only was she in a strange place, but that her mother was dead, too?'

'No, but . . . surely honesty is the best policy? Aren't you breaking the trust between you by lying?'

Rosie smiles, but it's a sad expression. 'Close your eyes.'

'What?'

She reaches for my forehead, then drags her fingers over my lids until I see black. 'Now imagine that when you open your eyes, you're in a completely unfamiliar place. You don't recognize anything, you don't recognize me, and you can't find anyone you know. You're scared and confused and disoriented. You ask to be taken home, and someone you don't recognize tells you *this* is your home and you're not going anywhere. Every time you ask for your mother, someone tells you she is dead. And because you can't retain that information for long, you have to hear it again and again and again. How would that make you feel?'

Rosie speaks gently, without judgment, but still, the words feel like a sucker punch. When I open my eyes, they're full of tears.

'In the morning, Anna won't remember that I promised to take her home. All she will know is how she feels. And with any luck, she'll be feeling safe, secure, and happy.' Rosie watches me, looking for comprehension in my face. 'We can make each moment frightening for her with the truth. Or we can lie to her and make each moment happy and joyous. I know what I'd prefer if it were me.'

20

I arrive at work four minutes late the next morning, which isn't disastrous apart from the fact that my eyes feel scratchy and I can't stop yawning. It had been a late night. Through the window, I can see Angus in the garden with Clem on his heels, catapulting questions at him. He smiles at something she says, then points off at a bush in one corner of the garden. I am grateful that he likes kids, or at least appears to, because this morning I can use all the help I can get.

I rub my eyes and look at a bowl of fruit on the counter, trying to remember what I'm supposed to do with it. After a few minutes, I yank open the refrigerator and bury my head, hoping the cool air will snap me awake.

'I hear there was some commotion last night.'

I grab a carton of milk and reverse out of the refrigerator. Eric is leaning against the doorjamb.

'Morning,' I say. 'Yes. Rosie told you?'

Eric nods. 'I'm sorry Anna disturbed you.'

'Don't be.' I set the milk on the counter. 'Actually, I can't stop thinking about it. She was quite upset.'

'It's very sad,' Eric says. 'A tragic disease, Alzheimer's.'

'It is. Last night Anna asked for her mother. She also kept asking, "Where is he?"'

'She did?'

I nod. 'Clearly she was talking about Luke. And I wondered, I mean, is there any reason why she can't at least visit him?'

'Why do you think she was talking about Luke?' Eric asks.

'I don't,' I admit, 'but who else would she mean?'

Eric shrugs. 'You said yourself that she asked for her mother, who is long dead. "He" could have been her father, her brother. Anyone. Anyway, it's the families' decision to keep the doors locked at night. There's nothing we can do.'

'Yes, but—' A thought rushes at me. Eric said Anna tried to kill herself and *then* they started locking the doors, but what if that wasn't the sequence of events? What if the suicide attempt was *because* they locked the doors? 'Was Anna's suicide attempt before or after you started locking the doors?' I ask. I pause only a second before continuing, so certain I'm right. 'It was after, wasn't it?'

'No,' Eric says, frowning. 'I don't think so.'

'Oh.' I pluck a pear and an apple from the fruit bowl and begin slicing them, trying to hide my disappointment. 'I just thought it might have explained things. I mean, if I were separated from the one I loved, I'd probably—'

'Loved?' Eric exhales. 'Eve, falling in love requires memory, communication, reason, decision making. It's very unlikely that people with dementia have these capabilities.'

I think about Rodney and Betty, the couple Rosie told me had held hands every day. *They* didn't need memory to have a connection.

'But—'

'Look,' Eric says, 'this job can be difficult. These people are at the end of their lives, and it's sad. Particularly for Luke and Anna, being so young. But in order to do this job, you need to keep a certain distance. You are, first and foremost, a staff member here. And while it's wonderful that you care so much about the residents, your job is to cook and clean. So leave things to the night nurse from now on, eh? After all, that's what she's paid for.'

'Okay.' It's hard, but I force myself to meet his eye. 'I will.'

Eric claps his hands, indicating a change of topic. 'Anyway, I should get my day started.' He turns toward the door, then pauses. I have an almost overpowering urge to give him an almighty shove to get him out of my sight.

'So we're clear about Luke and Anna, then?' he says.

'Perfectly clear,' I say, even though the one thing I am *not* clear on is Luke and Anna.

21

Anna

Twelve months ago . . .

'P-promise me something,' Young Guy says as I pull a sheet over my chest. We're in my bed, a squeeze for two grown bodies, but we are managing pretty well. I don't know what time of day it is, and I don't care. I don't have anywhere to be. I have *Alzheimer's disease.*

'Sure.'

He watches me carefully, his face becoming hard-lined. 'Promise we'll . . . be together. R-right until the end?'

I smile, because I can't help it when I look at him. 'I can't promise that. And neither can you.'

'I c-can.'

'Okay, you can. But just because you say it doesn't make it so. When we get worse, they could separate us very easily and we'd have no idea.'

'We would.' He props himself onto an elbow. 'We'll . . . make an order. Do not s-separate.'

'Like "do not resuscitate"?'

'Y-yes.'

I laugh. 'Who will we leave the orders with?'

'Eric. Our f-families.'

'Come on! We'll be so gaga, they could put us in cardboard boxes and we wouldn't know. They could call the family dog Anna, and you wouldn't know the difference.'

Luke doesn't laugh.

I groan. 'You make me feel like such a black cloud, you know that? I'm a positive person! Around you I'm like . . . Negative Nora.'

I hope Luke is right, that we will know each other. But I'm not convinced. I've already forgotten so much. 'When I stop remembering you, I want to go. To flick a switch and end it. Why stay any longer, you know?'

'N-never s-say—'

'Why not? Do you really want to keep going to the miserable end, when your entire body has forgotten how to function and you piss and shit your pants and some stranger has to clean it up? That's what you want?'

He nods.

'Even if you don't remember me?' I ask.

He gets that look in his eye like he's looking right through me, past my skin and hair and bones and right through my chest, into my soul. 'I w-will.'

'Were you always so sweet, or is it the dementia?'

He dips his head. 'P-promise me we'll be together in the end,' he says. 'No switching a button, no ending it. Promise?'

I groan. But his face is determined. There's no arguing.

'Fine,' I say.

'Say . . . it.'

I roll my eyes. 'I promise. We'll be together in the end. Batshit crazy. And together. I promise.'

In the morning, after Young Guy has stolen across the hall into his own room, I sit at my table. My notebook is in the drawer and I get it out. Briefly, my mind wanders to the last time I sat here to write. Things feel very different now. This time, I'm writing a letter to myself. My future self.

November 1, 2013

Dear Anna,

Today you made a promise. You promised the young guy with the tea-colored eyes that you would stay with him until the end. No cutting out early, no taking the fast exit. It's hard to believe you agreed to that, right? I can hardly believe it as I write this.

So why did you agree?

You agreed because this guy is the one you didn't know you were waiting for. You agreed because, as it is, you're not going to have long enough together. And you agreed because this guy is a pretty good reason to hang around.

Soon you won't remember this promise – that's why I'm writing this down. So if you are reading this now, there's something else you should know: Anna Forster never breaks a promise.

Anna

22

None of the residents said anything the first time Young Guy held my hand in the big front room, but I know they noticed. Baldy flew into a coughing fit. Southern Lady's eyes narrowed, then widened. Really Old Lady smiled, but then, she always smiles. (She probably wouldn't smile if she knew what we got up to at night.) But after a while, they start to like it. *I* start to like it. And, it might be dementia, but I can't actually remember a time before his hand rested on mine.

Today it's the usual suspects in the big front room. And the guy who does the garden. Every now and then, he comes inside with flowers and hands them out. The ladies love that. But today the garden is covered in white stuff, so he must have gotten the flowers sent from somewhere warm.

'Gabriela!' he says when Latina Cook-Lady walks past. He hands her a special bunch of flowers wrapped in brown paper. 'Congratulations.'

She gives him a big, happy smile. Today she announced that she has a baby in her belly, and everyone is really excited. I know I should feel excited, too.

Next he gives me a flower. 'How are you this morning, Anna?' he asks.

'I'm okay.' I feel bad for not remembering his name. I do, however, remember the name of the flower. 'Lovely alstroemeria.'

His face tells me he's impressed, and I feel pleased.

'Well, well,' he says, 'you know your stems. Let me guess, you used to be a florist?'

'Do I look like a florist?'

He considers that. 'Now that you mention it, no. What *did* you do?'

'I was a paramedic.'

I may as well have said that I was the person in charge of the United States. Southern Lady's mouth pops open, her husband's eyes widen, Baldy even stops chatting to his imaginary wife.

'You know what a paramedic is, right?' I say, chuckling. 'I didn't say . . .' I try to conjure up the title for the person who goes to the moon, but it's temporarily – or permanently? – just out of my reach, 'you know, a space person.'

'It must have been exciting,' says Really Old Lady. 'Speeding around in those buses with sirens and the lights flashing.'

'Traumatic, more like it,' Baldy says. 'Who do you think scrapes the bodies off the street after they leap from those tall buildings?'

'There was some of that,' I say. 'But it wasn't all sirens and dramatics. There was a lot of looking after people who'd had too much alcohol to drink. A lot of routine transfers from places like Rosalind House into the hospital.'

Or the place where they keep dead people, I don't say. The residents start to look a little bummed, so I decide to afford them what they are looking for. 'But it had its moments. Once I had to help restrain an A-list famous person who went off on a drug-fueled rampage in a hotel room. And' – I can't help a smile at this one – 'I delivered a baby once, right on the floor of a shop-center place.' I can still see the slimy little thing – a boy – peering up at me from between his mother's legs. The newspaper had run a story on it, but I'd let Tyrone pose for the picture. The bright lights liked him more than they liked me.

The residents coo and I sit a little taller. It's been a while since anyone has listened to me like this. Like I know what I'm talking about. 'And there was one time—'

'*There* you are, Grandpa!' We all turn to look at a young girl with spiky yellow fuzz on her head, hovering in the doorway. 'Sorry to interrupt. I just really need to talk to my grandpa.' The girl is looking at Baldy, but then her eyes scan the room and stop at me. 'Oh. Hello again.'

It's weird. She's definitely looking right at me, but she doesn't seem even slightly familiar. She must have mixed me up with someone else.

'I'm glad I ran into you,' she says. 'I wanted to thank you. Your advice worked.'

I study her. She's too young to be a friend of mine, and if Baldy is her grandfather . . . I don't get it. No, I definitely don't know her.

'I came into your grandmother's room, remember? A few months ago? I took a wrong turn on the way to the bathroom and found you, and we started talking and you gave me some wonderful advice—'

'I'm sorry,' I say, 'I think you've mixed me up with someone else.'

Baldy, suddenly, is beside the girl. He pats her shoulder.

'I'm *sure* it was you,' she insists. 'You must remember. I told you that Grandpa was worried I'd be cursed if I got married, and you told me to tell him that I'd rather have a year of true happiness than die without knowing what happiness was. And it worked, we're getting married, right here in the garden of Rosalind House next year!'

As someone with Alzheimer's, I'd be lying if I said it didn't feel good seeing a 'normal' person get confused. *See*, I want to say, *it can happen to anyone.* This young woman seems perfectly together, of sound mind, and still, she is confused.

'My grandmother isn't a resident here,' I tell her, grateful for this nugget to hold on to, proof that I'm not the one who is confused. 'I am.'

There's a strange sudden stillness in the room. The girl's gaze bounces to Baldy's, then slowly slinks back to me.

'I . . . see,' she says finally. Her cheeks are a little pink, and I hope I haven't embarrassed her. 'I must be thinking of someone else.'

A few minutes after Baldy has gone off with his grand-daughter, Young Guy and I trundle toward my room. We make the decision to do this without a word, just a look and a nod. Like an old married couple. Given the fact that we're not likely ever to be an old married couple, I'm glad we're getting the opportunity now. White flakes are fluttering down outside, and it's cozy in here. As we walk, he takes my hand. I've never been the sentimental type, but the hand-holding is growing on me.

Baldy and his granddaughter are in the entry-hall bit. If Baldy ever possessed the ability to whisper, he has lost it now, and I hear the words 'dementia' and 'sad'. They're talking about us.

'I just feel so sorry for them,' she says. 'They're so young.'

I keep walking. I understand that people feel sorry for us. I'd probably feel the same if it had happened to someone else. But Young Guy stops, and because of our interlinked hands, I stop with him. Baldy and the young woman look at us.

'You don't need to feel sorry for us,' Young Guy says. 'We're a l-lot luckier than most.'

Then he gives me a little tug and we walk together to my room.

23

Clementine

Our guests are lined up against one wall of the gymnasium. Mom is at one end, wearing jeans and flat shoes. Even though we were allowed to invite anyone we liked, most of the boys have brought their moms and the girls have brought their dads. I'm the only girl who has brought her mom.

'Good evening, everyone,' Miss Weber says. She's wearing a dress, like most of the moms, and pink shoes with ribbons that tie around her ankles. 'Thank you so much for coming to our Family Dance Night. We've been working very hard on the decorations. Doesn't the room look great?'

Our guests clap. I notice Miranda's dad is holding a bunch of flowers. Reds and purples and whites.

'We would like to thank the Heathmonts for donating the materials for our banners and artwork, and the Andersons for providing the trestle tables. And to everyone who brought along cakes and cookies today.'

I grin at Mom. She brought red velvet cupcakes with

creamy vanilla icing – I can see them on the table, stacked up into a triangle. Mom's red velvet cupcakes are the best.

'Soon we're going to start the dancing, but first, I thought you might like to hear some singing. We've been practicing very hard, haven't we, class?'

Last year we sang a song, too. I can't remember what it was. But I remember looking out at Daddy in the crowd. The other parents were whispering and nudging and taking videos on their phones, but Daddy just watched. Afterwards, he said he didn't need to record it on his phone, because it was already recorded in his memory forever.

This year we sing 'Firework' by Katy Perry. When we're finished it's time to dance with our special person. Freya's dad picks her up and she wraps her legs around his waist. Miranda's dad spins her around in circles so her skirt floats all around her. Legs stands on her dad's feet. I put my arms around Mom's waist and we sway a little.

'Sorry,' Mom says. 'I'm not a very good dancer.'

Afterwards, Mom talks to Harry's mom, and Harry and I eat red velvet cupcakes and Harry gets vanilla icing on his nose.

'Harry!' I say, giggling. 'You've got—' I'm laughing too hard to finish.

Harry laughs, too, even though he doesn't know what's so funny. 'What?'

'Your nose!'

'Oh!' He wipes his nose, but only gets a little bit of icing off. The rest is still there. We laugh so hard that Harry's face goes bright red.

Then Miranda and Freya come over with their dads.

The dads shake hands and smile at Harry's mom. They look at my mom, but they don't shake her hand or smile.

'Our dads don't like your mom,' Miranda whispers. She's standing beside me, helping herself to a red velvet cupcake.

'Yes, they do,' I say.

'They don't,' Freya says. She also has one of Mom's cupcakes and she takes a bite. 'They really don't.'

I look over at Mom. Harry's mom has started talking to someone else, and my mom is standing by herself. I remember her standing by herself at the school gates.

'Why don't they like her?' I ask.

'Because she is dith-spicable,' Miranda says. 'That's what my dad said.'

'Dith-spicable,' Freya repeats. 'Just like your daddy.'

Harry frowns. I start to feel hot. I don't know what 'dith-spicable' is. But they are standing really close, and I want them to go away.

'She isn't.'

'She is,' Miranda says.

Mom looks over at me. At first her eyes are happy; then she starts to frown. Maybe she sees my face getting hot? She takes a step toward us.

'She isn't dithpicable,' I say to Miranda. 'You're dith-picable!'

And I start hitting and scratching at Miranda and I don't stop until I'm crying and strong hands are pulling me away.

24

'I think a few days at home would be the best thing,' Ms Donnelly says. 'Not as a punishment, just for her . . . well-being. So she can have a little one-on-one time with Mom.'

Ms Donnelly is the principal of the *whole* school and we are in her office. She's not pretty like Miss Weber – she has short gray hair and big black glasses and she wears brown skirts. Miss Weber is here in her office, too, and so is Mom. After I finished hitting Miranda, Miss Weber quickly brought us in here, away from the shouting and the crying.

'Of course,' Mom says. 'I mean, I'm working at the moment, but I'll figure something out.'

'Just for a few days,' Ms Donnelly says. 'We don't want to disrupt Clementine's routine. We understand that she has been through a lot these past few months.'

I look at my fingernails. There is dried blood under some of them.

'So,' Ms Donnelly says. She opens a folder, and I see it has my name on it. CLEMENTINE BENNETT. As she looks down at it, her glasses slip down her nose. 'You're living . . .

on Forest Hills Drive? Number 82?' Ms Donnelly looks up.

'Yes, that's right,' Mom says.

Mom's cheeks go pink and Ms Donnelly frowns. No one says anything for a few seconds.

'I see,' Ms Donnelly says finally, closing the folder again. 'Well, as for this incident, I've spoken with Miranda's parents. Mrs Heathmont was quite upset, which is understandable, considering Miranda received quite a few scratches. But she and her husband have agreed that they will not take any further action so long as Clementine apologizes to Miranda.'

I look up. Mom, Ms Donnelly, and Miss Weber are all staring at me.

'Clem?' Mom says. 'Did you hear what Ms Donnelly said?'

I frown. 'What does "dith-spicable" mean?'

On the way home, I think of Miranda's face all scratched and punched up. I think of Miranda's dad with the bunch of flowers and Legs dancing on her daddy's feet. I think of 'dith-spicable'.

'So?' Mom says. Her knee is bouncing up and down. 'Are you going to tell me what happened?'

'Miranda just made me mad, that's all.'

'What did she do to make you mad?'

'Stuff.'

Mom looks at me quickly, then back at the road. 'Was she talking about Daddy?'

'I don't want to tell you,' I say.

'Why not, Clem?'

I sigh crossly. 'I'm not Clem. I'm Laila.'

Mom blinks. 'Okay. Why don't you want to tell me, Laila?'

'Because,' I say. 'I don't want to hurt your feelings.'

I look out the window on my side. For a while, Mom doesn't say anything. Then we stop at the traffic lights.

'What if you told someone else?' she says slowly. 'Another grown-up, someone you don't know. You could tell them exactly how you feel, and you won't have to worry about their feelings. How does that sound?'

'Okay.'

'Good,' she says. 'Good.'

'Mom?'

'Yes?'

'Are we going to have a little one-on-one time?'

She smiles. 'We sure are. You can come to work with me and be my very special helper.'

I smile, too. I'm a good helper. I'll help Mom set the table and we'll make peanut butter Bundt cake for the residents. Peanut butter Bundt cake was Daddy's favorite.

'Mom?' I say.

'Mmm?'

'I don't want to say sorry to Miranda.'

We're at home now. Mom stops the car and turns off the engine. She turns to face me. 'I think it would be good if you did, hon.'

'Why?'

'Because you hurt her. And if you hurt someone, you should say you're sorry.'

204

'But Miranda hurt me,' I say, 'and she doesn't have to say sorry.'

Mom opens her mouth, but before she can speak, I crawl into her lap and burst into tears.

25

Eve

It's hard to describe the joy I feel when I pull my first carrot out of my Rosalind House vegetable patch. It's a sunny day, and despite a brisk breeze, the whole gang is out here – Clara and Gwen, Luke and Anna. I've come to think of the vegetable patch as 'our patch', and I think they have, too. We've been working hard all morning, and now Anna and Luke sit on the edge of the garden bed, enjoying the sunshine while Clara and Gwen drink lemonade under the tree. The air smells of earth and herbs. The only sound of significance is the shear of the secateurs as Angus cuts stems.

Clem is out here, too. I think of her yesterday, clawing at Miranda. It was so out of character. Apart from when she was a toddler (and even then, it was only with good reason), I'd never seen Clem hit another child. Now, looking at her, it's hard to imagine. She watches Angus intently as he explains the different kinds of flowers and how to make them last. Whenever he is around, she seems to gravitate toward him. He is sweet to her, but it makes me wonder – what is she lacking? What can I do to help fill the hole?

I'd spent the previous night searching for a child psychologist for Clem, and I'd managed to get an appointment next week, but in the meantime, her mental health was in my hands. And it wasn't only her mental health in jeopardy. I couldn't stop thinking about how Ms Donnelly looked at me as she recited my address. Did she know something? If she did, I could only hope that she was too distracted by everything that was going on with Clem to figure out what.

I pick some sprigs of rosemary for the roast lamb and some mint for the ice water. Bert won't like it; he told me off last week for 'fancying up the water' (with lemons, that day), but he's going to have to live with it. It's a minty-ice-water kind of day.

'Is this enough flowers for you, Eve?' Angus asks. His arms are laden with chrysanthemums, lilies, and hibiscuses – enough to fill an auditorium.

I laugh. 'You're kidding, right?'

Angus doesn't laugh, but his eyes crinkle in the corners, and I guess this is the best I'm going to get. His cool, silent thing is starting to grow on me. Richard was quick to smile, to compliment. After a while, with someone like that, it starts to lose its value. 'If there are leftovers,' he says, 'just take them home. Put them in your bedroom.'

The word 'bedroom' makes me blush.

'My mother used to say that a woman should always have flowers in her bedroom,' he says.

'Did she say why?'

Angus typically just shrugs. But I notice his cheeks are a little pink, too.

A sudden flash of movement to our left steals our attention. An enormous dog has bounced into the yard with its owner on its heels.

'Rupert! *Rupert!*'

Angus puts down the flowers and goes to help. The dog seems to think it's a game. It bounds this way and that, like a toy attached to a spring. Luke, who'd been sitting on one edge of the garden bed near Anna, stands, while Anna shrinks behind her hands. That's when I remember: Anna is afraid of dogs.

Angus has herded the dog toward the gate, but just as the owner is about to grab its collar, it bounds away, across the lawn. Anna lets out a shriek. The dog heads toward her but before it gets there, I leap, catching the dog around its waist. I roll to the ground. I might as well have tackled Angus. It's heavy – really heavy – and wriggling. I pull tight around its belly. My breathing is ragged, and something doesn't feel quite right in my elbow, but I'm not letting go.

A moment later, Angus grabs the collar and passes it to the owner.

'Sorry,' the man says. 'So sorry.'

Angus helps me to my feet. I glance over toward the vegetable patch to see how Anna is faring and my breath catches.

'Angus,' I say. 'Remember when you told me that Luke used to protect Anna from the dogs when the pet therapy people came to visit?'

'Yeah.'

'You also said you weren't sure if people with dementia were capable of having real feelings for others.'

He cocks his head, panting. 'Yeah, I think I said that.'

I point at the vegetable patch, where Luke is crouching in front of Anna. His arms are outstretched and she is tucked in, safely, behind him.

'What do you think now?'

After the dog commotion, Clem asks if she can head inside and watch some TV. Once she is settled, I get out the cleaning cart and get busy. I spritz, wipe, dust, and vacuum until my arms feel like a pair of noodles. And the whole time, I'm thinking about Luke and Anna.

What I would *give* to know what was going on inside their brains! Eric said *'Falling in love requires memory, communication, reason, decision making,'* but did it, really? After seeing Luke today, I can't help but think that love is more like a river – it wants to flow. And if one path is blocked off, it simply finds another.

By the time I get to Anna's room, I'm exhausted. I get out the duster and idly wander around, pushing dust this way and that. It's on the lower shelf of her dresser, under a carpet of dust, that I find her notebook. I recognize it – it's the one Anna had stuck my photo in on my first day. My instinct is to open it, but with my fingers on the inside of the cover, I hesitate. I ought to respect her privacy. I return the newly dusted notebook to the shelf.

And immediately snatch it back.

Maybe I'll just read the first page and see what it says? Then, before I can change my mind, I toss it open.

November 1, 2013

Dear Anna,

Today you made a promise. You promised the young guy with the tea-colored eyes that you would stay with him until the end. No cutting out early, no taking the fast exit. It's hard to believe you agreed to that, right? I can hardly believe it as I write this.

So why did you agree?

You agreed because this guy is the one you didn't know you were waiting for. You agreed because, as it is, you're not going to have long enough together. And you agreed because this guy is a pretty good reason to hang around.

Soon you won't remember this promise – that's why I'm writing this down. And if you are reading this now, there's something else you should know: Anna Forster never breaks a promise.

Anna

There's a tap at the door and I jump.

'Just me.'

It's Angus, holding up my basket, which contains precisely one carrot. 'I thought you might be needing this. Sorry, did I scare you?'

I point at the notebook. 'Look at this.'

Angus comes closer. I give him a minute to read.

'See!' I say. 'She *does* love him. And he loves her, that's obvious after today.'

Angus frowns. 'You know . . . I did read once about a woman with dementia who didn't remember that she'd ever been married, but when someone showed her her wedding dress, she burst into tears. The article said that the memory center of the brain is right next to the emotion center, so the emotional power of the dress was still there, even though the memory was gone.'

'So maybe Luke knew he had to protect Anna from the dog, even though he didn't remember why . . .'

'Blows your mind, doesn't it? The way it all works – the heart, the brain.'

'It does,' I say. 'It really truly does.'

Angus's gaze floats over my face, and the twinkle is replaced by something . . . more intense. A frisson of energy runs through me. 'Angus—'

'Shh,' he says, and then Angus's arms circle my waist and we are kissing. He smells of the grass. His arms hold me upright, and it's a good thing because I'm a feather in a cyclone – powerless, light, swept away. It feels so strange, and so, so right.

'Mom?'

I stumble backwards. Clem is in the doorway. 'What are you *doing*?'

'Nothing.' I push back my hair, straighten my ponytail. 'Angus was just . . . returning my basket.' My head is spinning, and the proximity of Angus isn't helping. 'Are you hungry, honey? I was about to go make a snack, would you like to—?'

'Were you kissing?' Clem asks.

I flick a glance at Angus. He looks apologetic, and also a little dazed. Like I feel.

'Why don't we go into the kitchen?' I say to Clem.

'*Were* you?'

I don't know what to say. My head feels full of air; my mouth is suddenly dry.

'You were,' she says finally. 'I *saw* you.'

'Yes,' I admit, 'I was.'

Clem's jaw becomes tight. It occurs to me that this is the opposite of how things were supposed to go. I am her mother. In six or seven years' time, I am supposed to catch *her* kissing a boy. I am supposed to give *her* the third degree.

'I don't want you to kiss anyone,' she says. 'Ever. Again.'

I feel a surprising urge to cry. Mostly because her request, unfair as it feels, is wholly appropriate. Her father died only four months ago. *Four months.* Did the fact that he had done terrible things reduce my mourning period? Or the fact that I found Angus impossibly attractive?

'Okay, Mom?' she says.

'Clem—'

'It's *Alice.*'

'Okay, Alice.'

'So you won't kiss anyone ever again?'

I glance at Angus, and he shrugs. It's a shrug that says, *Don't worry about me. Do what you need to do.*

I wish there were a handbook for parenting daughters whose whole world had been turned upside down in the past few months. A girl who had been having trouble at

212

school and who, in time, would have to come to terms with the fact that her father wasn't the man she thought he was. Then I realize I don't need a handbook, because I already know what it would say. 'Yes. Never again.'

I take Clem's hand and lead her out of the room, leaving Angus standing there. And, no matter how much I want to, I can't bring myself to look back.

26

That afternoon, Clem and I make a peanut butter Bundt cake. I wait for her to bring up my kiss with Angus again, but she doesn't, and I don't either – kids talk when they're ready – but the quiet worries me. Even before she could speak words, Clem was loud. As a baby, she'd sit up in her high chair at the kitchen bench while I cooked, making high-pitched baby noises and banging toys and laughing toothlessly. As I watch her serious little face, I have such a pang for *that* Clem, I almost double over.

We put the cake in the oven, and Clem makes herself scarce before cleanup – at least in that regard, nothing has changed. When she's gone, I finally allow myself to look for Angus through the window. He's bent over a garden bed, his gloved hands buried in dirt. It makes me sad to think those hands will never be on me again.

When the last of the dishes have been washed up, I go looking for Clem in the parlor. Instead I find Anna. Her chair is right in front of the window and her hands are on the glass.

'Hey, Anna,' I say. 'Everything okay?'

She doesn't respond. She feels the corners of the window, then slams a fist into the middle.

'Anna?'

She spins around, clearly annoyed at the interruption. 'What?'

'What are you doing?'

'Nothing.'

'Do you want me to open the window?'

Her eyes flicker to me, and her frustration turns to curiosity. 'You can open it?'

'Of course.'

I roll her chair back so I can have a better look. The window is double-hung and floor-level. Eric told me that, since Anna's fall, the top-floor windows have been bolted shut. These windows do open though, so I slide the top pane down an inch, letting in a slow breeze. 'There.'

Anna looks puzzled. 'But . . . how do I get out?'

'Oh, you want to go outside? We can go out the door. Here, I'll take you.' I reach for the handles of her chair but she shakes her head.

'No. I want to go out *there*.'

She sounds stubborn, almost whiney. Her jaw is set.

'Why do you want to go out the window?' I ask.

'Because . . .' She swallows. 'I've had enough.'

She crosses her arms and stares at the window resolutely.

I follow her gaze. There's a slight ledge and from her vantage point, in her chair, it looks like a drop. I wonder if Anna thinks this is a second-floor window. If she thinks that by going out it, she'll fall.

I've had enough.

I squat beside her. 'Why have you had enough?'

A rogue tear slides down her cheek.

'Because of Luke,' I hear myself say. 'Because you are being kept apart from him?'

She looks at me and I can't tell how much she is following.

'What if you weren't kept apart from him?' I ask. 'Would you still want to go out there?' I gesture at the window.

Her eyes are two pools of pale green emotion. I think of Luke crouching in front of her when the dog came into the yard. Of Anna asking, 'Where is he?' Of the looks between them. The love that so clearly still exists. And suddenly I understand what she's been asking me all along.

'You wouldn't, would you?' I say to myself. Then I look her squarely in the eye. 'In that case I'm going to help you.'

That night, Clem and I stay a little later than usual. She doesn't have school tomorrow, so I don't see the harm in letting her watch a little TV while I finish things up. The residents all head off to bed – they may be early risers, but in this place everyone is asleep by 8:15 p.m. Once the dinner has been cleared up, I grab my purse and start down the hallway. The dishwasher is humming, the floors are clean(ish), and the meals have been planned for the week. Clem is in the parlor in front of the TV, and I am outside Anna's door.

I think of Richard, hanging from the ceiling beam in his study. I think of the moment I found him, the words that hung around me, useless and unsaid, the actions that

216

floated in the air, undone. It was too late. But it isn't too late for Anna.

I step forward, suddenly emboldened. I'd told Anna I'd help her. And I will.

27

Anna

Eleven months ago . . .
There are three doors in my room. One leads to
the hallway, one to the bathroom, one to the closet. Each
morning I pick one, a lottery of sorts, figuring I have a
one-in-three chance of finding my clothes. At first I used
to put the effort in – to use logic and reasoning and memory.
The bathroom would probably be closer to the bed, that
sort of thing. These days, though, it's basically a crapshoot.

'Eeny meeny miney—' I point to door number two.
'Mo!'

Young Guy (who showed up in my room a few minutes
ago to take me to breakfast) flicks open the door, revealing
a toilet. 'Better luck next time.'

Some days, it drives me fucking crazy when I can't find
things. A few weeks ago, or maybe it was a few days ago,
I picked up a glass thingy and hurled it against one of the
doors because I couldn't find the bathroom. When you
need to pee as often as I do, you don't have time to mess
about, looking for the toilet.

'That one is definitely . . . the hallway,' I say, pointing to door number one. I have no idea if this is right, and I can't be bothered to look for clues. But we've already found the toilet-room, so I figure I've got a good chance.

He peels open the hallway-door, revealing a row of clothes hanging from a pole-thingy.

'Damn!' I say, but as he pulls an item off the thingy (an item that may or may not be weather appropriate), I laugh. There was a time when I had no desire to live beyond a point when I couldn't tell what was behind a door. But today I'm very glad to be alive.

We're in the upstairs room again. Young Guy dips the stick-thingy on the record player and music starts playing. I wonder how long we will be able to find our way to this place, this upstairs room. It feels like *our* place. The idea that we won't be able to remember it seems somehow more tragic than not being able to remember my own name.

He holds out his arms. 'W . . . would you like to . . . ?'

'What?'

He moves his arms and his hips jauntily. I know what he's suggesting. I'm supposed to walk into his arms and hold his hands and jiggle about to the music. I can't think what it's called either.

He tries a few times to produce the word and then grimaces. 'You kn-know,' he says finally, with effort. His eyebrows crease uncertainly. It also makes me laugh.

I stand and shuffle into his space, but instead of taking

his hands, I lay my cheek right against his chest. Together we begin to move.

'Yes,' I say. 'I do know.'

It's that day when people visit. I hate that day. And I'm not the only one. Really Old Lady hates it because she rarely gets a visitor. Baldy doesn't like it, because the middle-of-the-day meal is served earlier, and according to him, Myrna doesn't like her schedule being messed with. More and more, I'm seeing the plus sides to Myrna. In fact, I think I might befriend her myself. *Sorry, can't play bingo today, Myrna doesn't like it. Not my fault,* I'll say. *Myrna's.*

Jack usually comes on his own these days, or with just one of the little boys. I haven't seen his wife in a while. Even so, I find his visits stressful. Here, at this place where I live, when I forget something or say something weird, people either don't notice or don't react. But when I say something weird in front of Jack, he looks confused. Corrects me in a slow, simple voice. *'Don't you remember, Anna, it was Aunt Geraldine?'* or *'Yes, Anna, you already said that.'* Worst of all is the long silence followed by the nod. The look that says, *I have no idea what you're saying, but it's not worth my time to try to figure it out.*

Today, I'm feeling pretty anxious. Not just because it's the day when people visit but also because of Luke. (I know his name is Luke because he introduced himself to Jack a few seconds ago.) Luke has had the gloriously misguided idea that we should introduce each other to our families – you know, like a regular couple. Sometimes he has some pretty messed-up ideas. I told him that. I think.

So we're in the big front room. Jack is sitting opposite us, staring at our joined hands. I have no idea what I am supposed to say. Eventually I decide, as I do so often these days, to say nothing. I have Alzheimer's, after all. Surely that gets me out of uncomfortable small talk?

'This m-m . . . ust be weird for you, Jack,' Luke says finally. He's trying hard, and though his words are slightly labored, he's doing a wonderful job. 'I'm sure you . . . thought your days of meeting your . . . twin sister's boyfriends were over.'

Jack's eyes seek mine, a little incredulous. I force a smile.

'If it makes you feel any better,' he continues, wobbling on the word 'better'. 'I can promise I'll be the l . . . last.'

I can't help myself, I laugh. For someone with dementia, Luke is pretty smooth. He smiles a little shyly and glances at me. I'm impressed. I haven't heard him speak so many words without pausing in a while. But Jack doesn't so much as crack a smile.

Luke, I notice, keeps glancing at his hands. He has a few little tics, but this one is new. It's not until he tips his palms upward that I notice the blue ink scrawled across them. I see the words *Jack, twin,* and *boyfriend.* My heart breaks a little.

Jack looks like he wants to respond, but he's thinking very carefully before he does. I'm happy to wait. But before he can get his thoughts together enough to speak, a woman sweeps into the room, kisses Luke's cheek, and falls into the sitting-thing beside Jack.

'Sorry I'm late,' she says. 'You must be the brother. I'm Sarah. The sister.'

This woman is as blond as Luke is dark. She wears jeans and a thin-jacket with lots of shiny stuff at her wrists and neck. Her face is upturned, suggesting friendliness. She looks from Luke to me and then finally to Jack. 'So? They've told you?'

Jack stares at her. 'You *know* about this?'

'Of course. Luke tells me everything.'

'Terrific,' Jack mutters. 'Anna tells me nothing.'

'Look, there's no reason to be upset,' she says. 'My brother is a wonderful guy.'

Luke's sister sounds remarkably calm, even happy. This, I know, will rile Jack no end.

'I'm sure he is,' Jack says. 'I just don't want him taking advantage of my sister so he can live out his last wish to have a girlfriend.'

There's a short silence. 'Luke's had plenty of girlfriends,' the sister says. 'He doesn't get into anything unless he is serious.'

'Great!' Jack says. 'That's just great.'

'Besides,' she continues, 'why shouldn't they have a little happiness in here?'

'It all depends,' he says, his voice a little louder now, 'on what kind of happiness they are having—'

'They're adults! It's none of our business what they do!'

'Whose business is it if Anna gets pregnant? Hmm?

222

Theirs? Maybe they could raise the baby together in this place? You're right, this is a fantastic idea—'

Jack's face is red and his voice is loud. The sister's face closes over. I shrink back into my sitting thing, away from them.

'St-st-st . . . *Stop it!*'

I blink up at Young Guy, who's standing now. Jack and the sister are wide-eyed, blinking but silent. It's lovely, the silence. I'm grateful to Young Guy – I want to say thank you, but the words drift away from me before I can catch them and use them.

'Anna?' A helper-lady jogs into the parlor, frowning. She doesn't usually jog. Or frown, for that matter. She squats beside me. 'You have a visitor.'

I hear, but it doesn't make sense. Don't I already have visitors? 'I'm sorry.'

Jack's eyes are focused beyond me, and for this reason, I turn around. There's a tall man behind my chair, dressed smartly in black pants and a white shirt. A thick brown coat is tucked under one arm. The man is, all at once, familiar and unfamiliar.

Behind me, I hear Jack clearing his throat. 'Dad,' he says. 'You're here.'

28

Anna

Dad isn't an attractive man. He has height, but the skinny kind, rounded at the shoulders so he curves forward like a wilting flower. His eyes are pale blue and his gray-orange fuzz is combed to hide a bald spot. All this information is apparent to anyone in the room, though. The things that I *should* know about Dad – the day of his birth, his baseball team, whether his stoop is old or new – are not there. Or perhaps they are, but deep down, hazy, as though he were a character from a novel I read a few years ago rather than the man who gave me life. He looks at me closely, perhaps for signs of my dementing. I wonder if he's finding any.

'Anna,' he says, 'I can't believe it.'

At the sound of his voice, my brain releases a select few, seemingly unimportant memories. The way he used to eat ice cream with a fork. The way he used to drink his . . . morning caffeine drink . . . so hot, it should have taken the skin right off his mouth.

'What are you doing here?' I ask.

'What do you think?' he says. 'I came to see you.'

Jack walks out from behind me, reminding me that he is here too. 'Dad,' Jack says, 'I'm not sure this is a good idea.'

Another memory is niggling at me, but just out of my reach like an itch I can't scratch. It's as if my brain has pulled a curtain over the memories area. And not even the VIPs are getting in.

'Dad,' Jack tries again, 'how 'bout we go outside?' Jack catches Dad's elbow, not waiting for an answer.

I look at Dad, at the jacket under his arm with its wide, diagonal hip-pockets.

'Chocolate cigars!' I cry.

Dad stops. 'You remember those, huh?'

I am practically jubilant at unearthing this memory. Chocolate cigars. They were always in Dad's pocket when I was a kid. *'Take a load off,'* he'd say to Jack and me, handing us one each and igniting it with his thumb-lighter. *'Have a cigar.'* I have to fight a smile and remind myself that the man with the chocolate cigars in his pocket is the same man who up and left his wife when she got sick. The same man who left me.

'I don't have any today, I'm afraid,' he says. 'But if you'll see me again, I'll bring some next time.'

'Dad!' Jack says. 'You can't just show up here and—'

'It's okay,' I say. 'I'll talk to him.'

Jack looks uncertain. 'Are you sure?'

I nod. 'Let's go to my room, Dad.'

It feels strange saying the word 'Dad'. I haven't called anyone that since I was a teenager. As I start down the hall, I pray that I can find my way, and for once (hey, the gods aren't usually that kind to me) I'm shown some mercy. Inside, we sit.

'So . . . you have it, then?' Dad says. 'Alzheimer's?'

'Yes.'

'Why didn't you tell me? I would have supported you.'

'Thanks,' I say evenly, 'but I don't believe you.'

He nods. 'I deserve that. And anything else you have to dole out. I've already missed so much. Now, even if it's insults, I don't want to miss another second.'

I stare at him, all self-assured. I can't believe he has the nerve to show up here like this, after all this time. Did he think that I would just open my arms and let him back in my life? And why would he want to be back in it, anyway? If he ran away from a wife with Alzheimer's, what did he want with me? 'What are you doing here, Dad?'

'I let your mother push me away when she got sick,' he says after a moment. 'I've always regretted it. And I've no intention of letting history repeat itself.'

I stare at him.

'I'm not making excuses,' he says, 'just trying to explain. Your mother was a proud woman. She didn't want me to watch her decline. I never intended to leave you and Jack, but—'

'Surely you didn't expect us to have a relationship with you after you abandoned our Alzheimer's-ridden mother? The irony is that you were the one who taught us to have more integrity than that.'

'I messed up. And you paid the price. But there's nothing

226

you can say to stop me coming back, Anna. I am going to repair our relationship.'

'Repair our relationship?' I snort. 'Don't hold your breath.'

He stands. 'I've no intention of it. At my age, holding one's breath is a bad idea.'

I feel a surprising urge to laugh. But I refrain. That could be construed as letting him off the hook. 'Suit yourself.'

Dad plants an awkward kiss on my forehead, and then shuffles toward the door. I want to tell him to get out. I want to tell him to stay.

'When I found out I had Alzheimer's, I left my husband,' I blurt out, when he reaches for the door handle. 'The marriage wasn't happy, and Alzheimer's seemed as good a reason as any to call it a day. So we're alike in that way, I guess. Running away when things get tough.'

Dad's eyes have become soft and shiny. 'That doesn't make us alike, Anna. You left an unhappy marriage when you were most vulnerable, which shows courage. I left a woman and two children when *they* were most vulnerable, which shows the opposite. A better man would have stayed.'

'Are you a better man now?' I ask. I'm angry at myself when I realize my face is wet.

'Trying to be.' He laughs softly, shakes his head. 'And looking at you, honey, perhaps I did do something right.'

*

227

That night, Young Guy buries his head in my hair, and I wrap a leg around his waist and pull him closer. It's mostly dark, but a thin line of light shines in from somewhere.

Wow. I blink into the semidarkness. That's . . . weird.

I blink again. There's a person in the bed next to us. Actually, more than one person – there's *people* – moving briskly under the covers.

'Holy—' I push him off and jump up. The people next to us do the same. 'Who the fuck are they?' I whisper.

Am I hallucinating? But no . . . they're right there. They're black, not just their skin but their eyes, their hair – *all of them*. I *must* be hallucinating.

'Do you see that?' I say to Young Guy. *'There!* Look!'

I fling out an arm, and one of the phantom people flings their arm out at the same time. I jump backwards. At that exact moment, so does she.

Young Guy slides slowly out of bed and stands beside me. He looks as freaked out as I feel. This is . . . too strange. I turn to face the black woman and she matches my stance. I wave. She waves. Slowly, the pieces click together. I edge forward, reach out to touch the face of the black person in front of me. It's smooth, flat. And then, *ching.* The penny drops.

'The people,' I say, 'the black people . . . they're us. They're our shadows.'

For a moment, all I can do is stand there. Holy moly. I actually thought my shadow was some kind of crazy mutant alien. Is that how far gone I am? Young Guy's hand curls around mine, and I realize it is shaking. And not just that – he's making a noise, too. In the dark, it's hard to tell what he's doing, but finally, I realize. He's laughing.

Chuckles start to bubble up in me too, slowly at first, and then a full-on manic giggling explosion. Beside me, Young Guy laughs. And so do our shadows.

I jolt awake. Something isn't right. Young Guy's cheek is resting on my torso just below my chin and . . . Skinny is towering over us.

'I just found them like this,' she is saying to someone. Her face is bent and twisted and her voice is high-pitched. 'I don't know where Rosie is. Carole, would you just *find Rosie?*'

'Bert's twisted his ankle,' someone else says. 'She's bandaging it.'

Skinny pulls back the thin-blanket that's covering us and peers under. 'They're partially clothed, at least. Thank God! Oh, Anna's awake.'

I lie very still as the guy with the mustache comes into view. His eyes roll over my body slowly. 'Are you all right, Anna?' he asks.

I nod, shrinking farther under the thin-blanket, wishing they would get out of my room.

'Did you know Luke was here with you?' he asks, his eyes still wandering.

I glance at the top of Young Guy's head and then back at the man. 'You know I have dementia, right? I'm not blind.'

Mustache Man's eyes narrow. He wipes at his forehead with his arm.

There's something majorly unsettling about lying flat while people hover over you, but Young Guy is heavy on my upper torso, so I'm stuck.

'We'll have to call her brother,' Skinny says. 'And Luke's sister. Do you want me to do it?'

'I'll do it,' Mustache Man says, but he keeps looking at me. 'Anna, do you need help getting dressed?'

I shake my head so hard, I get dizzy.

'Fine. Trish will wait outside until you're dressed and then bring you to my office, okay?'

I don't really want to get dressed or go to Mustache Man's office, but I don't see what choice I have, so I nod.

'Good,' he says, exhaling. 'Then we can sort this whole thing out.'

Mustache Man and Skinny finally leave and I shimmy Young Guy's head off my body and rise into a sitting position. That's when it dawns on me, what Skinny and Mustache Man want to sort out. It's *us*. Me and Young Guy.

29

Eve

As I push Anna's door open, my whole body is trembling. Questions – and doubts – loop in my head so fast, I feel giddy . . . Will she be awake? Will she be startled? Will she remember our conversation? The last thing I want is to terrify her. But before I can rethink anything, Anna sits up in bed.

'Hey, Anna,' I whisper, taking a couple of cautious steps toward her. Like any person woken at night, she blinks, rubs her eyes. Assesses her surroundings. Looks at me warily. 'I'm Eve,' I say. 'Would you . . . um . . . like to see Luke?' I smile, hoping his name will stir something in her. It doesn't.

She frowns. 'Who?'

My confidence, if I ever had any, deserts me. 'Um, well . . . he has dark hair, brown eyes . . .'

I trail off, give her a minute. But she just continues to look blank.

'You know what?' I say. 'Why don't you just go back to sl—'

'Rosie!' Bert's voice rings into the silence suddenly. I stifle a gasp. 'I need to use the gents'. Come and give an old man a push out of bed.'

My gaze bounces to the door, which is open. I dart for it, pushing it shut just as Rosie comes up the corridor to help Bert. I say a silent prayer that Anna doesn't choose this moment to freak out. It works: she remains quiet.

A few moments later, when I hear Rosie make her way back to the nurses' room, I notice Anna watching me. 'Who is Luke?' she asks.

I creep to her side uncertainly. 'Luke is the young guy,' I whisper. 'He has dark hair, brown eyes —'

'Is he cute?'

I chuckle. 'He *is* cute.'

'Okay. Then let's go.'

I wheel her to the door. There's no sound from the residents but I can hear Clem's TV program in the parlor and the low drone of infomercials from the nurses' room. This is our chance.

I hurry across the hall and I open Luke's door. Inside I flick on the bathroom light, casting a gentle glow into the room. The nerves, all of a sudden, are back. For me. Not for Anna. She looks around with the curiosity of a child, getting her bearings. I wheel her inside.

I know the moment she sees him, because she stills, and releases her breath softly. Luke blinks awake. He sees me first, then Anna. Maybe it's because I want to see it, but I swear, a bulb lights up within him. He lurches upright.

I push Anna over to Luke and help her move onto the

232

bed beside Luke. Then I back away. She plants a hand on each side of his face and he closes his eyes. They start to nod in unison – a strange, beautiful liturgical dance – then stop with their foreheads resting together. The empty space between their bodies, I notice, resembles a heart.

After a moment, Anna looks over at me. Her mouth moves ever so slightly, and a breath of noise comes, like a whisper that didn't work out. But I hear what she's trying to tell me all the same. *Thank you.*

The next morning, I stand in the kitchen, yawning. In theory, I'm washing the breakfast dishes, but in practice, I'm just staring out the window, where Angus is doubled over in a garden bed. The ground is going to freeze soon, and he's working hard at putting the plants to bed. Even from the back, there's something sexy about him. I try to ignore it, but it's like trying to ignore the sunset during an evening stroll on the beach. Not happening.

Perhaps feeling my stare, he turns. Quickly I focus on the blackened char on the base of the saucepan I am washing. I haven't spoken to Angus since Clem saw us kissing. I've barely *looked* at Angus since then. I have, however, thought about Angus since then. When I look back at the window he is standing up, walking toward the house. A moment later, he's in the kitchen.

'Hey,' he says.

'Hey,' I say. Clem is in the parlor, and I silently pray she won't choose this moment to come tumbling in.

'I just wanted to show you this.' Pinched between

Angus's thumb and forefinger is a tiny green sprig. I gasp. 'Cilantro?'

'Just about enough to feed a baby Smurf. But yes.'

'Wow.' I remove my gloves and lean over to smell it. 'Mmmm. I've never had any success growing cilantro.'

'You've never tried with me before,' Angus says.

I blush, wondering if Angus is thinking the same thing as I am: That there's something else I've never tried with him. Why on earth am I thinking *that*?

'Well, thanks for showing me,' I say.

'Actually, I was wondering if I could tempt you to have a rest from cooking one night?' he says. 'Maybe let me cook for you?'

'Oh.' I laugh. 'Thanks, but it *is* my job. And I don't think Eric would be very happy if—'

'Not for the residents,' Angus says, chuckling. 'For you.'

I feel the heat rise in my cheeks. I want to say yes. But . . .

'You'd rather not,' he says.

'It's not that. It's just—'

'Clem.' He nods. 'I get it. It's okay.'

'I'm sorry, Angus.'

'It's fine.' He hands me the cilantro and smiles. 'For you.'

'Thank you.'

I turn back to the sink, shove my hands into the rubber gloves. I know I'm doing the right thing, but sometimes the right thing feels so wrong. I'm still pondering this a few minutes later when I hear footsteps behind me.

'Eve! *There* you are.'

234

I turn. Eric is standing in the doorway to the kitchen. My heart sinks.

'Do you realize it's nearly ten o'clock?' he asks. His face is ruddy and his hair a little unkempt.

I glance at the clock. He's right. By ten o'clock, according to my manual, the breakfast dishes are supposed to be done and the residents' rooms should be made up. I doubt, in all the months I've been here that I've met that timeline, but I was late this morning, and my corn fritters took three tries to get them right, so today I'm definitely behind the eight ball.

'Shoot!' With my forearm, I push the hair out of my face and start on the last pot. 'Sorry, Eric. I'm almost done here.' There's a tray of orange and poppy-seed muffins cooling on the kitchen table and I gesture at them. 'Have a muffin, Eric. Fresh from the oven!'

I force a smile, but for the first time, Eric doesn't return it.

'Eve, I'm concerned that you're getting your priorities out of whack. Your role is a cook-housekeeper. And the housekeeping side of things, to be honest, is not up to scratch.'

This hits a nerve. 'In fairness, Eric, I'm *filling in* doing the housekeeping. And it's actually a lot more work than I expected.' I put the pot in the drying rack and turn around. 'I thought you'd have found someone by now. I can't imagine it is a difficult role to fill, and it's already been months—'

'Actually there's been a change of plan in relation to that position,' he says. 'I've just heard from above that the budget has been cut, and the cleaning is going to be a permanent part of your role now.'

I blink.

'I know it's not ideal,' he says, 'but that's our reality. We're cutting costs.'

Eric isn't quite meeting my eye. I get a funny feeling.

'Why are we cutting costs?' I ask. 'I'd have thought that with the amount that the residents pay, there would be a good profit to be made here. I mean, the food budget is already tiny—'

'The decision has come from above,' he says. His tone is sharp and final. 'If you're not up for it, I'll find someone else.'

'I . . . I didn't say I wasn't up for it.'

But that's exactly what I want to say. I want to tell Eric to stick his cleaning job. I want to literally throw in the (dish) towel. But without this job I have no address in Clem's school district, and the last thing she needs, especially now, when she is having trouble, is to be moved to another school.

'So,' he says expectantly. 'What do you say?'

'It's fine, Eric. I'll do the cleaning permanently,' I say through my teeth.

'Glad to hear it.' Eric finally picks up a muffin and takes a bite. 'It's very good,' he says on his way out the door. As he walks away I notice his smile, the one he was curiously missing a few moments ago, is back.

My visits to Anna become a nightly occurrence. The routine is pretty simple: Every night after dinner, I go into

236

her room and take her for a little walk. Rosie is busy at that time of night, and Trish and Carole have left for the day, so it's surprisingly easy. Once Anna is in Luke's room, I clean up the kitchen or watch a little TV with Clem, and ten or fifteen minutes later, I wheel her back again.

It's not an ideal scenario. I worry that Clem will come looking for me, or that Luke or Anna will become agitated, or that Rosie could go into Anna's room and find her missing. But it's only a few minutes, I tell myself. And a few minutes can mean the difference between life and death.

The first few nights go smoothly, and during the day-time, Anna has seemed more cheerful. Luke has been more engaged, too. But each night I have to start from scratch, introducing myself to Anna, asking her if she'd like to see Luke.

'I wondered if you'd . . . like to see Luke,' I say when I arrive in her room tonight. 'Luke is the young guy. Dark hair, brown eyes—'

'Cute?' she says.

I grin. 'Very cute.'

I've come to enjoy the repetition of our nightly ex-change. Night after night, Anna reacts to the same situ-ation exactly the same way. There's something wonderful about it. What else is wonderful is that she's never resistant to visiting Luke. As soon as I mention him and give a few details, her whole demeanor lifts. How, I wonder, if she doesn't remember him? With no logical explanation, I'm forced to conclude that some part of her remembers. The heart, perhaps.

My least favorite part is getting her to leave Luke's room again.

'We're busy,' Anna says one night, when I try to retrieve her. 'Go away.'

'I need to take you back to your room, Anna. You can come back tomorrow.'

'No,' she says a little more aggressively. 'You come back tomorrow!'

I feel desperately unprepared for this. On the heels of panic, I remember Rosie's words. 'We can make each moment frightening for her with the truth. Or we can lie to her and make each moment happy.'

'Don't you want to get a good night's rest before your trip?' I ask.

Anna looks at me. 'My motorcycle trip?'

I nod. 'You leave early tomorrow.'

Anna looks momentarily annoyed, then sighs. 'She's right,' she says to Luke. 'I shouldn't ride on just a few hours' sleep. I guess I'll see you when I get back.'

And she leaves with me.

The fourth time I go into Anna's room, she's agitated. The lighting in her room is low, and she keeps looking over her shoulder. I introduce myself as loudly as I can without waking the other residents, then stand in her line of sight. She ignores me, glancing over her shoulder again. It takes me a moment to realize it is her shadow she's worried about.

'Don't worry about her,' I say, jabbing my thumb at the shadow. 'She's not coming.'

238

Anna looks at me and sags, clearly relieved. 'Phew,' she says.

Our visits become the highlight of my day. Perhaps it's because of the quiet or because it's just the two of us, but conversation is easy. Sometimes we chat for a while before I take her to Luke's room. I tell her about Clem and about Richard. About what a terrible cleaner I am. Sometimes Anna just listens; sometimes she talks. Anna's memory isn't there, and some of her judgments are a little off . . . but more and more, I'm hit by a feeling that Anna and I are becoming friends.

The next night, when I go to Anna's room, it's as if she's been waiting for me. She's in her wheelchair by the door, looking expectant. 'I'm ready,' she says before I say anything.

I approach slowly. There's a clarity to her that I haven't seen before. Rosie told me this could happen – that sometimes, for a short time, people come back. She never did tell me for how long.

I kneel in front of her. 'Do you know where we're going, Anna?'

Tears shimmer in her eyes. 'To see him.'

'That's right. We're going to see Luke. Is that what you want?'

She nods. I half expect her to wheel herself to Luke's room; that's how present she seems. Instead, she takes my hands. 'Thank you,' she says.

I try to respond but my words get stuck in my throat, underneath a deadweight of emotion.

'I won't remember this, will I?' she says.

I shake my head and she nods, lets out a long, wobbly breath. I see so much courage in that breath. I see the person Anna was. No. The person Anna *is*.

'Oh well,' she says. 'Live for the moment, right? It should be easy when that's all you've got.'

'Anna,' I say, finding my tongue. 'For the record? You might not remember this. But I promise you that I'll never forget it.'

30

By the time I haul myself out of bed the next morning, Clem's already dressed and sitting on the couch. It's her first day back at school. She's chosen an interesting outfit: stripy leggings, tutu skirt, a green long-sleeved T-shirt with DIVA written across the chest. And her sparkly sneakers. I pause when I see them. They're hot pink with flashing lights that trigger when she jumps and they were a gift from her father for her seventh birthday.

'You okay, hon?' I ask, dropping a slice of raisin bread into the toaster.

Clem nods, still staring.

'You looking forward to seeing Legs today?' I ask.

'Yeah.'

'And you're going to say sorry to Miranda?'

Clem sighs. 'Yes.'

'Good girl. It's never okay to hit someone, is it?'

She shakes her head. At the sight of her solemn little face, the noose in my stomach that I associate with mother's guilt pulls tight.

'I'll be waiting outside when class is out, okay?'

'Okay.'

'And what will you say if someone says something about Daddy?'

'He was *my* daddy, so I know better than you,' she recites, just like we practiced.

'That's right,' I say. Clem keeps staring at her shoes. 'And Clem?'

I brace, waiting for her to tell me that her name is Sophie-Anne or Laila or Alice. But this time she lets it slide.

'Yeah, Mom?'

'When you say sorry to Miranda, be sure you keep one hand in your pocket, so you can keep your fingers crossed.'

Clem looks up, blinks. And finally, she gives me a big, beautiful smile. At the sight of it, the noose around my stomach releases. A little.

Of all my tasks at Rosalind House, I hate ironing the most. Firstly, I have to do it in a little cupboard of a room, with a fold-down board and an iron that fills the entire space with so much condensation that my hair frizzes. Secondly, it takes an exorbitant amount of time to do one shirt, even very badly. Thirdly, because I have a knack of zoning out to pass the time, I tend to have a fairly high incidence of, well, incidents.

This afternoon, I stand in the doorway to Bert's room. He stares at the iron-shaped mark on his shirt and frowns. 'It's not good enough, Eve. It's really not good enough.'

'I know. I'm sorry. I'll buy you another shirt.'

'I don't want another shirt. I want *this* shirt. With no mark.'

'It's just . . . I'm not a great ironer, is all.'

'You young folk, you're so slapdash! You don't take the time to do things properly.' He tuts and shakes his head. 'Now, Myrna . . . she could iron. Never once made a mark on my shirt. Not once!'

'I'm sorry,' I repeat, because there's not a lot else to say. I can't ask Myrna for an ironing lesson. I look out the window for Angus, and instead, I see Trish wheeling Gwen across the lawn in the whipping wind. That woman is crazy for fresh air, walking her in this weather. I look back at Bert. 'Maybe I should ask Gwen for some tips?'

Bert shrugs, all indifferent, but a pair of rosy circles appear on his cheeks. 'I suppose you could.'

'She's very sweet, I'm sure she'd be happy to help.' I eye Bert closely. 'Don't you think she's sweet, Bert?'

He keeps his head down. 'Wouldn't know.'

'She thinks you're sweet.'

His eyes bulge. 'Excuse me?'

'Gwen,' I say. 'I think she likes you.'

Bert clears his throat, and it turns into a coughing fit. I pat him firmly while using the opportunity to tuck the ruined shirt into the back of my pants, out of sight.

'So?' I make my voice a little singsongy. 'What do you say? You and Gwen?'

'Don't be ridiculous,' he says. The rosy spots have disappeared from his cheeks and he's all business again. 'And stop trying to distract me! Next shirt you ruin, I'm telling Eric. No excuses.'

'Right,' I say. 'Okay.'

With that, I trundle out of the room. But when I glance back from the doorway, Bert has swiveled his chair and is looking out the window. At Gwen.

At 3:30 P.M., when Clem bounds out of the school gates with a smile on her face, I think I might weep in relief. I've always thought Legs was a sweet kid, but when I see her little hand wrapped around Clem's, I have an overwhelming desire to sweep her into my arms and kiss her.

On the way home, Clem is a lot cheerier than on previous days. She tells me how she went right up to Miranda and said sorry, and how afterwards Miss Weber said it was a very brave thing to do. Then she tells me that Miss Weber said she could sit next to Legs all day. I decide I'd quite like to kiss Miss Weber, too.

That night, after Eric, Carole, and Trish have left, I go right to Anna's room. It's earlier than usual, but since it was Clem's first day back at school, I want to get her home so we can spend some time together before she goes to bed. Now, if I can just give Anna and Luke a little glimpse of each other before I go, I'll have all my ducks in a row.

There are a few residents still milling around, and Rosie is in the kitchen making a coffee. It's not ideal, but it will have to do.

'Hi, Anna,' I say, closing her door behind me. She's by the window, gazing out at the night. 'It's Eve.'

She looks over her shoulder, frowns. 'Hello.'

'I'm a bit early,' I whisper after I explain that we're going to see Luke. 'My daughter is having a tough time at school, so I want to get her home so we can hang out a bit.'

Anna doesn't usually respond beyond the odd yes or no when I talk about my life, but I get the feeling she likes to listen. More and more, I've been confiding in her – complaining about the cleaning, telling her my little worries. She doesn't remember what I've told her on previous visits, but she often manages to keep up pretty well with the conversation we're having.

'I haven't been the best mother lately,' I tell her.

She looks at me. I hesitate.

'Okay,' I say, 'I have a confession. I kissed the gardener.'

I watch Anna for a reaction, but her expression remains neutral.

'Actually, he kissed me,' I correct. 'But my daughter saw us. She asked me to promise never to kiss anyone ever again.'

Anna takes a minute. 'Did you promise?'

I smile. She *is* following. 'I did.'

There's a couple of seconds' silence, but I can tell by the way Anna's forehead is pinched that she is still with me. So I wait.

'Is he cute, this gardener?' she asks, after a few moments.

'Gorgeous,' I say miserably.

'Then you'll have to break that promise.'

I chuckle, but Anna remains deadpan. It makes me laugh more.

'Life is too short not to kiss,' Anna says.

'Maybe you're right,' I say, wiping my eyes. I go around the back of her wheelchair and take the handles, still

245

grinning. Then I check that the hallway is clear and hurry her across to Luke's room. Once they're settled, I head to the parlor to check on Clem.

'Are we leaving?' she says, looking up from the TV.

'Not yet. Just have a couple more things to do.'

'Mo-*om*!'

'Sorry, hon. I won't be long, I promise.'

She sighs, looks back at the TV. I glance at my watch. It's been only five minutes. That will have to do for tonight.

'Where are you going?' she asks as I leave the room.

'To take out the trash. I'll be right back!'

I pass Rosie in the corridor. When she has disappeared into Bert's room, I slip into Luke's. Anna is on Luke's bed, where I left her. It's usually like this. They just talk, kiss, touch. Apart from my first night at Rosalind House, when I found them in bed together, the relationship seems fairly innocent.

When Anna hears me, her head snaps around. 'Don't you knock?' she says, frowning.

'Sorry,' I whisper, closing the door behind me. 'But it's—'

Anna holds up a palm. 'We'd like some privacy, please.'

Anna's voice is loud, but I fight the urge to shush her, certain it would only irritate her more. 'We need to go, Anna. You have a motorcycle race tomorrow—'

'Cancel it,' she snaps. Then she turns back to Luke.

'But you've already paid your entrance fee. And—'

'I. Don't. *Care.*'

I feel a flicker of panic. 'Okay,' I say. 'No race, then.

246

But can you keep your voice down because . . . Jack is asleep.'

The other day I'd said 'the residents' were asleep, and she'd become upset, asking '*What residents?*' When I mentioned Jack, though, she'd quieted.

Not today.

'*Fuck* Jack.' As she says it, Anna gives me a look of pure hatred. I stand there, wondering what to do.

'Mom. Mom! Where *are* you?'

I hurry into the hallway, closing the door behind me.

'*There* you are!' Clem says. 'You said you were taking out the trash!'

'Sorry, hon, I had a couple other things to do first.'

'What things?' Rosie says, coming down the hall with a mug in her hands. She joins Clem and me in a three-point circle in the corridor. 'I can finish them for you. You two go home.'

Clem beams.

'Oh no!' I say. 'It's cleaning stuff. I couldn't ask you to do that, Rosie. Clem, I'll just be another few minutes.'

'Believe it or not, I *can* unpack the dishwasher and take out the trash,' Rosie says. 'I can even wipe down a counter. Go on. I insist.'

'But—'

'She insists, Mom.' Clem is holding my purse, and her own bag is perched on her shoulders. Her hand slips into mine. 'Come on. Let's go.'

'Okay,' I say, but my voice is as thin as the strip of light I can see coming out from under Luke's door. 'Okay. We'll go.'

Rosie smiles and I take my purse from Clem, put it over my shoulder. I thank Rosie and wish her good night. And then there is nothing left to do but leave.

31

Anna

Eleven months ago . . .

I was right about Mustache Man. When he said we were going to "sort this whole thing out" he *did* mean Me and Young Guy. As for the "sort" part – that must have meant he was going to call Jack and the sister. Now all of us gather in a small room and they shout over our heads as if we aren't even here at all.

'They were in bed together,' Jack cries.

'Yes, Trish found them this morning,' Mustache Man says. His eyes dart around like flies in a jar. 'But Anna didn't seem distressed.'

'Am I supposed to be grateful?' Jack says. 'How could you let this happen?'

'What do you suggest?' the sister cries. 'That we tie them up like dogs?'

'For God's sake,' Jack says. 'Did I say that? Surely there's a middle ground between tying them up and letting them roam wild.'

'We don't tie anyone up at Rosalind House,' Mustache

Man says, wiping his brow for the fiftieth time. 'And no one is roaming wild.' He looks at me. 'The last thing we want is to take away your freedoms, Anna, or yours, Luke. We want you to be happy.' He looks at Jack. 'And safe.'

I roll my eyes. Mustache Man should be a diplomat.

'So why don't we discuss that and see if we can find a solution that is comfortable for everyone?' he says.

I tell Mustache Man that Young Guy and I are comfortable with the current arrangement, and Jack groans. 'I don't doubt that Luke's comfortable with it,' he says, and then the sister starts going crazy again.

I put my hands over my ears, but it doesn't stop the noise. It feels like a radio is on in my head, loud, on a talk-back channel in a language I don't understand. If they'd speak one at a time, and slowly, I might be able to keep up, even join in. Like this, I've got no chance. So when Mustache Man asks if Young Guy and I would like 'a little break', I don't see any point in protesting.

'I'm scared,' I say to Young Guy when we're in the big front room, sitting side by side on the . . . giant long chair. My head is resting against him.

'What . . . w-why?' he asks.

'I don't know.'

With him, I don't waste brain energy on trying to say the right things or making sense of my feelings. I simply say what's on my mind. Sometimes it feels scary, being so stripped bare with someone. Sometimes it feels good.

'I do know that I'm happy now,' I say. 'So if we keep doing this, we'll be okay.'

250

He pulls me tighter and I hear what he is no longer able to tell me: *Yes. We will.*

There's a new guy at Rosalind House. Old, obviously. Mostly bald. Wearing a bow tie with a short-sleeved shirt. He's tall and skinny at the head and shoulders and wider around the middle and legs. Mr Pin, I dub him, because he reminds me of a bowling pin. He obviously isn't happy to be here, but I think we can all sympathize with that.

He noses his pushy-wheeler into the big front room, muttering as he goes. The woman who follows him bears a striking resemblance, only with more hair and fewer liver spots. Probably his daughter or granddaughter. Maybe even a young wife. Once, I was pretty good at telling people's ages at a glance. These days, well . . . Take this woman, for example. She could be thirty-five or sixty-five. Together, they head for the floral armchair by the bookcase.

'Can't sit there,' Baldy says, before Mr Pin even gets close. He taps his head in the direction of the chair without so much as lifting his eyes from his book. 'That,' he says, 'is Myrna's chair.'

'Excuse me?' Mr Pin says.

Baldy repeats himself.

'Well, as Myrna isn't currently sitting in it, I'm sure she won't mind.' Mr Pin rotates with his walker, ready to plant his bony butt right on Myrna. The room silently goes on full-alert.

'Are you blind?' Baldy splutters. 'She's right there.'

Mr Pin looks at the empty seat and then at Baldy.

251

Finally, he looks at his young look-alike. 'Louisa,' he says, 'do something.'

'I'm sorry, sir,' Louisa says to Baldy in an over-the-top polite voice. 'You must be mistaken. There's no one sitting here.'

'There *is*,' Baldy says. His voice is typically grumpy, but there's a waver to it. 'Myrna's sitting there. And she'd appreciate not being sat on.'

In a place like this where nothing ever happens, this sort of confrontation is as good as a Fourth of July fireworks display. People appear from all over the place, coming to check out the action. Even I feel a little thrilled. But also worried. Like something bad is about to happen.

'It's the only seat available,' Mr Pin says. He starts to remove his outer-shirt thingy, and the color leaches out of Baldy's face. 'So unless you can—'

Before I know it, I'm out of my chair and standing beside Baldy. I may not love the guy, and I definitely think he's bonkers, but Mr Pin is new, and I can't help feel a certain loyalty.

'Roast night tonight, Myrna,' I hear myself say. I stare at the empty chair, trying to bring up an image of an old lady in my mind's eye. 'Your favorite.'

The entire room is silent. Mr Pin freezes with one arm out of his outer-shirt thingy.

Baldy stares at me, then gives me a slight nod. Mr Pin looks at us for a moment, then starts to lower himself into the chair.

'P-Pet therapy t-today, Myrna,' Young Guy says suddenly. 'You can hold a h-h-hamster!'

252

All the heads in the room spin toward Young Guy. Baldy finally starts to crack a smile. Mr Pin stands and squints at the chair, confused.

'It's all right, love,' Baldy says to Myrna. 'No kitchen mice at pet therapy.' He shakes his head and laughs. 'When we were first married, I came home one day to find her standing on the kitchen bench after seeing a mouse. She was white as a sheet. Been there for hours, she said. They didn't have cell phones in those days, of course.'

'That happened to Clara once, didn't it, love?' Southern Lady's husband says. 'She said it was the size of a cat! I came racing home from work, and it was no bigger than my thumb.'

Southern Lady – Clara – crosses the room and, elbowing Mr Pin out of the way, she perches on the arm of Myrna's chair. 'It *was* the size of a cat, Myrna,' she whispers, elbowing Myrna's nonexistent shoulder. 'These men have no idea what we put up with.'

We form a little circle around Myrna's chair, and I can't keep the grin off my face. Baldy, I notice, is also grinning, and so is Young Guy. He offers me a wink.

Mr Pin and the young woman shuffle away from the chair. Away from me, probably. Away from the lot of us.

The 'solution', apparently, is to have Young Guy and me followed. Since our meeting with Mustache Man, every time I so much as *look* at Young Guy, he is whisked away. At mealtimes, Skinny goes into passive-aggressive over-drive. '*There's a lovely view of the garden from this seat, Anna,*' she'll say if I sit next to Luke. '*Why don't you pop over here?*' I politely decline, of course, and generally she won't force it, but it's a small win. We have no time alone together. At night, the nurses roam the halls, which limits our meetings. When it's the nice nurse – Blondie – she looks the other way for a few minutes before moving us along. Anyone else, and we're practically mown down before we crack open the door.

I had it out with Jack, of course. I don't remember the details, but I do remember shouting until he threatened to request a sedative. Jack worked in a court as one of the arguing people, but up until recently, I could argue him under the table. Not anymore. He was fast – really fast – ready with a reply before I'd even thought of the question. He also knew how to work the emotions. He didn't just yell at me – no, that would have made it too easy to hate him – he cried, the son of a bitch. Real streaming tears. Told me this was *killing him*. 'Funny that,' I'd told him, 'because this memory-disease is killing me. And for the first time in forever, I wish it would hurry up and get it over with.'

32

Anna

Ten months ago . . .

You know what's sadder than the fact that I haven't laid a finger on Young Guy in forever? Soon I won't know him. Yeah, that'd be true even if it wasn't for Project Watch Us All the Time, but in light of Project Watch Us All the Time, well . . . not even a super-strength pink pill can make me feel better about that.

But time ticks on, slower than before. Every now and again, I think about that window in the upstairs room. About how I could go up there and end it, just like that. Then I see him in the big front room or out on the lawn, and I decide: Not today. I won't do it today.

I'm flat on my sleeping-bench, where I've been all day. What I'd give for a drink of water! I threw up this morning and I can still taste sick in my mouth. I'm hungry, too, but every time I try to think what I'd like to eat, I think I might be sick all over again. So I just stay where I am, on my sleeping bench.

When Skinny walks in, I give her the barest glance, then look back at the wall. She'll just be reminding me about fresh air again. Fuck fresh air.

'Coming?' she says. 'It's about to start.'

'What is?'

'The wedding.' Skinny's voice is over-the-top patient, making clear the fact that she has told me this before, perhaps very recently. 'Bert's granddaughter's wedding. In the garden.'

She looks at me, frowns. 'Where are your clothes, Anna?'

'Where are yours?' I say, although it's silly because her clothes, quite obviously, are on her body. Mine are not. I'm sitting here in a top-thing and a pair of sleeping-pants. 'Anyway, I was just about to get dressed,' I say.

That part is true, at least. I *was* about to get dressed, a little while ago. But when I couldn't find my clothes, I lost interest and started looking at the wall. 'Someone has hidden my clothes,' I tell her, awash with new frustration. 'Or stolen them. It was you, wasn't it?'

Bitch.

'Your clothes are right here, Anna, in your closet. Why don't I help you?'

She opens a door and, like magic, there they are! It pisses me off. I really hate it when Skinny is right.

She pulls out a long shirt with no sleeves. 'How about this? This would be nice for the wedding.'

I look at the thing she's handed me. 'Is it warm out?'

She hands me another thing, this one with long sleeves and open at the front. 'You'll be fine with this cardigan on top.'

To her credit, Skinny is surprisingly efficient at getting me dressed. She even brushes my hair and pins it back and then smiles and tells me I look very pretty. It annoys me, her showing this nice side after hiding my clothes like that. But it's also really handy not having to get dressed by myself, so I guess we're Even Steven.

Outside my door, in the long thin room, I see him. Skinny must see him, too, because she takes my elbow and starts dragging me toward the back door. As I pass him, the backs of our hands touch for an instant and I close my eyes. When I open them again, he's gone.

It looks like a fairy threw up outside. White flower-leaves are sprinkled over everything: the grass, the chairs, the green arched thingy out front. The chairs are divided in the center by a pink floor-rug that is also sprinkled with – you said it – white flower-leaves. From somewhere or other music plays. I recognize the song, I think.

I'm starting to wonder what all this is about when someone explains there is a wedding about to take place. Baldy's granddaughter's. All the people who live here are seated at the side of the garden; so are the staff. Latina Cook-Lady sits on one side of me. Her belly is big and round now, and she rests her hand on it. In her other hand is a sandwich that smells like pickle and cheese. It's making me hungry.

Everyone oohs and ahhs, but I'm underwhelmed. For my wedding to Aiden, I wore a short black thingy and red pointy shoes, but this, I guess, is most women's dream. Baldy walks the bride down the aisle on his pushy-wheeler, for which he earns a standing clap. I admit, judging from

257

all the flower-leaves, I'd written the bride off as a super-ficial Barbie-princess-wedding kind of girl, but when I see her, edging down the aisle next to her elderly grandfather, she earns back a modicum of my respect.

It's not until the couple are exchanging their vows that I realize Young Guy is beside me. His head hangs forward, blocking the sun from my face. And I definitely still know him. For now.

'Well, well,' I say, wondering why someone hadn't whisked him away. 'Skinny must have got laid.'

We both glance at her, at the end of the bench, dabbing her eyes. Her mind was clearly elsewhere.

His hand clasps mine.

We stay like that through the ceremony, as the music – Pachelbel's Canon, according to the folded paperthing-amajig – plays around us. And before I know it, I'm picturing *our* wedding. What it could have beenlike. What it *should* have been like, if it wasn't for the stupid brain-disease. Then again, if it wasn't for the stupid brain-disease, we would never have met.

When the wedding guests move on to the party, Latina Cook-Lady brings out the bread with fillings and bubbly water and we eat and drink outside. Even Skinny and the other lady – Fat? – eat out here with us. No one talks – it's as if we've been put under a spell. Maybe it's witnessing someone at the beginning of their lives that has made us reflective of our own lives, at the end.

That night, when I extend my arm under the thin-blanket, *he's* there. How, I have no idea. After the brief hand-holding at lunch, Fat and Skinny didn't leave us alone. Every time he looked at me, one of them was in my face, suggesting Scrabble (whatever that is). But tonight Blondie is on duty. She must have allowed him to take liberties.

He half sits, half lies on the sleeping bench and looks at me. 'I w-wish this were the beginning,' he says. 'Like for the c . . . c . . . couple who got . . . marr . . . married.'

In the moonlight, I see tears in his eyes. It's the first time I've heard him talk in . . . I don't know how long.

'I was thinking that, too,' I say. 'Imagining what our life would be like. We'd have a house, our own house, with no . . . helper-people.' I pull myself up on one elbow. 'A cottage with a spare room that we'd say was a study, but we'd both know it would be the baby's room. You'd pretend the idea of a baby terrified you when it actually thrilled you.'

He smiles. A tear slides from the corner of his eye.

'We wouldn't have one of those after-wedding vacations because we're flat broke, but you'd surprise me with a flying balloon ride over the city.'

'I'm . . . don't . . . heights.'

'Which makes it all the more sweet,' I say. I'm starting to enjoy this fantasy.

'We'd have a cat,' I say, and Luke pouts. 'Who we'd call Dog. After we'd been married for a little while, I'd go off that drug that stops babies from being made, reasoning that it could take months or even years to make a child, and then we'd find out the very next month that we *had* made a baby. The baby is a boy and we'll call him—'

He holds up his hand, stopping me mid-sentence. 'Only . . . one baby?'

'I'm nearly forty. It's unlikely we'll have an army.'

'Then—' He stops. It's getting harder for him, this speaking. '—a girl.'

I roll my eyes, even though I'm delighted that he is joining in. 'Fine. A girl then. She has your eyes—'

'And your . . .' He frowns, then grabs a piece of my hair and tugs it.

'Curls,' I say, 'which she hates!'

He grins, indenting a dimple.

'She has you wrapped around her little finger,' I say.

He chuckles. And I can see it: Him and me and our little girl. And it's the funniest thing – when I wrap my arms around my stomach, I can actually feel a little bump.

33

Eve

It might be futile, but the night after I leave Anna and Luke in the room together, I allow myself to hope. Maybe it will all be fine? Maybe Anna and Luke will fall asleep in each other's arms and I'll be able to move them back in the morning before anyone notices? Maybe I've done them a service, allowing them to have an entire night together – probably the last they'll ever have?

I arrive as early as I can manage. The residents' doors are all shut. The place is in silence. A good sign. I tap on Luke's door quietly and hurry inside.

My heart sinks. It's empty.

Anna's room is empty, too. I creep around, looking for signs of them, but they are nowhere to be seen. Finally I go to the nurses' room. As I enter, Rosie glances up. Anna and Luke sit opposite her, in a pair of armchairs.

'Morning, Eve,' she says. 'Why don't you sit down and tell me what is going on?'

It could be worse, I tell myself. It could have been Eric who caught me, not Rosie. Then again, Rosie is probably the closest thing I have to a friend right now, apart from Anna, and I don't feel good about betraying her.

'How long has this been going on?' she asks when Anna and Luke are back in their rooms and we are in the hall.

'A couple of weeks.'

'A couple of weeks?' Rosie puts a hand to her temple and starts to pace. 'Are you *crazy*? Do you realize you could get fired for this?'

'Only if you tell Eric.'

She stops pacing. 'Are you serious?'

'I know you should tell Eric,' I say. 'But I'm hoping you don't.'

Rosie is incredulous. 'Why shouldn't I?'

'Because Anna and Luke should be allowed to be together. And you know it.'

Her eyes flash. I'm taking a risk, saying this. I don't know for sure that is how she feels, but it's a pretty strong instinct.

'So what have you been doing, exactly?' she says. 'Going into Anna's room every night, dragging her out of bed, and wheeling her into Luke's room?'

Sounds pretty crazy when she puts it like that. 'Pretty much.'

'And then?'

'I leave her there for a few minutes, then bring her back. But last night, you interrupted, so I couldn't take her back.'

'So you don't usually leave them overnight?'

'No.'

Rosie seems relieved to hear this. She thinks for a

minute. 'And . . . are they happier when they see each other, do you think?'

'*Infinitely* happier.' A feeling of hopefulness starts to bubble up. 'And they've been so much more settled during the daytime—'

'Just to be clear, Eve, you shouldn't have done this. You took this whole thing into your own hands, and it could have had disastrous consequences for everyone.'

'What *kind* of consequences?' I ask. 'And don't give me the whole issue of consent, because I don't buy it. Clearly both Anna and Luke would consent to this! I even—'

'I agree they would consent,' Rosie says quietly.

My mouth is already full of a retort, but suddenly, I stop. 'You do?'

She nods. 'But, Eve, if we're going to do this, we're going to do it my way.'

I blink. 'You mean . . . ?'

A small smile appears on Rosie's lips. 'Yes, we're going to do it. But this time, we're going to do it right.'

From that night on, it's Rosie's rules.

Each night, Rosie locks Anna's and Luke's doors, and around five minutes later, before I leave, I unlock them again. It's semantics, but it makes Rosie feel better to be able to tell Eric she has locked the doors if she's asked a direct question. Then, once everyone is asleep, Rosie goes in and ushers one over to the other. She lets them have a visit, but she keeps the doors open and checks in on them regularly. This, she said, was a nonnegotiable part of the arrangement, and though I didn't entirely understand it, I

263

didn't care. Anna and Luke are together. I am keeping my promise.

Today, I'm wheeling the cleaning cart down the hall when I run into Angus. He's holding an armful of flowers.

'Hey,' I say.

'Hey,' he says.

'You have some dirt on your face.' I reach out, wipe it off his cheek. Then I quickly take my hand back.

'Gone?' he asks.

'Sorry. I'm clearly the mother of a young child.'

He laughs and I feel an overwhelming wave of pure lust.

'Does the offer of dinner still stand?' I ask suddenly. Perhaps it's the laugh, or maybe the fact that Anna and Luke's connection has renewed my faith in love, but the words just tumble out of me.

'Sure,' he says, startled. 'Absolutely. But what about Clem?'

'Clem wants me to be happy,' I say. 'And life is . . . well, rather short. Isn't it?'

Angus's eyes twinkle. 'That it is.'

'So, how's Thursday night?' I ask.

'Thursday night is good,' he says, and he tucks a flower behind my ear.

I make a mental note to thank Anna.

At 3 P.M., I wheel the cleaning cart into Clara and Laurie's suite. I'm supposed to make up all the residents' rooms after breakfast each morning, but at this stage, it's more of a goal than a reality. And with everything else that's going on, it's fallen even further down my list of priorities.

I start with the bathroom to get it out of the way. I hate the bathrooms. The smells, the streaks, the smudges. I spray the shower screen, wipe the vanity. I pour a little bleach into the toilet, leave it for a minute or two, then flush it down. I rehang the towels squarely and neatly. The floor looks clean enough, so I leave it alone. Finally, I pick up the used towels and carry them out to the hamper.

It's a legal requirement that each resident has a separate room, but because Clara and Laurie are married, they converted one bedroom into a living room, with a sofa and television and dressing table. When I get out of the bathroom, Clara is sitting at the dressing table, looking at the photographs that litter the countertop.

'It's just me,' I say. 'Shall I keep cleaning, or would you like me to come back later?'

Clara glances over her shoulder. 'Oh, go ahead, honey, don't mind me.' She picks up a photo frame, looks at it, puts it down again.

I wipe down the tables, vacuum the floor, make up the bed. Then I get out my feather duster. 'Okay if I dust?'

'Of course.'

I pick up a photo in a heavy silver frame to dust underneath. As I put it down, it catches my eye. 'Is this you and Laurie?'

'Our wedding day.' She throws me a smile. 'Laurie and I have been together sixty-one years.'

'Wow. What a wonderful achievement.'

It *is* an achievement; I've always thought so. All

marriages, even good ones, involve a lot of work, a lot of compromise. It says a lot about a person, I think, if they make it to the end with the one person.

Then, as it happens every so often, I'm thinking about Richard.

'I'm sorry,' Clara says. 'I shouldn't be saying this, with your husband and all.'

'It's all right. I like hearing about happy endings. Even if I don't get to have one.'

'Oh, honey.' She sighs. 'There's nothing happy about endings.'

I replace the photo. Clara doesn't seem herself. She's holding a string of pearls in one hand, rolling a single fat pearl between her fingers, and I notice that she looks terrible – somehow puffy and gaunt all at once. Her makeup is too dark for her complexion, and her pink lipstick bleeds into the lines of her mouth.

'Are you all right, Clara?' I ask.

'Course I'm all right, honey,' she says. 'Just . . . a headache, is all.'

'Shall I get Laurie for you?'

Clara makes a gesture with her hand, dismissing the idea, and I catch a waft of her scent: lavender and talcum powder. 'Do you have any sisters, Eve?' she asks.

'Me?' I say, surprised. 'No. No brothers or sisters.'

'You're lucky.'

'*Lucky?*' I laugh. 'Do you know what it's like eating your dinner every night for twenty years under the watchful eye of two parents who have nothing they'd rather do than talk – at length – about *your* day? With no one to interrupt, no one who's failed a math quiz to steal their attention. Just you. And them. What I would have done for a sister!'

From the way Clara smiles, I think I've got her. But then she says, 'Sisters aren't always the way they look on TV, Eve, with all the hugging and the sharing secrets and the swapping clothes. Sometimes sisters can be treacherous.'

I think back to the day in the parlor when Laurie said Clara's sister was coming to visit. Clearly things aren't particularly harmonious between the two of them.

'Have you ever wondered if your whole life was a lie?' Clara asks.

'Yes,' I say.

She looks at me, nods. 'Yes, I s'pose you have.'

My cell phone rings in my pocket and I snatch it and glance at the screen, ready to silence it. Then I notice the call is coming from Clem's school. 'Sorry, Clara, I have to take this.'

'Yes, of course. Go ahead, honey.'

I punch the button. 'Hello?'

'Mrs Bennett, this is Kathy Donnelly from Clementine's school. I'm afraid we have a little problem.'

34

Clementine

'Clementine, it's Miss Weber. Can you open the door, sweetheart?'

I put down the toilet seat and sit. I'll wait here until everyone has gone home, and then I'll come out. By that time, Mom will be here, and she'll take me home and I'll tell her I never want to come back to school again.

'It's just me,' Miss Weber says. 'All the other kids have gone back to class. Why don't you come out and tell me what happened?'

'I don't want to.'

'Clementine, *something* must have happened for you to lock yourself in here. I want to help you, but you have to talk to me. Did someone say something to upset you?'

'Yes.'

'I'm sorry to hear that. Can you tell me what they said?'

Your daddy was a bad man. Everyone hated your daddy.

'They told lies.'

'What kind of lies?'

There's writing on the toilet door:

Jenny and Katie woz here.
Ella ~~*stinks*~~ *smells nice.*

I suddenly want to write something. *Miranda stinks.* Or maybe, *Miranda is a liar.* But I don't have a pen.

'Clem?' It's another voice; not Miss Weber. Immediately I feel a rush of tears.

'Mom?'

'Yes, it's me.'

Everyone hates your mom, too.

I throw open the door and run headlong into Mom's belly. 'What is it?' she says, cradling my head. 'What happened?'

'I haven't gotten to the bottom of it yet,' Miss Weber tells her. 'Something happened at lunchtime. Clem didn't come back to class, and I found her in here. I've tried to get her to talk, but she hasn't said anything except that someone said something to upset her.'

Mom stands back and looks at me. There is a wet patch on her shirt from my tears. 'Who said something to you?' she asks. 'Was it Miranda?'

I'm crying too much now to get any words out, so I just nod. Mom kneels down in front of me and makes her voice all quiet. 'What did she say, hon?'

I know how he died. He wasn't old or sick.

'I want to go home,' I say. 'Can we go home?'

'I'd really rather know what happened,' Miss Weber says.

'Then we can deal with it. If Miranda did say something to Clem, I'll talk to her, talk to her mother—'

I squeeze Mom's hand. '*Please* can we go?'

'Actually, Ms Donnelly wanted to speak to you, Mrs Bennett,' Miss Weber says to Mom. 'She said it's important.'

Mom's face goes white.

'*Please!*' I cry.

Mom looks at Miss Weber. Finally Miss Weber nods.

'Tell Ms Donnelly I'll call her,' Mom says.

Miss Weber gets my bag and then walks with us to the parking lot. At Mom's car, she squats down and gives me a hug. 'We'll work this out, Clementine. It makes me very sad to think that someone has upset you. I'm going right back to class now and I'm going to talk to everyone about how we shouldn't say things to upset our friends.'

'Even if they're true?' Mom says quietly.

Miss Weber and I look up, but I don't think Mom is talking to me. Not to Miss Weber either. She's just kind of talking to the air.

On the way home, Mom calls Eric to say she's not coming back to Rosalind House. She says she's sorry, but it's a family emergency. I want to tell her that I don't mind, that I like being at Rosalind House, but then she says, 'I'm taking my daughter home, and *that's that*,' and hangs up the phone.

At home, Mom makes her homemade mac 'n' cheese, and she lets me eat it on the couch.

'I know you don't want to talk about it,' she says, sitting

beside me. 'But I would really like to know what Miranda said to you.'

'I don't want to tell you.'

'Okay,' she says. 'Well, is there anything you want to *ask* me?'

I dig my fork into my bowl. 'Was Daddy a bad man?'

I don't look at her. She is quiet for a few seconds, then I *do* look.

'Daddy *did* do some bad things,' she says finally.

'What things?' I ask.

'Well. He took other people's money and he lied about it.'

'Oh.'

I start to look down, but Mom lifts my chin and looks into my eyes. 'Is that what Miranda said? That Daddy was a bad man?'

'And . . . other stuff.'

'What stuff?'

I push my macaroni around, say nothing.

'You don't want to tell me?' Mom says, and I nod. 'Okay, you don't have to tell me now. But maybe later, when you've thought about it, you might tell me then.'

I swallow. 'Yeah, maybe.'

I don't feel like eating anymore, so Mom and I watch some TV. I don't really pay attention. I'm thinking about what Mom said. *Daddy did bad things.*

Later, when we're in bed, I'm still thinking about it. Mom falls asleep quickly and I watch her for a while. Her eyes are closed and her mouth is open.

'Mom?' She doesn't answer, so I tap her shoulder. 'Mom?'

Her eyes fly open and she jerks upright. 'What is it? Are you all right?'

'Miranda said Daddy killed *himself.*'

Mom blinks; then her eyes get wide and sad. She sits up.

'Did he?' I ask. 'Kill himself?' I wait with my heart booming in my chest.

Mom tries to cuddle me, but I sit back. I need to see her face. Finally she says, 'Yes, Clem. He did.' Her eyes are shiny. She reaches for me again, but I move even farther back.

He *did.*

Daddy killed himself. Daddy was a bad man.

I dive under the covers and cry and cry.

35

It's hot in Dr Felder's office, hot enough to make me want to go back out into the rainy, horrible day. Outside, people scrunch their faces against the wind. Mom is waiting in the room outside. I had an appointment with Dr Felder anyway, she said, but we were able to move it up, probably because I cried so much last night. Last night, I thought I might never stop crying. Then, this morning, I stopped crying all at once, like I'd suddenly run out of tears.

Dr Felder is a therapist. She has spiky black hair and red glasses that hang on a chain around her neck. Her nails are painted red, and she has lots of silver rings on her fingers. She also has a lot of toys. A huge dollhouse with lots of rooms, and lots of dolls to go inside it.

She sits on the beanbag next to me, her hands folded in her lap.

'How are you today?' she asks.

'I'm okay.'

'Would you like to play with something?'

'No.'

'How about we just talk, then?'

I trace a line in the swirly carpet with my finger, say nothing.

'Is there anything you'd like to talk about, Clementine?'

I miss you every single day. I miss the way we used to play.

'No.'

'Sometimes it can be hard to talk,' she says. 'Particularly about things that are painful. But it's important we talk about things, or they can become stuck inside us. You know that feeling people get in their bellies, when they're feeling sad or worried about something? It can feel like butterflies or a clenched fist or sometimes it can even make you feel a little bit sick?'

I know the feeling she's talking about. It's the one I get when Miranda is around.

'That's what happens when you hold feelings inside,' she says. 'If you talk about what's bothering you, sometimes that feeling won't feel quite so bad. And sometimes, it will even go away entirely.'

'My daddy killed himself,' I say.

'I'm sorry,' she says. 'Do you miss your daddy?'

I shrug. I *did* miss him. Now I don't know.

'Sometimes,' Dr Felder says, 'when you lose someone suddenly, the hardest part is not being able to say the things you need to say to them.' She looks at me. 'What would you say to your daddy if he were here right now?'

'I'd tell him I was very angry with him.' I look at Dr Felder's face, at her funny glasses and spiky hair, and I wonder what she will think about this.

274

But she doesn't seem to think anything. 'What are you angry about?' she asks.

'I'm angry that he left us.'

'That's understandable.' Dr Felder is quiet for a bit.

'And I'm angry that he is a bad man.'

'Oh?' Dr Felder's eyebrows rise up. 'Why is he a bad man?'

'He did bad things. With people's money.'

She nods. 'It must be hard for you to hear that your dad did bad things.'

'It is,' I say. 'I thought he was a good daddy. I thought he was the best daddy in the world.'

Suddenly, the tears come back.

Dr Felder takes a box of Kleenex from her desk and holds it out. I take one.

'Is there anything else you'd like to say to your dad, Clementine?'

I think of a night not long before Daddy died, when Mom went out late. Daddy and I ate pizza and then he let me put pink lipstick on him and clips in his hair. When it was time for me to go to bed, he promised he would keep the lipstick on until Mom got home so she could see it. In the morning, he told me he *did* keep it on, that Mom thought he looked *very pretty*. I giggled.

Now I wonder if he was telling the truth.

'No,' I say. 'Nothing else.'

36

Eve

That night, I sit on the sofa with a large glass of white wine in my hand, rehearsing.

Hello, Angus.

Welcome to my home.

Won't you come in?

It is supposed to sound sensual, but it all sounds ridiculous, coming out of my mouth. I'd spent the last hour going back and forth about whether I should even be going ahead with my date at all. But every time I pick up the phone to cancel, Anna's voice speaks to me. And I put the phone down again.

At 7:30 P.M. on the dot, I pick up my phone again. It's late notice, but I'll fake an illness or something. But before I can dial Angus's number, it starts to ring.

My heart flies into my throat. I'd received two phone messages today, one only an hour ago, from Ms Donnelly at Clem's school. Her message simply said to call her back, but her voice was clipped – the voice of a determined debt collector. She must know something. I picture her at her desk behind her thick glasses, circling our address in red pen, and I want to curl up and cry. But when I look at the phone, it's Mother's number on the screen. I exhale in relief.

'Clem?' I say.

'Hi, Mom.'

'Are you having a good time at Nana and Papa's?'

'Yeah.' She giggles. 'Papa keeps saying he's not ticklish, but he is.'

In the background, I hear Dad insisting that he is not, in fact, ticklish. This is followed by loud (obviously false) laughter on his part and real laughter from Clem. It warms my heart.

'Clem?'

'Yeah?'

A crackling sound, like a radio between channels, blasts into the room. The buzzer.

'What's that?' Clem asks.

'Oh, a delivery, probably,' I say quickly. 'Anyway, Nana is dropping you home early in the morning, so I'll walk you to school, okay?'

'Okay.'

I exhale. I'd been expecting some protest at the word 'school', but she seems in good spirits. 'Okay. Have sweet dreams, hon.'

'I will. Bye, Mom.'

With a racing heart, I buzz Angus inside. Then I glance in the mirror. I wish I'd gone for the jeans and soft black sweater instead of the cleavage-hugging red wrap-dress, but it's too late now. I peel open the door, and Angus is standing there, holding a brown bag full of produce and a small bunch of pink roses.

'Hi,' I say. So much for my sensual welcome.

'Hi,' he says.

I smile. We stand there a minute.

'Can I come in?' he asks.

'Oh! Sure.' I giggle and open the door farther. What is it about Angus that makes me behave like an imbecile every time I see him? 'You can put the bags in the kitchen over there. Thanks again for getting the groceries.'

Angus heads straight to the kitchen, and I follow. 'Where I come from, you don't ask a woman if you can make her dinner and then ask her to buy the groceries.'

Angus unloads the bags onto the bench and I quickly realize that with Angus and all his groceries in the kitchen, there's not enough room for much else. Including me. I stand there awkwardly for a moment until Angus clears a small amount of bench space and pats it.

I hesitate.

'Go on. I like having someone to talk to while I cook.'

I continue to hesitate until Angus grips my waist and lifts me onto the bench. He immediately starts to unpack the bags, nonchalant, but the gentle gesture leaves me scrambling for breath for several seconds. Angus doesn't seem to notice. I watch him pull items from the bags. Parsley. Spinach. Potatoes. His hands, I notice, are impressively clean. I suppose I'd have expected a residue of dirt that was impossible to remove, but his gardener's nails are cleaner than my own.

'Shall I open this?' I say. I gesture to the beading bottle of white wine on the counter.

'I'll do it,' he says, fishing out a Swiss Army knife from his pocket. I slide off the bench and reach around him for glasses. For a delicious instant, my front presses lightly against his back.

'How was your—?' I start, at the same time as he says, 'Long day?'

'Sorry,' we say in unison, and then, 'You go. No, you go.'

Angus pours our drinks, and I take a large gulp of wine. Then another. Angus and I usually have a fairly easy, comfortable relationship at work, but what if we are a disaster socially? If this evening goes awry, I can kiss our comfortable work relationship good-bye! I watch Angus as he reaches for my chopping board. His expression is pleasantly neutral, but then, he has the advantage – having a meal to prepare, busy-work to keep his hands occupied and his head from over-analyzing it all.

'Nice place,' he says after a lengthy silence.

'Yes,' I say, surveying the expanse of brown décor. 'I'm sure brown is coming back into fashion – I'm just a little ahead of the trend.'

Angus chuckles. 'I love what you've done with the kitchen,' he says, taking a piece of whitefish out of a cool bag and resting it on the chopping board. I laugh and give him a friendly punch. He catches my fist and holds it for a long moment. A pulse of electricity runs through me.

'What are you cooking?' I ask, breaking the charged silence.

'Sea bass. And potatoes.'

I smile again. No jus. No ancient grain salad or Vietnamese greens. Just fish. And potatoes. Which, if done properly, is a meal entirely unto itself.

Angus finds a peeler in a drawer and declines my offer to help. In my kitchen, he seems so confident, so relaxed. His peeling hand is completely steady and smooth as it glides over the potato. But when I look down at my own hand, holding my wineglass, I notice it's shaking just the tiniest bit.

We eat dinner at the small round table and afterwards move to the couch. There, Angus reclines, pulling me – in a way that is both natural and entirely terrifying – into the crook of his arm. For no reason in particular, I think about Anna and Luke. Did they once have evenings like this? Well, perhaps not exactly like this, but I can't help picturing them together, on the couch in the parlor, talking, holding hands, enjoying each other. They *deserve* to have nights like this.

'Well,' I say, relaxing against him. '*That* was delicious.'

'I was pretty nervous,' he admits. 'I haven't cooked dinner for a chef before. I was hoping to impress you.'

'You did,' I say. 'The last person to cook for me was Clem, and that was toast and a cup of tea on Mother's Day.' I smile. 'This was very special.'

'How's Clem doing?' Angus asks.

'She's . . .' I start to reel off the standard response – she's coping, she's strong – but I stop myself. 'Actually, I have no idea. She's up and down. I'm worried about her.'

280

'She's a great kid, Eve.'

'Even though she told me I could never kiss you again?'

'Yeah, that was a shame,' he says. 'But I like her. She's feisty and she says what she thinks. But she's also kind, which not all seven-year-olds are. The other day, after May's visitors left, Clem sat beside her for a while and held her hand.'

I smile because I remember Clem doing that. Afterwards when I asked her why, she'd said, *'I think May feels lonely after her family leaves.'*

'She *is* special like that,' I say.

Angus grins and taps his head gently against mine. 'Anyway, I have some news.'

'You do?'

'My sister, Kelly, is pregnant.'

I jerk up, look at him. 'But I thought she couldn't afford to do IVF because of—'

'Not IVF. She became pregnant naturally. She's twelve weeks along. She had an ultrasound today, and it all looks good.'

I can't believe it. Guilt and relief and elation all swirl through me at once.

'The funny thing is that they did IVF seven times and never had any luck. Then, after five months of no treatment, she became pregnant naturally!'

'I've heard of that happening,' I say. 'It's almost as though the body needs you to relax and forget about it in order for it to happen.'

'And that wouldn't have happened if they hadn't lost their money.'

Silence. 'Oh, Angus, I don't think—'

'What your husband did was bad. But good and bad stuff comes out of everything. I don't have to tell you that, do I?'

He doesn't. I've thought about it; good coming from bad. After all, if I hadn't met Richard, I wouldn't have had Clem. And yet . . .

'I'm not sure Richard should be taking credit for your sister's pregnancy.'

'Maybe not,' Angus says, 'but it's a good reminder that people heal and move on with their lives. And they might even start a new chapter that they wouldn't have if it wasn't for what he did.'

'Yes. Maybe.'

'I must admit . . .' he says, reaching out to stroke my cheek, 'I'm hoping that you and I are starting a chapter right now. And while I'd never wish what happened onto you or Clem, I have to say, I'm very glad to be sitting here with you right now.'

'Well,' I say, 'I'm *not* glad we're sitting here.'

He raises an eyebrow. 'Oh?'

'I'd be much happier if we were lying' – I point over Angus's shoulder toward the bedroom – 'right over there.'

Angus's eyes follow my finger; then they start to twinkle. He stands, lifting me with him. 'Your wish is my command.'

37

Anna

Nine months ago . . .

'Put this on,' Dad says, handing me a pair of blue doo-dahs for my legs. His cheeks are flushed, and that's when I realize I'm naked, apart from a white sheet. He digs back into my closet and pulls out a pair of underthings. 'And this. I'll be in the dining room.'

I don't move. I'm perfectly happy right where I am.

'What are you going there for?' I ask.

'Lunch.' He doesn't say *remember?* but the way he looks at me, I guess he must have said this before. 'The cook has made tostadas or enchiladas or something.'

'She only ever makes tostadas or enchiladas or something. What I'd really like is a big, juicy cheeseburger with a side of fries.'

Dad smiles. 'I'll save you a seat.'

He leaves, and I look at the things in my lap. With a strange, almost scientific awareness, I realize I have no idea what to do with them. The blue things go on my legs – I know that much. But there are three holes, two small and one large, as well as a long thing with silver teeth and a big silver circle. Pockets and seams are everywhere. What am I supposed to do with it all?

I lean back, resting my head against the back of the sitting thing. I could easily sleep, right here, for hours. Is it really only the middle of the day? The light outside, hazy and foggy, indicates that it is. And so does the gnaw in my belly. It's a little paunchy now, my belly. So much has changed about me lately, it's no wonder I don't recognize myself.

Finally I stand, and when I do, my left side starts to tingle. My mind runs over the possibilities. Pins and needles? Heart . . . explosion? Dead leg? I shrug off the thought. No use panicking myself. I have a brain-disease. What are the chances of that white, jagged stuff striking twice?

I sit back down, tired, but a horrible feeling nags at me – a feeling that I should be somewhere else. Then again, I live in a home for old people. Where could I possibly need to be?

I close my eyes and go to sleep.

'Anna.'

When I open my eyes, Dad is standing over me. On autopilot, I rub my eyes and stretch. Funny what my brain will do for me. It will stretch without any request, but when I desperately want it to conjure up information, nothing. 'What?'

'Lunch.' His voice sounds irritated, which is strange. He must be really hungry.

'Oh. Good. I'm starving.' As I stand, a pile of clothes

slides off my legs, and I realize I'm wearing only a white sheet-thing. A *towel*, that's what it is. 'I'd better get dressed. You go ahead, I'll meet you there.'

A flash of pink comes to his cheeks, then just as quickly, it blanches away. He looks unexpectedly, impossibly sad. 'It's okay,' he says. 'I'll wait.'

On the table next to my sleeping-bench, I have quite the collection of things. Flower-leaves. Rocks. Movies I'll never watch. A book that Dad left here last time he visited – I might tuck it away before he comes back, a keepsake. Maybe I'll write it in my notebook to tell Jack. *Stole Dad's book.* What's he going to do? I have the brain-disease.

A drip of something rolls down my forehead. It's stifling in here. Boiling hot. I hoist myself off the sleeping-bench. There must be a cool-machine around here somewhere! Or a whirly-spinner that blows air around. Or a wet cloth or something I can put on my head. I walk over to the hole in the wall and put my face to it, but there's no wind. No relief.

'Anna?' says a man's voice. 'What are you doing?'

I spin around. 'Jack!' It feels like forever since I've seen him. 'Thank the Lord. Where is the cool-machine? Is it summer?'

Jack watches me for a disturbingly long time. 'Yes,' he says. 'It's summer.'

He cuts across the room to the hole in the wall and slides it open. I laugh. *Silly me. It was closed!* Then he unbuttons my woolly overshirt and takes it off. Pulls something else over my head. 'There you go. That should cool you down.'

Jack is wearing a shirt, short leg-pants, and shoes that hardly cover his feet. With my things off, already I start to feel cooler. 'Ah,' I say, 'that's better.'

A little boy steps out from behind Jack and grins, all coy and cheeky.

'Hello, young man!' It's hard not to smile at his little elfin face. He reminds me of someone – a cartoon character – Richie Rich or Dennis the Menace or something. Just the sight of him makes me feel happy. 'What's your name?'

The little boy looks at Jack, and Jack nods. 'It's . . . Ethan,' he says.

'That's a cool name,' I say. 'Nice to meet you, Ethan.'

The little boy's smile disappears. Jack is still smiling, but he's always had a terrible poker face. When we were little, if one of us had to lie to Mom and Dad, I always told him to wait in the bedroom. For that reason, Mom always demanded Jack be the one to tell the version of how the vase got broken, or whatever scuffle we found ourselves in. Now, although his tone is patient and friendly, his face is stiff.

I don't feel so happy anymore.

'I think you should go now,' I say, turning my back on them. I focus on the hole in the wall, the open hole. The air that drifts in and out is warm and dry. Because it's *summer*.

'But we just got here—'

'I'm tired,' I say. 'I want to sleep.'

I wait a moment. But when I look over my shoulder, they're still there, limp, like those dolls on sticks who need someone to pull their strings. What are they called? I scrunch up my face, trying to bring up the word. It's on the edge of my tongue.

I spin around. 'What the fuck are those little dolls called?'

The words sound ugly, and the little boy flinches. There are tears on my face, and I feel like I might be sick. I expect the little boy to flee from the room but instead he forges toward me, closer and closer, until I'm the one who flinches. When he's an inch away, he tugs me down and wraps his little arms around my neck. 'It was nice to meet you, Anna,' he says. He's a hard, wiry little boy, and he smells like sunshine and dirt. 'I love you.'

'I love you, too, Ethan,' I say without thinking. And in a second or two, I'm happy again.

38

Eve

My feet barely touch the floor as I serve breakfast, and it's not helped by the fact that I have a clear view from the dining room to the garden bed where Angus is working with a shovel. I'm grateful, at least, that it's cold out and he's wearing several layers of fleece. If this were a shirt-off kind of day, I'd have barely been able to restrain myself. Clem sits up at the table with the residents, buoyed by her night with her grandparents. With any luck, her mood will extend into the school gates and through the day.

I collect an empty toast rack from the center of the table and am about to head back to the kitchen when I catch the tail end of a conversation among the residents.

'—apparently, he just wandered into Bert's room,' May is saying to Gwen and Clara. 'Who *knows* why his door was unlocked . . .'

My ears prick up. 'What did you say, May?' I ask. 'Who wandered into Bert's room?'

Bert whacks down his spoon. 'Well, it wasn't Elvis Presley. Now, can everyone just stop talking about it?'

'It was Luke,' May whispers. 'Apparently, his door was left unlocked and he got disoriented and walked into Bert's room in the middle of the night. Bert woke the whole place up with his shouting but by the time Rosie got there, Luke was gone. We all went looking for him and Laurie found him in Anna's bed.'

It takes everything I've got not to drop the jug of milk in my hand.

'Does Eric know?' I ask.

Clara nods. 'Bert told him the moment he walked in. Rosie's in his office right now.'

'Eric's here? I didn't see his car?'

'He has a new one,' Clara says. 'That shiny silver one, out front?'

I blink. 'That's *his*?'

Clara shrugs. 'The retirement world clearly pays well.'

I run down the hall and don't bother to knock on Eric's door, just fling it open. 'It wasn't Rosie!' I say. 'It was me!'

It's not until I'm standing there that I realize I have no idea what Rosie has told Eric, what lie she might have spun or angle she might have played – an angle that I might have just ruined. I lift my chin, trying to look confident, but Eric's eyes focus on my shaking hands. 'Come in, Eve,' he says. His face is red and cross. 'Shut the door.'

Both Eric and Rosie remain silent as I sit in the empty chair.

'So *you* unlocked the door?' he says.

I steal a glance at Rosie. 'Yes.'

'Why?'

'The thing is,' I start, 'Anna and Luke love each other. I found a letter, you see, in Anna's notebook – it says Anna promised to be with Luke until the end. And then, a couple of weeks ago, I found Anna by the window and—'

Eric strums his fingers on the desk. 'Can you excuse us, Rosie?'

Rosie leaves. I want to slump, but I sit tall, as if pulled skyward by an invisible string.

'Eve—'

'I've googled it!' I get to my feet. 'Research shows that people with dementia do much, much better when surrounded by those they love. A lot of people with dementia are old and don't have any loved ones left, but Anna and Luke *do*. They have each other. So, to separate them is just . . . tragic. Can you imagine if the love of your life were in the very next room, but no matter how you tried, you couldn't get to her? Wouldn't you be suicidal?'

'So you just decided to take it upon yourself to unlock Luke's door last night and see what happened?'

I pause. *Last night.* He only knows about last night.

'Well, yes.'

Eric stands and walks around the desk, stopping right in front of me. 'Do you understand how serious this is? If Luke had become agitated or confused, our residents could have been in danger. If someone were hurt, Rosalind House would have been liable. I have enough people breathing down my neck without having to worry about

290

this.' Eric sighs, stares off. 'Let's say your theory is correct – Anna was blissfully happy with Luke. Why would she try to kill herself?'

My mouth is open, ready to counter any argument he might have . . . but this is the *one* piece of the puzzle I still haven't figured out. If they didn't start locking Anna's door until after she tried to kill herself . . . why did she do it?

'Exactly,' Eric says when I come up with nothing. He wanders back to his side of the desk. 'I'll have to let the families know what's happened,' he says. 'If Anna's family is concerned that she's been taken advantage of, they might ask for a medical examination for Anna to establish if she was overpowered or forced. Next time you think about helping her, think about sparing her the trauma of that sort of examination, if you know what I mean.'

I feel the sting of his words, but I take the 'next time' as a good sign.

'It goes without saying that this is a one-time warning. And I'd be very sorry to lose you.'

'I'd be very sorry to go,' I say.

As I turn to leave, I notice Angus through the window, digging in the garden. And I realize I'm telling the truth.

39

Clementine

On the way to school, Mom worries. Her face is a frown and she says if anything at all happens, I should tell Miss Weber to call her and she will come and get me right away. I worry, too. I don't want to see Miranda or hear her giggle or hear her say things about my dad. What I *really* want is for her family to move away so she doesn't have to be at my school anymore.

Mom talks to Miss Weber for a few minutes at drop-off, and then she kisses my head even though she'd already done that twice already. She asks if I'm ready, and I fight my tears and say I am. Then I spot Ms Donnelly coming toward us, and Mom leaves in a hurry.

Now, we're in the gymnasium because it's too cold to be outside. The gymnasium smells like feet. I'm on the floor, playing patty-cake with Legs, when I hear Miranda.

'Well, *look* who is back!' Miranda walks in between Legs and me. We let go hands – but it's too late, Miranda's falling. She lands with a smack.

'Are you all right?' I ask.

Miranda doesn't look at me, just gets up quickly and grabs Legs's hand. 'Come on, Legs! Don't play with Clem. She *attacks* people.'

I frown. 'No, I don't!'

'Liar,' Miranda says. 'You flicked a twig in my eye *and* you scratched me at the dance.' She says this quickly, like she's been practicing it. 'And now you just tripped me.'

'I don't attack people,' I say quietly. 'I only attack *you*.'

Legs covers her mouth because she is giggling.

Miranda's face moves like she's chewing it from the inside. 'Anyway,' she says, 'my mom has spoken to Ms Donnelly, and if you do attack me again, you'll be kicked out of the school.'

Legs's eyes widen. I wonder if it's true or if Miranda is making it up.

'Anyway her daddy was a jerk,' Miranda says to Legs. 'So *she* must be a jerk, too.'

I get to my feet. I want to slap Miranda's face and tell her *she* is a jerk. But I don't want to get kicked out of school so I push my hands into my pockets.

'Do you know how her daddy died?' Miranda's voice is really loud. Her face is pinched, like she's trying not to smile. I want her to shut it. I want to make her shut it.

Miranda puts her arm through Legs's. 'He *killed* himself,' she says in a loud whisper, and she juts out her chin and smiles.

'Shut up!' I yell, and my hands rise up out of my pockets, forming fists. They shoot toward Miranda. I don't care that she is telling the truth. I don't want Miranda and her jutting chin to say it.

Miranda's eyes go wide and scared. But I don't hit her.

'You didn't know my daddy,' I say, and I run out of the gymnasium, out the side door, and I don't stop running until I get to Rosalind House.

When I arrive at Rosalind House, I go right out to the garden. Angus is out there, digging in a garden bed, so I stay hidden behind the tree. The wind blows right through my coat and chills my bones. I shiver.

'Dad?' I close my eyes. 'I want to talk to you.'

I let my mind go all empty. Then Daddy starts to form in front of my closed eyes. His face, his black hair.

'Daddy!'

I can see him only when my eyes are closed. His legs are crossed at the knee, and I remember how I used to sit on his foot and bounce like I was riding a horse.

I start to smile, and then I remember. 'I am very angry with you, Daddy. You stole people's money, and now everyone hates you.'

I think of Dr Felder when she asked if there was anything else I wanted to say to Daddy. I decide there is.

'Because of you, Mom doesn't have anyone to talk to in the playground when she picks me up. And Miranda keeps saying nasty things to me. And we live in a horrible apartment that smells like salami! And . . . you *killed yourself*. That makes me angriest of all. Sometimes,' I say, 'I think I hate you.'

There are tears on my face and I want a hug, but I can't hug Daddy, and anyway he is a bad man. So I just cry more.

I keep talking, telling Daddy everything I want to say. When I am finished, I feel a little better.

When I open my eyes, I see Angus, across the lawn. He's standing up, talking to Mom, standing really close. Then Mom leans against him and Angus puts his arms around her. I watch them. She tips her head up so she is looking at his face and he pushes a piece of her hair behind her ear. She smiles. Then he puts his hands on her face and kisses her.

40

Eve

I tell Angus everything. How I started opening Anna's doors, how Rosie had joined me. I tell him about my friendship with Anna, and about Eric finding out. Angus's eyebrows rise a couple of times, but his eyes are soft. He puts his arms around me, tucks a piece of loose hair behind my ear. Then he gives me the softest, most wonderful kiss.

'So that's it,' I say.

I wonder what Richard would say if he saw me now. His Eve, whose biggest stressor was what to cook for dinner, has real problems.

'So what are you going to do about Anna?' Angus asks.

'I honestly don't know. I can't lose my job – it's the one thing keeping Clem at her school—'

Angus stares at me.

'Oh. I didn't tell you that part, did I?'

He feigns exasperation, shakes his head. Then he smiles. In the cold garden, it feels so good to be in his arms. I think of last night – of the things we did to each other, and I start to fantasize about pulling him into the shed and maybe . . .

'Mom?'

I whirl around. Clem is standing there, her cheeks swimming with tears.

'Clem.' I race to her. 'What are you doing here? Why aren't you at school?'

She takes a step back, looks at Angus.

'You saw,' I say.

She nods.

'Clem,' I say. 'I . . . I can explain.'

A tear wells and falls onto her cheek, and then another one. 'It's okay.'

'Honey, I'm so sorry.'

I half expect her to walk away or yell or stare at me in disgust. But her utter lack of expression is more unsettling than any of it.

'Can we just go inside, Mom?' She shivers inside her coat. 'I'm cold.'

'Yes, of course. Let's go inside. We can talk there.'

'Mom?'

'Yes?'

'I don't want to talk about' – Her gaze flickers to Angus – 'that. Is that okay?'

'Of course,' I say, surprised. 'That's okay.'

I put my arm around Clem and glance at Angus. He nods soberly. It might be the last time we share a look, I realize. It might be the last time we share anything.

*

297

Clem sits in the kitchen on a stool while I call her school. They are very apologetic, clearly concerned I'll be litigious, but they don't need to worry. Especially since if anyone has anything to feel guilty about, it's me.

'So,' I say to her after I hang up. 'What happened at school?'

Clem looks at her lap. 'Miranda was saying stuff.'

'What stuff?'

'She said that I attack people, and if I attack her again, her mom will get me kicked out of the school.'

I think of Ms Donnelly's messages that I still haven't returned. And it occurs to me that I might very well get Clem kicked out of school myself.

'Well, you aren't going to attack her again, are you?' I say.

'No.'

'Well, then, you don't have to worry. And I'll speak to Miss Weber, okay?'

Clem doesn't say anything.

'Okay, hon?'

'Okay.'

I start to get suspicious. Had she already done something? But before I can ask her, Eric walks past the kitchen, jolting me out of our little world. I glance at the clock. 'Shoot! Clem, I have to do some cleaning. Would you like to help?'

She shakes her head.

'Do you want to go to the parlor and watch TV?'

'Can I just stay here, Mom?'

She looks so tiny up on her stool, legs dangling, and I

have a sudden pang of yearning for Richard. Before he died, if Clem was having a problem, I'd call him.

'*Put her on the phone,*' he'd have said, and then would have had her giggling within seconds. For all his foibles, he was a good father.

But Richard isn't here so instead, I grab the cookie jar from a shelf. 'Course you can. Here. Eat as many as you like.'

She looks at the jar and finally smiles.

'I won't be long,' I say.

I get my cart and drive it past the parlor. Bert is reading the newspaper aloud. Anna and Luke gaze out of different windows. Laurie and Clara sit side by side, in separate chairs. It's funny, usually Clara and Laurie sit in the love seat with an arm linked, or hands intertwined – some sort of physical contact. The fact that they aren't touching now makes me look twice. On the second look, I realize what's amiss.

It's not Clara.

Suddenly I remember how my conversation with Clara ended last time. '*Sometimes sisters can be treacherous.*'

I head straight to Clara and Laurie's room, give her door a gentle knock. 'It's only me,' I call. 'Can I make up your room?'

'Thanks, honey,' she says. 'Come on in.' Clara's voice sounds weak and quiet. I find her reclined in bed, in the dark.

'Would you like me to open the curtains?' I ask, and she nods. I set down my bucket and pull back the curtains, securing them with ties. 'Is that your sister in the parlor?' I ask.

'Yes. That's Enid.'

'I thought she visited only once a year.' I realize, a moment too late, that I'd learned this particular piece of information while eavesdropping on Clara and Laurie a few months ago in the parlor. But Clara doesn't seem to notice.

'She does. But I asked her to come again.' Clara sighs. 'You may as well know. I'm dying.'

I pause, half-bent to dip my cloth into the bucket.

'I've been giving myself breast examinations every month for forty years. Mama had the cancer, too, you see. She wasn't interested in going to see a doctor.' Clara chuckles blackly. 'Mama died, of course. And I always said if I found a lump, I'd cut it out faster than you could say "cancer". But when I went to the doctor, he said it was too late. Ironic, huh?'

'I . . . I'm so sorry.'

Clara *pffts*. 'Sorry isn't worth the paper it's written on. What matters is action. Righting the wrongs. You know what I mean?'

I frown. 'I'm not sure I do.'

'A long time ago, Eve, I did something terrible to my sister. Betrayed her in the worst way. Now I have to make amends.'

'Make amends . . . how?'

'I'm going to give her Laurie back.'

I stare at her. 'What?'

Clara looks out the window. 'Laurie grew up in the

300

house right opposite ours. By the time he was sixteen, any fool could see he was sweet on Enid. I used to watch them through the window, Laurie chopping wood for Mama while Enid sat on a tree stump beside him. But Enid was a lady. She didn't giggle or flatter Laurie. To anyone else, it would have looked like she wasn't interested in him. Not to me. Sisters know these things.' Clara shakes her head. 'Then, one day, Enid was given the opportunity to go away with our church, to be a missionary. She was a giver, Enid – that kind of thing was right up her alley. It all happened quite fast, someone had dropped out or something, and she didn't get a chance to say good-bye to anyone. And when Laurie came around the next day to chop wood, well . . . I told him she'd gone away.'

I blink. 'But that's hardly a betrayal—'

'In our day, if a young woman went away suddenly, it meant she was in the family way.' Clara smiles ruefully. 'Let's just say I did nothing to dissuade Laurie from that belief.'

'Oh.'

'While she was gone, I sat with Laurie while he chopped firewood. And, unlike Enid, I smiled. I giggled. I couldn't help it. I told myself I was better for him than her. By the time Enid came back, Laurie and I were engaged. As soon as he saw her, I knew the feelings were still there. I still see it, whenever she's around.'

Sisters can be treacherous. It all makes sense now.

'So . . . what are you going to do?' I ask.

Clara looks away from the window and straight in my eye. 'I'm going to make things right. While I still can.'

'But . . . how can you possibly do that?'

Clara clasps her hands together in her lap and gives a light shrug, like it's the most obvious thing in the world. 'I'm fairly sure dying should do the trick.'

I leave Clara's room without so much as vacuuming and pause at the entrance to the parlor. Clem is in there now, talking to Bert. The two of them seem to have developed quite the friendship. May has fallen asleep in her chair and Gwen is knitting. But my eyes lock on Laurie. Clara's sister has disappeared and he's sitting alone. I lower myself into the chair beside him. 'I just saw Clara.'

He looks up, scans my face. 'She told you?'

'Yes.'

'I still can't believe it,' he says, looking back at his lap. 'My Clara. I always thought she'd outlive me by twenty years.'

'I'm sorry, Laurie.'

He dismisses my apology with a wave of his hand. 'We've been lucky, Eve. We've had a long marriage. Four sons. A long life.'

'A happy life?'

He glances up, surprised. 'A *very* happy life.'

'Tell me,' I say, sliding forward in my chair until my knees nearly touch his. 'Tell me why you chose Clara. What was it about her that made you decide she was the one?'

A smile inches onto his face. 'Clara made me feel like the only man in the world. She still makes me feel like that. No one else has ever come close to making me feel as good as Clara. No one is stupid or blind enough, probably.'

'No one?'

Laurie is still for a moment. He sweeps a gray strand off his temple. 'Well, there was one other person, if I'm being honest. A long time ago. She was very different from Clara.'

I think I might be treading on thin ice, but I have to ask. 'Any regrets?'

He frowns at me, less annoyed, more curious. And I find myself holding my breath. 'When you get to my age,' he says, his face softening, 'you don't waste time with regrets. In the end, you just remember the moments of joy. When all is said and done, those are the things we keep.'

And just like that, I let go the breath I'd been holding.

That afternoon, as I'm making up Bert's room, a memory comes at me. Clem was a tiny baby, and I'd been up half the night with her. I'd woken first thing in the morning with a start – full of the terror reserved for new mothers. The bed beside me was rumpled and empty, and so was Clem's crib.

I followed the tune of 'I'm a Little Teapot' to the downstairs bath, where Richard was stretched out in the water, cradling Clem's tiny, nearly sleeping, body. He glanced up, smiled, and kept on singing. I still remember his face, saccharine but warning, making clear that stopping the song would be a disastrous option.

So I sat on the edge of the bath and sang, too.

Every time the song came to an end, we'd pause, holding our breath, and every time her little eyelids fluttered, we broke back into song. In the end, I took off my pajamas and got into the bath, too. After about an hour of it, Clem fell asleep.

Another memory comes at me after this one. Then another. The way Richard used to bring home recipe books when I was ill. The time we were on holiday in Vietnam and he tried to get me tampons from three different pharmacies that didn't understand a word he was saying. The night he waited up to show me the lipstick that Clem had put on him – because he'd promised her he would.

After all was said and done with Richard, I couldn't regret my life with him. There were moments of joy. There was *Clem*.

I finish arranging the pillows on Bert's bed and then fall into the armchair by Bert's window. And for the first time since Richard died, I cry for him.

41

Anna

Eight months ago . . .

One day Jack arrives to take me somewhere. I don't care to venture what day it is, since even if I did have the capacity to figure it out, who really cared? We go to a room with chairs around the edges, and I pick up one of the thin books to avoid speaking to Jack. I don't like talking to Jack. I'd never tell him that, because I know he's trying. He keeps the conversations simple and slow, the topics basic. But it's impossible not to feel his scrutinizing, like I'm taking an exam. I concentrate so hard on not saying something stupid that I become stuck in my head and completely forget what he asked in the first place. And I fail.

With the thin book in my lap, my first thought is . . . all the *writing*. Even on the cover, bright pink and orange headlines slash the page. There are several pictures, too, of famous people I don't recognize. How do people make sense of this? Did I used to read these? I put it back on the glass tabletop and instead stare at the television, muted, in the corner. That's when I feel a kick in my belly. Latina Cook-Lady must have served one of her spicy dishes today, judging by the way my belly is moving.

'Anna Forster.' A woman stands in the doorway, her thick black hair streaming over one shoulder. I recognize her. It's my family doctor – Dr Li.

I feel a genuine smile as I stand. I am going to greet this doctor by name. A small, verging-on-pathetic win, but a win for a person with Alzheimer's. A win for me.

'Yes,' Jack says, standing also. 'Nice to see you, Dr Li.'

It really, *really* pisses me off that he beats me to it. I punch Jack hard, in the shoulder. I feel his head swing toward me, slack-jawed, but I don't even look. I just walk past him and Dr Li and into the exam room.

'So, Anna . . .' Inside the other room, Dr Li, at least, addresses me. 'How have things been?'

I stare at her for a long time. The last thing I want is for Jack to answer for me, but I can't for the life of me figure out how to answer her question. *How have things been?*

'She does better with more specific questions,' Jack says finally. 'Yes or no. One- or two-word responses.'

This is true insofar as Jack is concerned. Jack never gives me a chance to say anything more than two words. But with Young Guy, I say a lot – at least, I did. Perhaps Jack is right? Perhaps I am a little out of practice? Either way, I can't be bothered explaining. Instead I scowl at Jack and he winces, preparing to receive a punch. I laugh out loud, which probably makes me look a bit crazy.

'I see,' Dr Li says, and scribbles something on a white

306

square. Then she looks back at me. 'Are you feeling well today, Anna?'

'I'm very well.' I raise my eyebrows at Jack. That was definitely more than two words.

'Have you been taking all your medication?'

'Yes.'

'There's a nurse at her facility that administers her medication,' Jack says, 'so she's definitely taking it.'

Dr Li looks at the white square. 'So . . . Aricept, vitamin E?'

I nod. If that's what's written on her square, that's probably right.

'And Celexa,' Jack adds. 'I think that's it.'

'Any side effects? Dizziness, headache, agitation, sleeplessness?'

'Normal night-restlessness,' Jack jumps in. 'Sleeps during the day, awake a lot at night.'

'Is that right, Anna?'

Dr Li looks at me expectantly, so I nod. She consults the white square again.

'Aricept can cause sleep difficulties in some people,' she says. 'I can add a sleeping tablet to your medication to help with that. Would you like that, Anna?'

'Sure.'

'Good,' she says, scribbling on a different square. Then she lifts her head. 'So, how's your mood?'

'It's been better.'

'Any depression, anxiety, feelings of helplessness?'

'She does seem to be down lately,' Jack says. 'Especially compared to a few months ago. To be honest, I'm

307

concerned about the speed of her decline. Do you mind if I speak here, Anna? I want to make sure the doctor understands what is going on.'

I don't know why he's asking now since he's done all the speaking since we arrived. But I nod.

'Anna's made a . . . friend in there,' he says to Dr Li. 'A guy, also with dementia. And it turns out they've been sexually involved.'

Dr Li's eyebrows jump. 'I see.'

'I don't know what to do. I want Anna to be happy, but how can I trust this guy? He has *dementia*. I want to believe that Anna could stop him from doing anything she doesn't want to do, but . . .' Suddenly I realize Jack is crying. 'It's all happening so fast. She's not the Anna she used to be.'

'I understand,' Dr Li says. 'It must be very difficult for you.'

'A year ago, to the unknowing eye, Anna seemed normal. A normal forgetful person, but you could have a conversation with her. She could have dinner with the family or talk on the phone. But when she came to our house in September, she was only there for four hours before she went berserk and we had to bring her back. I visited her last week, and she was in her room in a sweater, jacket, and boots with the window closed while it was ninety degrees out. It takes her a good five or six seconds to answer a question, and sometimes she doesn't bother at all.' Jack hangs his head, and his shoulders begin to shake. 'Anna was always the one who protected me when we were kids. Now I want to make sure I protect her.'

Dr Li glances at me, presumably to see how much I am taking in. The answer is all of it. Every word.

'I'm sorry,' I say. I concentrate on my words to make sure this comes out right. 'It sounds horrible, what you said. I know I'm . . . not getting things right anymore, I'm getting confused and doing strange things. But I'm . . .' I pause to wipe my face. 'I'm still here. It's just – you have to look a little longer and harder to find me.'

Out of the corner of my eye, I notice the doctor push her chair back, trying to pretend she's not there. Jack slides forward in his chair and looks at me. And for the first time since I checked into that place with the old people, maybe for the first time since I was diagnosed with Alzheimer's, Jack sees me.

42

Eve

'Clem's not talking.'

It's late afternoon, and I'm pressed into a corner of the cleaning cupboard, on my cell phone. I've already told Dr Felder about Clem running away from school and seeing Angus kiss me in the garden. So far, Dr Felder has just listened. It's nice, the way she listens. It makes me realize how much I've missed having someone to talk to about Clem.

'I've tried bringing it up, but she says she doesn't want to talk about it.'

'Then you should listen to her,' Dr Felder says. 'Believe it or not, people – even kids – are pretty good at knowing what is best for them. If she doesn't feel like talking, it means her subconscious is still processing everything. And that's perfectly fine.'

'I know, but I worry. Clem is a *talker*. Usually my biggest problem is how to get her to *stop* talking.'

'Clementine will talk again. And when she does, she'll know that she can go to you. In the meantime, you should think about what you're going to say to her when she *does* go to you. She'll definitely have questions, particularly about her father's death, and his business activities that she perceives to be "bad". She'll want to know how you are processing all of it. Have you considered having any therapy yourself, Eve?'

'Me? Oh no. I'm just worried about Clem.'

'I know. But sometimes the best way to look after other people is to look after yourself. Think about it, Eve.'

'I will.'

After I hang up the phone, I check on Clem in the parlor. She's where I left her, beside Bert, talking. Clearly her desire not to talk doesn't extend to him. The parlor has filled up in the last few minutes. Twelve out of the thirteen residents are in there, just staring at Clem as though she were the *Mona Lisa* herself. It's like her presence has set off a radar – *child nearby!* – prompting them to wake up from their naps or send home their visitors and shuffle into the communal space. In fact, the only resident not in the parlor is Anna.

I'm in the hallway dusting the side tables when two men come out of her room. I recognize the young one as her brother, from a photograph in her room. And the older one bears such an uncanny resemblance to Anna that it has to be her father.

'Hello,' I say, smiling. 'You must be Anna's family. I'm Eve. The cook.'

'Jack,' says the brother. He shakes my hand, but he seems distracted.

'Peter,' says the father.

'How was Anna today?' I ask.

'Not bad,' Peter says. 'Today was a pretty good day. She actually made a few jokes.'

'She does have a sense of humor, doesn't she?' I say. 'She had Luke and me in stitches the other day.'

I watch Jack and Peter closely, so I notice when a shadow crosses Jack's face.

'They seem to have a special relationship, those two,' I continue. 'Anna and Luke.'

'Well, it was good to meet you, Eve,' Jack says, and starts for the door.

I almost cry with frustration. Does he not care about the connection Anna and Luke have? Or does he simply not believe it? Suddenly, I have an idea.

'Oh, before you go,' I call after them. 'There's something I think you should see.'

By the time the men have turned around, I'm already reaching for my purse. I'd tucked Anna's notebook in there earlier, to use as evidence with Eric if I needed it. I push it into Jack's hands.

'What's this?' he asks.

'A letter. Anna wrote it to herself last year.'

Anna's father takes the notebook and reaches for his glasses in his breast pocket. As he does, Jack scans the page with quick, darting eyes.

'It's quite romantic,' I say nervously, 'the two of them finding love in here.'

I'm certain this letter will invoke a positive reaction in Jack. Maybe even cause him to change his mind about locking the doors. But instead, his face clouds over.

312

He takes the notebook from his father and closes it in one hand. 'Do you mind if I take this,' he asks me, 'or will Anna miss it?'

'I . . . I'm not sure,' I say. 'I should probably put it back, just in —'

'I think it's better if I take it.' His voice is firm. 'Thanks, Eve.'

I'm stunned. He gives me a long, steady look. 'I suspect, having read this, you've got ideas of what you would do for Anna if you were in my shoes,' Jack says. 'But if you were in my shoes, you'd realize that fantasy scenarios don't exist for Alzheimer's disease. Your loved one is counting on you to keep them safe when they've lost the ability to do it themselves. And if you had all the information, you'd know that if I were to do what it looks like Anna wants, I wouldn't be keeping her safe.' Jack remains calm and articulate as he delivers his speech, but I notice the color rising in his cheeks. 'Anyway, it was nice to meet you. Dad? Let's go.'

As they turn to the door, I remain where I am, shaking slightly. What information didn't I have? And how could it possibly change everything to the point that they were willing to keep Anna unhappy rather than with the man she loved? I want desperately to ask Jack, to beg for the missing piece of the puzzle. But instead, I watch Anna's memories disappear – this time out the front door.

After Anna's dad and brother leave, I go to Anna's room, tap on the door.

'Hi,' I say.

'Hi,' she says.

She's sitting by the window in her wheelchair, next to an empty chair. I have the strongest urge to sit in it. I want to tell her everything. About Jack and her notebook. About Clem. About Angus. About Eric. Somehow, over the past few months, Anna has become the person I talk to about things. She's become my friend. But friendship works both ways. And today, I want to do something for her.

'Do you want to go and see Luke?' I ask.

It's only 5 P.M. but Eric left early. I answer the usual questions about who Luke is, and then I wheel her over into his room.

Luke is sitting on the edge of his bed, admiring a bunch of flowers on his bedside table. Angus had helped him arrange them earlier. He looks up and smiles shyly. And that's all the introduction they need.

When I return to the kitchen, my phone is ringing, and I snatch it up right before it goes to voice mail. 'Hello?'

'Mrs Bennett?'

'Yes?'

'It's Kathy Donnelly calling. From Clementine's school?'

I close my eyes. 'Ms Donnelly! I'm sorry I haven't returned your calls. It's just . . . been a little hectic around here.'

'I understand,' she says. 'Is now a good time to talk?'

'Actually, I—'

'I won't take up much of your time. I heard Clementine left the school premises unaccompanied today, and I was very concerned. I want you to know that we are taking steps to ensure this never happens again.'

Relief floods me. She's calling about Clem running away from school. Probably wanting to smooth things over. 'I appreciate that.'

'How is Clem doing?' she asks.

I glance around to make sure she's not nearby. 'Actually . . . she's been better. She's not herself. Quiet. Teary. But I'll get her through it.'

'I'm sure you will. It's not easy, being a single mother.'

The way she says it makes me suspect that she *does* know. And for the first time it occurs to me that Ms Donnelly, with her thick glasses and sensible haircut, might have a story of her own.

'Thank you,' I say. 'It's very kind of you to check in.'

'Actually, there's another reason I'm calling. It's about your address. It's listed here as 82 Forest Hills Drive.'

My stomach plunges. 'That's right.'

There's a pause. 'Hmm. It caught my eye because, before she passed away, my mother was a resident at a care facility called Rosalind House, which is at 82 Forest Hills Drive.'

I scramble for an excuse, something plausible that could explain this turn of events, but my mind is blank and she is waiting. Finally I open my mouth, and a huge sob comes out.

This is it. Clem is going to be kicked out of her school. She'll have to move mid school-year to a school in a rougher area with kids she doesn't know. Worst of all, she won't have Legs by her side anymore.

The silence, punctuated only by my sobs, continues for a perilously long time. I start to wonder if Ms Donnelly is even still there when she clears her throat. 'You know,' she says thoughtfully, 'I keep telling my optometrist that I need new lenses.'

I take a breath. 'Pardon?'

'My eyesight,' Ms Donnelly explains. 'It's *terrible*. I'm always reading things wrong. Perhaps you're not at 82 Forest Hills Drive. Perhaps you're at 83? Or 87?'

I swallow. 'Uh . . .'

'Yes,' she says. 'Yes, I'm sure that's what is says. Eighty-seven. I do apologize.'

'Ms Donnelly—'

'Please,' she says. 'Call me Kathy.'

'Kathy,' I say. If we weren't on the phone, I'd have grabbed Ms Donnelly and hugged her. 'I don't know what to—'

'It's not easy, being a single mother,' she says, and I hear the kindness in her voice. 'Tell Clementine we're looking forward to seeing her on Monday,' and she hangs up the phone.

That afternoon, when Rosie arrives, she looks terrible. Blue circles ring her eyes, and her lips are peeling. Clearly I'm not the only one this has been taking its toll on. She gestures for me to follow her into the nurses' room, and I do, passing Clem cartwheeling along the hallway on our way.

'I'm so sorry,' I say to Rosie as soon as the door shuts. 'I feel terrible.'

'Why? You took all the blame.' She lifts her bag off her shoulder and falls into a chair. 'I'm surprised to see you, actually. I thought Eric would have—'

'He gave me one last chance. He thought last night was the first time it happened.'

'Wow. That's good, I guess.'

'Did you know about Clara?' I ask.

Rosie's expression is guarded.

'It's okay, she told me she's dying,' I say.

Rosie's head falls back in her chair, and her eyes close. 'Yes, I knew. She has breast cancer. Very advanced.'

'How long has she got?'

'I'd like to say months,' Rosie says, her eyes still closed, 'but I suspect it's more like weeks.'

Even though Clara told me herself, it's still shocking to hear. Weeks. Could it really only be weeks?

'She wants to reconcile Laurie with her sister,' I say. 'Apparently, they dated before he met Clara and she's been carrying the guilt around all these years for stealing Laurie away.'

Rosie opens her eyes. 'I'm sorry to say it, but I doubt she'll get the chance.'

It isn't good news, not at all, but for some reason this pleases me. The idea of Clara handing her dying husband over to her sister in her final days is something I can't seem to stomach. 'So what happens now?' I ask.

'What do you mean, "what happens"?'

'With Anna and Luke,' I say. 'What happens now?'

'Well, we don't have a lot of choice, do we? We're going to have to keep their doors locked. We can't very well let them be together after what happened today . . .'

When I don't respond, Rosie looks up.

'Can't we?' I whisper.

317

Her eyes bug. 'You're not serious, Eve? After all this trouble? After Eric said this is your last chance?'

'I know it's not ideal but—'

'Eve, I *like* my job, okay? I can't put it at risk anymore, I'm sorry.'

'But . . . I promised her.'

Rosie looks like she wants to see through the skin on my forehead and into my brain, where perhaps she'll get a clue of what is going on in there. Perhaps for this reason, I decide to spit out the thought that's been spinning around in my head all day.

'It's just that . . . if another person kills themselves because I left when they needed me . . . It will kill *me*.'

43

Clementine

Cartwheeling makes your head hurt after a while. It's been almost twenty minutes, and May and Gwen are still watching. I'm starting to think that if I don't stop, we might be here all night. I tell them I have to go, and they give me a little clap and shuffle off. Then I peek around Rosie's door, looking for Mom.

'So what happens now?' Mom is saying.

Rosie says, 'What do you mean, "what happens"?'

'With Anna and Luke. What happens now?'

'Well, we don't have a lot of choice, do we?' Rosie says. 'We're going to have to keep their doors locked. We can't very well let them be together after what happened today . . .'

'Can't we?' Mom says.

There's quiet for a moment, then Rosie says, 'You're not serious, Eve? After all this trouble? After Eric said this is your last chance?'

'I know it's not ideal,' Mom says, 'but—'

'Eve, I *like* my job, okay? I can't put it at risk anymore, I'm sorry.'

'But . . . I promised her.'

It's quiet again. I wonder if they have noticed me standing there. But then Mom continues. 'It's just that . . . if another person kills themselves because I left when they needed me . . . It will kill *me*.'

I snap back from the door. The hairs on my arms and legs stand on end. *It will kill me.* The thought of Mom dying, too, is so scary I can't breathe.

It takes me a few moments to figure out what to do. Then I head for Eric's office . . . Miss Weber always says that if you find yourself in trouble, find someone in charge to help you. But when I get to Eric's office, he's not there. I climb onto Eric's chair. Next to the phone is a list of numbers, and I choose the one that says 'Eric's Cell'. As it rings in my ear, I look through the crack in the door. Rosie is arranging everyone's medicine in baskets on the cart. I want to scream, *What are you doing? Didn't you hear Mom say that something was going to kill her?* Then I hear a deep breath on the other end of the phone. 'Eric speaking.'

'Eric!'

'Yes.' A pause. 'Who is this?'

'It's me,' I say. 'Clementine.'

'Clementine? What are you doing in my office? Where's your mother? Is everything all right?'

'No,' I say in a small voice. 'Nothing is all right.'

'Clementine, honey, is your mother there?' he says.

'No!' I say. 'I mean, yes. But you can't talk to her. Eric,

I need your help.' I take a deep breath. 'Rosie said she has to lock Anna and Luke's doors, but Mom said she doesn't want to. She says, if she does lock them . . . it will kill her! And I don't want her to die. So can't we just unlock the doors? Please?'

I'm breathing hard now, but Eric is quiet. I wonder if he's still there.

Eric is quiet for a few seconds, which makes me nervous.

But finally, he says, 'Why don't you sit tight, Clementine, and I'll be right there? Then we can sort this whole thing out.'

The doorbell rings as soon as I put down the phone. Wow. Eric must have run the whole way. I zoom out of the office past Bert (who makes a noise like *geez* or *sheesh* or something), past Rosie and her medicine cart, and don't stop until I get to the door.

'Eric,' I say, throwing the door open. 'Thank you for—'

I freeze.

'Clementine, is your mother home?' Miranda's mom says, and then just pushes past me into the house. Miranda's mom is really fat, and her cheeks are pink from the cold. As I close the door behind us, I start to worry. What is she doing here? Did Miranda tell her about our fight this morning? She keeps walking farther into the house, staring at everything she passes – the lamp, the vase, the walkers lined up in a row.

Finally Mom appears. 'Andrea.' Mom's face goes pale. For a few seconds, I wait for her to say something, but Mom just stares at her like she's a talking goose.

321

'I got your address from the class list,' Miranda's mom says. 'I'm here to talk to you about your daughter. Today was the third time she hurt my daughter, and I wanted to let you know I'm putting in an official request to have her removed from the school.'

Mom looks at me.

'I didn't hurt Miranda!' I say. 'I promise, Mom.'

'Don't *lie*,' Miranda's mom says. She gets up close to my face, and her mouth is mean. 'I saw Miranda's knee, it has a huge bruise. You tripped her.'

'I didn't,' I say. 'She tripped herself.'

Miranda's mom opens her mouth again, but Mom steps between us. 'You heard Clem,' she says angrily. 'Miranda tripped herself. And I'll ask you not speak to my daughter. Speak to me.'

I want to hug Mom. Mom doesn't usually speak angrily to other grown-ups. I try to catch her eye to smile, but she just stares at Miranda's mom.

'How about I speak to you about this address you pro-vided to the school, then?' Miranda's mom says. She starts to walk again, peering around the corner at a row of walkers. 'Since this is obviously not your house.'

Mom doesn't move, but her face changes. No one says anything for a while.

'It's a residential care facility,' I say, to fill the silence. 'Mom is the cook. We live in an apartment. It's small and brown, and there's a pizza shop right underneath!'

Miranda's mom is still looking at the parlor, but now she spins around. There's a moment of silent grown-up

322

language, where they speak with their eyes instead of their mouths.

'So you don't live here?' she says to Mom. She's smiling a little, but it's not a nice smile. It's a tricky smile. 'Do you even live in the school district?'

I start to wonder if I've said the wrong thing.

'No,' Mom says. 'We *don't*. After Richard died, I couldn't afford a place in the area, and I didn't want to move Clem from a school she loved after she'd already lost so much. But the good news is, thanks to your daughter, Clem doesn't love her school all that much anymore.' I watch Mom, but she doesn't look at me. 'Now that I think of it, I should also thank *you*. Thank you for being such a narrow-minded, mean-spirited bitch. Thank you for having such a mean-spirited bitch for a daughter. It will make the move so much easier.'

I gasp and so does Miranda's mom. 'Bitch' is a bad word. And there's another noise, too – a scream. There's a crash, like glass breaking, and Mom turns and sprints down the hallway. At the same time, the door opens. And Eric walks in.

44

Anna

Seven months ago . . .

I'm lying on my sleeping-bench, daydreaming, when Jack appears in my room. His face is all wrinkled and lined and his hands are out in front like he doesn't know what to do with them.

'Anna, we need to talk.'

'Okay.'

'It's private. Let's go to your room.'

'This *is* my room.'

Jack wipes his face in his hand and presses his eyelids together. 'This is the parlor, Anna.'

'Oh.' I glance around. Yeah. I'm lying on the long chair-thing. 'Okay. Let's go.'

I'm glad Jack is here because I don't think I'd have found my way back. Everything looks the same. White walls, pale green furniture, hallways leading to doors. Doors to where? I wonder. Where oh where do all these doors lead?

Inside my room, we sit.

324

'Dr Li called this morning to tell me the results of your blood test,' Jack says. He's wearing a black thing, sliced in the middle with a white bit and a pink stripe. A *tie!* This is what he wears to work. Jack doesn't usually visit me on a workday. I wonder what he's doing here now?

'So?' I ask.

'You really have no idea what I'm about to tell you?'

'No.'

Jack sinks to his knees in front of me. I take his face in my hands. 'You look like Mom,' I say.

Jack smiles weakly. 'You look like Dad.'

'Remember when you told me that if I cut off all my hair, it would grow back straight?'

A small, surprised laugh explodes from Jack. 'You remember that?'

'What girl doesn't remember being bald?'

Jack looks at me for a long while. 'When it started to grow back, you had an Afro that would have made the Jackson Five proud. That was actually pretty cool.' He keeps looking at me, but his gaze slides toward my stomach, and his eyes grow sad. 'You're pregnant, Anna.' Jack puts his hand on my stomach, smoothing my clothes so they sit flat.

My belly looks round, like an upside-down bowl. Jack looks at it for another moment, then drops his head onto my knees. When he lifts it again, his cheeks are wet.

'You mean . . . there's a baby in there?' I point at the upside-down bowl.

He nods. I curve my hands around my belly, the way Jack did a moment ago. 'A baby?'

325

Jack closes his eyes. 'Oh God.'

I watch him. He looks upset. It makes me upset. 'You're worried because of the Alzheimer's.'

'Yes, Anna.' Jack can't even look at me. His brow is heavy and he keeps wiping it. It takes a moment for me to realize what he's worried about. I'm not going to be around for long. Who will look after my baby when I'm gone?

'You'll look after my baby, won't you?' My voice rises and cracks. 'After I'm gone. Will you bring it to live with you?'

Jack removes his hand and looks at me. For a moment, I think he's going to say something important; then he just sighs. 'Of course I'll look after the baby, Anna.'

'Okay,' I say.

'I need to talk to Eric,' he says after what feels like a long time.

'Okay,' I say again, because I also have someone I need to talk to.

Jack sighs a few more times and looks at me a lot. Then he shakes his head and leaves, using that power walk he has. It's pretty good, that walk. Intimidating. I want to tell him so, but he's gone. And anyway, I have somewhere to be.

And then, I'm out in the hallway again. White walls. White doors. Green sitting things. I pass a Latina carrying a pot of red food. The cook, I guess. She smiles on her way to wherever she's going. I whirl in circles, looking for him, trying to get my bearings. On my second turn around, I don't even know which door I came out of. When a bald man walks past, I sigh in relief.

'You okay, Anna?' he asks.

Anna! I give a little fist-pump. He knows me. 'Yep. Have you seen . . . um . . . ?'

'Luke?' he suggests.

I grin. That must be his name. Luke.

'No,' the man says. I decide to call him Baldy. 'He's not in his room?'

'Not sure,' I say. 'Can you take me there?'

Baldy is infuriatingly slow, but I tap along beside him because it's bound to be faster than finding his room myself. Anyway, I'm too happy to be by myself. *A baby.* I repeat it in my mind a few times. *A baby. Don't forget this, Anna. You have a baby inside your belly.*

But when we get to his room, it's empty. 'Crap.'

'Language,' the man tuts. 'I'm headed to the parlor. Would you like to come and look for him there?'

I'm about to say yes – after all, it has to be a better idea than stumbling around by myself with all these white doors – when it dawns on me. I know exactly where he is.

'Can you take me to the . . . stepping-blocks that take you to the next floor?'

He's grumpy, this old dude. He sighs, loud and inconvenienced, and then starts walking. After a couple of clanks of his walker, he turns and says, 'Well? You coming or not?'

Geez.

327

He takes me as far as the stepping-blocks and then says, 'You okay?'

'Sure am,' I say cheerily. 'Thanks!'

And then I'm climbing. A baby. Our baby.

He will be in the upstairs room, I'm sure of it. It's the perfect place to give him this news. I know it's not all happy. We're not going to live until our baby is a big person. But we'll have created life. Life that will exist after we've gone.

I climb up another set of stepping-blocks and walk into a thin-room with doors off it. One of the doors is open, and I peer inside. This is it! The room is full of large white mountains, but I ignore them and look for him. He's not here. I look again, and that's when I see the window-hole at one end. He must be through there.

I rush to the hole. I need to see him. As I walk through the hole, I bump into something. I have to duck down to get outside.

'Hello!' I call. The sun is blinding and hot. '*Hello*,' I say again.

I've forgotten his damn name again. I hear voices that sound like they're a long way away, and other noises, too. A bird. The hum of a car. The laugh of a child. A *child*. My hands find my stomach.

'*Where are you?*' I call.

'Jesus Christ.' The voice I hear is faint, like it's far away. 'That's a woman up there.'

'Where?' someone says.

'On the *roof*.'

'Oh my God!'

'Someone call 911.'

Although I can hear the voices, I don't know where they're coming from. And I don't really care. I still haven't found him. I need to find him before I forget. The ground below me feels uneven, like I'm standing on a slant. I wobble. Nothing around me is familiar. I don't think I'm in the upstairs room anymore.

'Anna!'

I recognize that voice. 'Jack? Where are you?'

'I'm down here,' he says. 'Don't jump. *Please!* I'm coming to get you.'

A sweep of wind goes by, and I extend my arms, trying to steady myself. But there's nothing to hold on to. Suddenly I see Jack. He's standing on the green, looking up at me. He's surrounded by people. None of them is the person I'm looking for.

'Where is he?' I ask.

'Luke's here, Anna!' Jack shouts. 'Just stay there, and I'll come and get you.'

I hear him yell to someone to get Luke. That's his name. *Luke.*

Jack is doing the thing when he is angry but he's trying to sound like he's calm. He is probably lying about Luke being there. I can't see him anywhere.

'Where?' I ask.

He looks around. 'There!' he says, pointing. 'He's right there. Now, I'm coming up.'

Jack disappears somewhere, and my eyes scan the green. I try to recall why I was looking for him. I hate it when this happens. I've got the feeling I went to quite a lot of effort to find him, and then . . . *poof*. It's gone.

I keep looking. Wondering. Then I see him, and it all falls away. My heart fills. And I step forward.

45

Eve

I follow the screaming all the way to Luke's room. I'm vaguely aware of Andrea behind me – she's never one to miss out on something interesting happening – but in the moment, I cannot find the will to care. What has happened?

When I get to Luke's room, Anna is crouched in a corner. The vase is upturned, and flowers and broken glass litter the floor.

'Hi,' I say, entering the room as fast as I can without being threatening. 'It's me, Eve. The cook.'

Anna looks up, her green eyes wide. I notice her palm is bleeding. Luke stands over her protectively. 'You've cut yourself, Anna.'

Anna looks at her hand as if this is news to her. Dark red blood rushes from the gash and drips from the crevices between her fingers. I realize, with a sinking heart, that she's going to need stitches.

'Is it okay if I take a look?' I ask.

She nods.

'Good. Why don't you sit on the bed? Luke – you, too.'

Anna sits, but Luke remains standing where he is. 'Okay,' I say, 'Anna, I'll just get something for your—'

'Eve? What on earth is going on?'

Eric appears in the doorway and my heart clenches like a fist. Behind him, in the hallway, Clementine and Andrea look on.

'Eric, I—'

'What were Anna and Luke doing in here *alone*?' he asks, incredulous.

I'm saved from responding by Rosie who appears from nowhere, shoving her way past Eric. She surveys the room and swears quietly. 'Eric, I need a towel,' she says. 'Two, if you have them. Quickly, we have to stop this bleeding.'

It takes Eric a few seconds to change his focus, but he finally grabs the towels. Rosie wraps Anna's hand in it. 'Point it up, Anna,' she says. 'It will stop the bleeding.'

Anna, it seems, cannot fathom these instructions, so Rosie does it for her.

'She'll need stitches,' Rosie says, confirming my initial thought. 'I can drive her to the hospital—'

'I'll do it,' Eric says. 'We need you here, Rosie.'

He looks at me, then jerks his head in the direction of Luke and Anna. 'So you still think they are better off together? That they're in love?' He adds a nasty, mono-syllabic scoff. I look at Anna and Luke, who are gazing vacantly into separate quadrants of the room, and I have to admit – right now, it's hard to believe they're in love.

And yet.

'I think you'd better go home, Eve,' he says.

'No. I'll go with you to the hospital. Or I can stay here with Luke. I'd rather wait until I know Anna's all right.'

'No.' Eric's voice leaves no room for doubt. 'You're going home.'

Rosie lets go of Anna's hand to grab some gauze, and immediately Anna's hand drops back to her side. I pick it up again for her, start to tell her I'll see her in the morning.

'No, you won't, Eve.'

I glance at Eric. He watches me for a moment, then throws up his hands. 'You can't honestly think you still have a job here?'

I stare at him, not comprehending.

'Wow,' he says. 'I'm sorry. But as of this moment, your employment is terminated.' Eric sounds mad and frustrated but also a little sad. This is how I know he means it. He walks over to Rosie's side, and she starts giving him instructions about Anna's cut – to keep the pressure on it, to keep it held up. It's as if I'm not even there.

After a moment, I feel a little hand pump mine. 'I think we should go, Mom.'

I blink at Clem. 'Yes,' I say after a moment. 'Yes. Okay.'

With a tug, Clem guides me out of the room. Andrea stands in the doorway, equal parts thrilled and perplexed. Her hands tremble, and suddenly I see her for exactly what she is. A frightened woman trying to take control wherever she can. Perhaps that's what we all are?

As Clem and I slope out of there, something that had been sitting in my subconscious finally filters through. As they sat side by side on the bed, Luke was holding Anna's (non-bleeding) hand.

46

Anna

S even months ago . . .
    'The patient has a displaced hip fracture and three cracked left-posterior ribs. No damage to the lungs. She has a broken clavicle, and she has sustained a mild concussion. The hip will make walking difficult, but her injuries are non-life-threatening. I understand she has dementia?'

'Younger-onset Alzheimer's, Doctor.'

Silence. 'And she was pregnant?'

'Eighteen weeks' gestation. Fetal death in utero.'

More silence. Then a sigh. 'Has the family been informed about the fetal death?'

The conversation lobs back and forth. I listen hard but I can't make much sense of it. All I can figure is that someone has been hurt pretty badly. I hope they're going to be okay. I also hope they'll leave my room. I'm tired and I want to sleep.

'The patient's brother has, Doctor. Unfortunately, the baby's father also has dementia.'

335

'A blessing in disguise?' the man's voice ponders. But no one answers.

Jack keeps telling me that I am at his house, but he's lying. I know what his house looks like, and this isn't it. For one thing, there are children everywhere. Not only that but it's also full of small plastic things that children play with. Jack doesn't really like kids, and he definitely wouldn't encourage them to go near his stuff. Besides that, the place is huge and made of marble. We're more likely to be in a shopping mall than we are at his house. I may have Alzheimer's, but I'm not completely nuts.

'Say something, Anna,' he says.

I keep staring out the hole in the wall.

'I'm so sorry,' he says. 'I never should have gone to speak to Eric. I never should have left you alone. This is all my fault.'

Jack is crying. I don't understand what he's talking about.

'Why would you do that? Nothing is ever so bad that you have to do that,' he says. 'Promise me you'll never do anything like that again?'

I don't say anything and Jack doesn't wait for me to.

'Now, on top of everything else, you can't walk. I should have figured out what was going on earlier. I should have stopped this before it got to this point.'

I stare beyond Jack because he's confusing me. But he doesn't go away.

'Are you not feeling well? Can you not talk? Blink once for yes, and twice for no.'

I close my eyes and keep them closed. It's a blessed relief.

'She hasn't said a word since she arrived. It's been over two weeks.'

No one other than Jack and I are in the room, so I can only assume Jack is on the phone. That, or I'm hallucinating. Which, I guess, is also possible.

'I have no idea . . . Nope . . . And she's regressed with her . . . bathroom habits, too. Yep. I've put her in Depends, but . . . yeah . . . yeah. I don't know what to do.'

He glances over at me. I look away.

It's strange, having someone speak about you while you are there. It happens a lot these days. It would be nice, I realize, to overhear *nice* things.

'Not much. She'll sit at the table during meals and pick at it, but . . . it's the not talking that is worrying me. Yeah. Nothing at all. She just sits in her chair, staring at the door.'

And what do you think that means, Jack? I silently ask him. *I want to go home.*

'Before the accident, she talked. Not so much as she used to, but she talked. Coherently. Now . . . nothing.' There was a long silence. 'Yes. Yes, okay. Tuesday at nine thirty? We'll be there.'

Jack pushes me into a room and sits beside me. Another person, a woman with black hair, sits behind a desk, puts her hands in her lap, and says, 'It's good to see you, Anna.'

'Thank you,' I say, the first words I've said in God knows how long.

Jack turns to face me, slack-jawed. I see betrayal in his eyes. *You spoke!*

Yeah, I want to say, but I can't be bothered. *I can talk. I'm just not speaking to you.*

'This is Dr Li, Anna,' Jack says.

'I know,' I say, even though I didn't know that.

The woman, Dr Li, scribbles something on a white square, then looks at me. 'I hear you had an accident, Anna. How are you feeling now? Better?'

I nod.

'Good. And your injuries. Your –' She glances down. '– ribs and your ankle . . . they're healing okay?'

I have no idea what she's talking about, so I just say yes. I want to keep talking to this woman. She looks at me and talks right to me.

'She can walk short distances,' Jack says, 'hobble from the couch to her chair or stand up in the shower. But the doctor said she'll spend most of her time in a wheelchair now.'

The woman nods. 'Have you been taking your medication, Anna?'

'Every day,' Jack says. 'I administer it.'

The woman nods. Then says to me, 'And you're living with Jack now?'

I shake my head. This, I know, is not right. 'I'm living at a huge place filled with people that feels like a shopping mall. Jack is there all the time. And I want to go home.'

338

'Home where?' the woman asks. 'To the residential care facility?'

I blink.

'Home where, Anna?' she asks again.

'To my . . . place.' It is beyond frustrating that I can't remember where home is. Here I am, being given the opportunity to say what I want, and I can't fucking remember. 'Jack knows.' I jab a thumb at Jack, but I don't look at him. The sight of him is enough to make me angry.

'Rosalind House,' he mutters. Even his mutter sounds irritated. I get the feeling he is as angry at me as I am at him.

'Rosalind House,' the woman repeats. 'Is that home?'

Rosalind House. I wait for a bell to ding or something to happen in my brain to tell me that, yes, Rosalind House is home. *Is that home?* I wait some more. Still no ding.

'I don't know,' I admit.

'It doesn't matter, anyway,' Jack says. 'I can't take her back there. Not after what happened.'

The woman takes the square things off her eyes and sighs. 'Have you discussed . . . the other thing?' she asks Jack. 'Does she have any memory of it?'

'I have no idea,' Jack says. 'As I told you, she hasn't said a word since she came back to live with us.'

'And the guy, the . . . father . . . has she seen him?'

'No. Of course not.'

The woman nods and is quiet for quite some time. Her expression is still – like she's worried or concentrating. I can't really tell which. 'Can I be frank?'

'I wish you would,' Jack says.

'I tend to share your worries about Anna's quick regression. She's had a trauma, so some regression is to be expected, but even to look at, she seems severely depressed. I can't help but wonder if she's missing her home. And, perhaps, missing this friend of hers.'

Jack makes a noise and shakes his head.

'You have her best interests in mind, I know that. What happened . . . all of it . . . must have given you quite the fright. But . . . if Anna were my sister . . . and she seemed happy there . . . I'd be trying to think of a scenario where I could get her there again.'

'You're not serious? Take her back to a place where she was impregnated, then tried to kill herself?'

'She doesn't have a lot of time left, Jack. A year, if that. If that's where she'll be happiest, why not?'

'Because it isn't safe!'

The woman nods. 'Obviously her safety is paramount, and you'd need to come to some sort of arrangement with the center to ensure that nothing like that would ever happen again. But, Jack, it's obviously what she wants.'

He looks at me. 'Is this what you want, Anna?'

'Yes,' I say, and this time, it's not just something I'm going along with. 'I want to go home.'

47

Eve

They say time gives perspective, and in a way it does. Christmas goes by. Clem and I spend it with Mother and Dad at their apartment. It's different from past holidays – sadder, because of the empty space where Richard should have been – but it was surprisingly nice, all of us tucked up in one little room, eating and drinking and being together. Clem didn't even seem to notice that she had only a few gifts. I'd been living paycheck to paycheck while working at Rosalind House, and now I wasn't really sure what I was going to do. A lot of places were closed for the Christmas break, so I was banking on finding a job in the New Year. In the meantime, Mother and Dad wrote me a modest check for a Christmas present, which I hoped would tide me over.

Angus and I stay in touch, mostly via text message. He understands that Clem is my focus. Sometimes after she's asleep, I lie on the couch and just talk to him on the phone. No matter what Clem is going through, I don't think she would mind us *talking*. Mother and Dad are wonderful, offering to cook, clean, look after Clem. I accept all offers, with the exception of Clem. The best thing to come out of my forced sabbatical is time with her.

I withdrew her from school before Andrea could launch an investigation, and the timing allowed us to have Christmas break and then start her new school afresh in the New Year. At the news she was leaving Legs, she'd kept it together quite well. In fact, when I told her we were going to have some time at home together, just the two of us, she actually seemed happy.

'Why did Daddy have to be a bad man?' she asks on New Year's morning, when I'm still yawning and stretching awake. Outside, fresh snow pats down for the third day in a row. We'd stayed up late to see in the New Year, watching movies and eating popcorn. Judging from the divots in my back, a few kernels still roam between the sheets.

'Sometimes I really *hate* him,' she says.

I think of my call to Dr Felder. This is it, I realize. She's having her moment. I roll to my side, then sit up. 'Sometimes I hate him, too.'

'You do?'

'I do. Sometimes I want to slap his face and scream at him, and other times I want to hug him and tell him how much I miss him.'

'Me, too.' Her face starts to crumple. 'I just . . . I don't know how to remember him, Mom.'

I pull her into my arms and kiss her forehead. 'You

should remember all of him. All the memories you have are still true, no matter what he did.'

'But—'

'They're all true,' I say firmly, almost as if I believe it. Maybe I do. I think of my conversation with Angus, about good things coming from bad. I think about Clara and Laurie, and the things we keep. 'Daddy hurt a lot of people, Clem. But Daddy did good things, too. He was thoughtful and kind. And he was a good daddy, don't you think?'

Through tears, she nods.

'So it's okay to remember that. Our memories are ours to remember any way we want.'

In Clem's eyes, the tears continue to fill and fall.

'Daddy loved you so much,' I say, and my voice cracks. 'If there is only one thing you remember about him, make sure it's that.'

Clem looks up at me. 'Can you tell me some stories of him? Some that I don't know?'

I wipe away a tear. 'Actually, I have a good one.' I sniff. 'About when you were a baby and I found you in the bath with Daddy. He was singing "I'm a Little Teapot" to you . . .'

Clem's mouth starts to upturn cautiously, as though she's not sure it's allowed. But after I've told the story three times, she's smiling properly. We stay there awhile, wrapped in each other, telling stories, laughing and crying. It's sad and it's horrible. But it's also nice, being together in our grief.

The next day, Clem and I walk to Buttwell Road Elementary. As the building appears in my line of sight, my heart is in my throat. Visually, it's not as appealing as her old school – it's a plain, single-level, redbrick building – but by and large, the kids look the same. As we walk into the playground, Clem squeezes my hand a little tighter. It'll be tough for her, starting halfway through the school year. A year ago, I wouldn't have worried, knowing Clem would be the most popular kid in the class by the end of the day, but now I'm not so sure.

We meet her teacher, a grandmotherly sort called Mrs Hubble, who puts her arm around Clem and instantly makes both of us feel better. She introduces Clem to a bouncy little girl called Billie with wild red hair, who will be Clem's special friend for the day. The two girls start talking right away. When it's time for me to go, I actually have to tap Clem on the shoulder. I half expect her to tell me, *Yeah, okay – you can go, Mom*, but she throws her arms around me and kisses my cheek.

I have to turn away so she doesn't see me cry.

Later that morning, Rosie calls to tell me that Clara is nearing the end. She says Clara was at the hospital but has returned to Rosalind House. *To die*, she doesn't say. She says she's spoken to Laurie, and he wanted to know if I'd like to say good-bye. I head straight over.

Rosalind House looks different under snow. Prettier, if that's possible. As I squeak along the snow toward the front steps, I remember Clara's pact to reconcile Laurie and her sister. And I hope that, as Rosie suggested, she hasn't had the chance.

I ring the doorbell and hold my breath, waiting for Eric. The last time I saw him, he was firing me. What would I say to him? But when the door swings open, an unfamiliar person stands there. A woman in her mid-forties with a bright smile and teased brown bob.

She smiles warmly. 'Hello,' she says. 'I'm Denise, the new manager.'

'The new . . .' I take this in for a second. 'What happened to Eric?'

'Come in out of the cold,' she says, and I do. She shuts the door and takes my coat. 'It's my second day,' she tells me. 'Do you have a family member here? We did send a letter explaining the change—'

'Oh no, I'm not family. I used to be the cook here. And the cleaner.'

Her expression becomes more guarded. 'Oh. Well, Eric is . . . no longer with the business.'

'No longer with the business? What happened?'

'I'm sorry, I really can't say.'

'Oh.'

'Can I help you with something? What was your name?'

'Eve,' I say, offering my hand. 'Eve Bennett. Actually, I'm here to see Clara. Laurie called me.'

'Of course,' she says. 'Come this way.'

We start down the hall. It's strange, being a visitor here. I remember my interview, when Angus led me inside to Eric's office. It feels like forever ago. As we walk, Denise waves at a family member coming out of Bert's room and helps a young woman pushing the cleaning cart to pick up the pile of towels she has dropped. (They'd hired a cleaner!)

I stop suddenly. 'Denise?'

'Yes?'

'Can you at least tell me . . . Eric wasn't . . . up to anything untoward, was he? With the residents? I mean, can you at least tell me that?'

She gives me a long, assessing look. Then she exhales. 'Let's just say that Eric was far too busy doing creative accounting to be bothering with much else. And that, at least, is something to be grateful for.'

Creative accounting? All at once everything clicks into place. The tiny grocery budget. The merging of the cook and cleaner position. Eric's fancy new car.

'That slimy rotten . . .'

As Denise's lips start to upcurve, I feel a rush of relief. And I have a feeling that Rosalind House is now in exactly the right hands.

When I enter Clara's bedroom, her eyes are closed. Laurie lies by her side, awake, staring as her face flickers and dances with new sleep. I watch for a moment from the doorway, then back away quietly.

'Eve.' Laurie spots me right before I disappear out the door. He smiles and starts to sit up.

'Stay where you are,' I say. 'Please. Seeing you two lying there, it gives me faith in love.'

Laurie ignores me and pushes himself upright. 'A pretty young girl like you, you shouldn't need help finding faith in love.'

I laugh. 'You might be surprised.'

Laurie watches me, waiting in that way I've become accustomed to these last few months. At Rosalind House, I've discovered a whole new way of being listened to.

'I don't want to talk about me,' I say. 'How is Clara?'

Laurie casts a glance down at her. 'It won't be long now.'

'Is she suffering?'

'I don't think so. She's asleep mostly. She's been saying some strange things.' He continues staring at her, adoring, but his expression is mingled with puzzlement. 'She told me about something she did, a long time ago. A secret she's been keeping.' Finally he strips his eyes off her and looks at me. 'A *confession*. She said she stole me from her sister – a hundred years ago, when we were kids.' His laugh is empty. 'She said her death wish was to put things right, to' – he laughs again – 'to reunite us.'

A knot ties itself, deep in my belly. She *did* tell him.

'It makes me sick to think that, when she knew she was going to die, *this* is what she was thinking about.'

'Is it true?' I ask. 'Did she steal you . . . from her sister?'

Laurie shrugs like it's the most insignificant detail in the world. 'Probably. But if she did, it was the best thing that ever happened to me. What upsets me most is that she thought this would undo everything we had. Sixty years of marriage. Every memory . . . every moment.'

I think of Richard. Of all the time we spent together that I'd rendered meaningless because of how things went in the end.

'And' – I swallow – 'it doesn't?'

'*Of course* it doesn't.'

'But if something starts on a lie—'

He makes a noise like *bah*. 'You might start something on a lie, or finish it on a lie, but that doesn't mean that everything in the middle isn't the truth.' He smiles a sad smile. 'Nothing can undo time.'

Finally, for both me and Laurie, the tears begin to roll. 'So what did you say?' I ask finally. 'Did you . . . grant her wish?'

He laughs. 'I told her I'm the husband, so my wishes come first.' He rolls back into a lying position and tosses an arm over Clara's waist. 'And my wish is to have the love of my life die in my arms.'

Clara didn't wake while I was there. I stayed for half an hour, then kissed her papery forehead and told her to say hello to Richard for me. Then I let myself into the hallway.

Pots bang in the kitchen; someone is obviously packing up the lunch dishes. Doing my job, probably a lot better than I did it. I think of Anna and Luke. Rosie told me on the phone that Anna had received seven stitches in her hand but she would be fine. I glance toward her room and shift my stance, wondering if I should pop my head around the door. She won't remember me, of course. But we'd had a rapport once. I can't help but wonder if we'll still have it.

Before I can decide one way or another, her door opens and her father walks out. 'Hello,' he says. 'It's Eve, isn't it?'

I hesitate on the spot. 'Er, yes. That's right.'

'I'm Anna's dad. Peter.'

'I remember,' I say. 'How's Anna?'

'Not great, today.'

'I'm sorry.'

'Actually, I was hoping I would run into you,' he says. 'Denise told me you aren't working here anymore.'

'No, I'm just . . . visiting.'

'Have you got a minute?' he asks. 'Could we talk?'

'Sure,' I say, surprised. 'In the parlor?'

'After you.'

In the chairs by the window, he pulls Anna's notebook from his bag. 'I was going to give this back to Anna today. It just felt like the right thing to do. Then I realized, if she reads it, it will just remind her of a promise she can't keep. So I kept it.' He looks at it sadly. 'But I'm starting to wonder if Anna should be kept from this man.'

'Why *is* she kept apart from him?' I ask. There's a note of begging in my voice. 'Can you tell me?'

His gaze drops away. 'I don't see why it's such a secret. Anna was pregnant.'

My mouth opens. I start to say *something*, but the words get stuck, and I can't seem to project them.

'No one realized, not even Anna, until she was nearly halfway through the pregnancy. When Jack found out, he sat down with her and told her – then he marched into Eric's office to unleash.' Peter pinches the bridge of his nose between two fingers. 'While Jack was with Eric, Anna took herself to the top floor of this building and jumped off the roof.'

349

I close my eyes. The final piece of the puzzle.

'Jack blames himself for leaving her alone after giving her that news, and he's adamant he's going to protect her from now on. He became the man of our house when I left his mother, so it's tough for me to come in now and tell Jack what's right for his sister.' His face is pained, like he might cry. 'But then I read this notebook, and it says she wants to live out the rest of her days with this man, no matter what comes—'

'And instead she's kept behind a locked door.'

He nods. 'If it were up to me, I'd want Anna to squeeze every minute of joy out of the days she has left. If that meant unlocking the doors, that's what I'd do. But I've tried talking to Jack, and it's falling on deaf ears.'

I think about what Peter said, but it doesn't make any sense. Anna could take birth control. The upstairs has already been blocked off for residents. Then I think about it again. *Jack blames himself.* Jack is adamant he won't let anything like that happen again. That makes more sense. Suddenly I realize I might be the only person who can get through to him.

'Would it be all right with you, Peter,' I ask, 'if I talked to Jack?'

The drive to Philly takes over an hour, but it feels like five minutes. As we drive, Peter tells me about his son. He uses all the adjectives of a proud parent – 'intelligent', 'funny', 'calm' – but also a few other words like 'headstrong' and 'stubborn'. And 'protective' – that's the one that frightens me the most.

When we pull into the driveway, Jack is out front, shoveling snow. Hearing the car, he turns. He looks at me for a moment; then his gaze shifts to his dad. It's accusatory. *What have you done now?*

'You remember Eve,' Peter says.

'Yes,' Jack says warily. 'Hello, Eve.'

'Eve is here to talk to you about Anna.'

'Is she all right? I heard she cut her hand—'

'Physically, she's fine,' I tell him. 'It's her emotional health I'm worried about.'

There is a moment's silence. A gust of wind flutes past, chilling me to the bone.

'I'm sorry, aren't you the housekeeper?' Jack asks.

'Yes, but I've spent a great deal of time with Anna over the recent months, and I care about her very much. Could I—?' I shiver and glance toward the door. 'Could I come inside?'

'What's this all about?' Jack asks, more to Peter than to me. Irritation, it seems, has taken the place of bafflement.

'I told you,' Peter says. 'It's about Anna. Come inside, Eve. This way.' Peter ushers me into the house while Jack reluctantly plants his shovel in the snow.

The house is magnificent. We walk into a high-ceilinged foyer with a marble floor. It reminds me more of a shopping mall than a house. Peter takes my coat and Jack shuts the door with a thud.

'All right,' Jack says. 'Let's get this over with.'

'This isn't an intervention, Jack,' Peter says.

'It better not be. Because this isn't a democracy. I have

351

Anna's power of attorney. So if this is about her boyfriend, forget it.'

Peter and I confer with our eyes. 'It's about the letter,' I say. 'Anna's letter.'

Peter gets the notebook out of his bag.

'Yes,' Jack says. 'I read it.'

'Then you know it says Anna and Luke agreed they'd stay together until—'

'I know what it says. I also know Anna has not been true to this promise, because she *did* try to kill herself. That is a fact.'

'That *is* a fact,' I say. Already I can see that I am at a disadvantage, arguing with an attorney. 'And I'll admit, I don't understand that part. Maybe we never will. But let's look at all the facts. When you took Anna out of Rosalind House, she became so depressed that, despite your reservations, you returned her there and saw marked improvements in just a few days.'

'So love can work miracles, is that what you're saying?' Jack laughs blackly. 'What do you want me to do? I took her back there, didn't I?'

'Yes, but they might as well be a world apart. Imagine the improvement if they were allowed to actually spend time together. If you unlocked the doors—'

Jack looks at me. 'This may come as a surprise to you, but I love my sister. She's the funniest, bravest, most extraordinary person you could possibly imagine.'

'I know she is.'

'She's also the most vulnerable person you could

imagine. And I am responsible for her. I let her down once. I'm not going to do it again.'

'I know you *think*—'

'Oh, you *know*, do you?' Jack's eyes flash. 'You know what it's like to have a loved one try to kill themselves because you walked out when they needed you the most?'

'Yes,' I say. 'Except in my case, they were successful.'

This stops him a second. Jack and Peter exchange a glance.

'You've probably heard of my husband, Richard Bennett?'

Jack stares at me. 'You're Richard Bennett's *wife*?'

I nod. 'You promised you would look after your sister. I promised I would support my husband in sickness and in health. And we did. Just because Anna and Richard made decisions we didn't understand when we weren't there, doesn't mean we let them down. It just means . . . they did something we didn't understand.'

I wait for Jack to lob back a retort, but he remains silent. Tears shine in his eyes.

'I admit, I still blame myself sometimes. But when I'm thinking clearly, I know that I had no control over Richard's actions. And though you may have some control over Anna's, she can still make her own decisions. And if I know anything about Anna, she'll make them, with or without your support.'

At this, a soft laugh comes from Jack. 'Wow,' he says. 'You *do* know Anna.'

'Keeping her away from Luke won't change what has already happened. But it might change what happens in the future.' I take the notebook from Peter and thrust it out for Jack to see. 'Anna *loves* this man. At this stage of their lives, they are all each other has left. Let her be with him,' I say. 'Because if you don't, you might just end up blaming yourself for that. And as Anna would say, life's too short.'

48

Clementine

When Legs visited yesterday, I thought I was going to burst with all the stuff I had to tell her. It's weird, not going to school together, but it's great to have so much to talk about. I tell her about my new teacher, Mrs Hubble, who is nearly as nice as Miss Weber, and my new friends, Billie and Scarlett and Pippa. What's so good about Legs is that she wants to hear everything. She's still my very best friend. She came to our apartment and we ate pizza and did each other's hair and danced around while we watched *Frozen*. Then Mom helped us make orange and poppy-seed muffins.

Today, Mom and me go to Rosalind House. The people at Rosalind House must not have many visitors, because when I walk in the door, it's like the man from the ice cream truck has showed up. Everyone grins like crazy. Angus is there and he gives Mom a kiss on the cheek when he thinks I'm not looking. It's a little weird, but it makes Mom smile. And I want Mom to smile. Anyway, Angus is pretty nice.

Mom scuttles off to see the new manager lady, and I do an Irish dance for Gwen in the hall. I give Laurie a high five and May a kiss. Then I have to excuse myself because, actually, I don't have all day.

Bert is in the parlor. *'There* you are!'

Bert looks up, blinks his yellow eyes, and after a million years, smiles. He needs to go to a dentist, but I don't tell him this, because it would be rude. 'Well, hello there, young lady.'

I guess Bert still doesn't remember my name. And for the first time in ages, this makes me a bit sad. 'I'm Clementine,' I say.

He nods.

I point to the chair next to him. 'Is Myrna sitting there?'

'No. Would you like to sit down?'

'Yes. I'd like to talk to you about something.' I settle myself in the chair. 'It's about Myrna.'

Bert's whiskery eyebrows shoot up. 'Oh?'

'Well, it's about Myrna *and* my daddy. You know how I've been talking to my dad sometimes, these last few months? Well it's been good, but I think I need to stop now. You see, I've got all these other people to talk to, like my mom, Legs, and my other friends. So I probably should talk to them, since they're alive and stuff. And I thought maybe you should stop talking to Myrna, too.'

Bert frowns.

'So,' I ask, 'what do you think?'

It takes him a long time to answer.

'You're very lucky to have all those people who love you,' he says finally. 'Your mom and your friends. But the thing about me is that I don't have a lot of people like that.'

'But you *do.*' In the very next chair, on the other side of Bert, is Gwen, so I lower my voice. 'How about Gwen? If you'd just speak to her, you wouldn't need to speak to Myrna.'

'I don't *need* to speak to Myrna,' Bert says. His voice is quieter than it was a moment ago. 'I *want* to. And I'm not willing to let her go. Maybe I'm a foolish old man, but' – he smiles – 'I'm an old dog, it's too late to start learning new tricks.'

I have no idea what he's talking about – dogs and tricks – but I'm pretty sure he's saying he wants to keep Myrna. I shrug. 'Well, if you're sure.'

'I am.'

I slide off the chair onto my feet. 'In that case, I guess I'd better get going. Bye, Bert.'

'I hope I'll see you again, young lady,' Bert calls after me.

When I turn back, Bert is giving me the biggest, brightest, crooked-toothed smile I've ever seen. If Myrna makes him feel like that, I decide, she can't be such a bad thing.

'Clementine,' I say. 'My name is Clementine.'

He smiles, nods, tells me he'll try to remember that. And as I walk to the garden, I decide I want everyone to call me that from now on.

The sky looks like a huge white sheet. I can't even remember the last time I saw blue sky. Out here in the garden, it's cold and the snow drenches right through my shoes. I know I don't have to be in the garden at Rosalind House when I talk to Dad, but there's something about this garden that feels right, even with wet feet.

'Daddy? I need to talk to you.'

I close my eyes and bring him into the center of my mind. He's sitting in a chair with one leg crossed over the other and watching me really close.

'I'm still angry with you,' I say, 'but I'm not *as* angry. Because everyone does bad things sometimes.'

Daddy doesn't say anything, but I know he's listening. His face looks like it did when he listened, tilted a little, soft eyes, smiling. I used to love it when Daddy looked at me like that.

'And you did good things, too. You were good at dancing. And . . . you used to sing to me in the bath when I was a baby.' My eyes get blurry and then I'm crying. 'I love you. But I'm going to stop talking to you now. And Mom and I are going to look after each other.' I feel a tug of hurt in my heart. 'If you ever need anyone to speak to, I'll be here. Or you can try ghosts.' Suddenly, an idea comes to me. 'Or Myrna. I don't think Bert would mind . . .'

I keep talking to Daddy for a little while, until my socks are wet through and I can't feel my toes. Then, slowly, I let him slip out of my mind, and I open my eyes. And right at that moment, there's a break in the white sky. And the sun comes shining through.

49

Eve

Three months later . . .

It's like a déjà vu. I'm standing in front of Rosalind House, my stomach a bundle of nerves. The only difference is, this time, I already have a job. Not at Benu or an up-and-coming Manhattan restaurant. A brand-new restaurant in the suburbs. It's not particularly fashionable and its patrons aren't photographed on their way in. The food is good, though, and I intend to make it better. I'm only the junior chef now. But that'll change.

At the moment, I do lunches at the restaurant, so I can drop Clem off at school every morning and pick her up every afternoon. We've moved into a house, a small one with two bedrooms, but Clem and I still sleep together most nights.

I've seen quite a lot of Angus, too, these past months. First a few trips to the grocery store, then a movie. Then another proper date. Then he started calling around the house every so often with a plant or some herbs. Clem has been warming to him. The pair of them started a vegetable patch in the garden at our house, and I've heard her giggling while they tend it together. Once, Clem even asked if he wanted to watch her Irish dancing.

Now, when the front door of Rosalind House swings open, Angus is standing there. I see him for only a second before he pulls me onto the step and into his arms. He bends to kiss me, but at the last minute he pauses, looks over my shoulder. 'No Clem?'

'She's at school.'

'Then—' He kisses me in a way that makes me think I might faint. When he stops, I feel boneless, like I might slide down his body and end up as a puddle on the floor.

'Well.' He smiles. 'Welcome to Rosalind House. Won't you come in?'

Inside, people buzz about. In the entrance to the parlor, I catch the pleasant scent of cinnamon and yeast, and I marry it to the plate stand of buns on the coffee table. My relief that they've found a good cook is only slightly marred by feelings of inferiority; after all, I never made cinnamon buns for visitors' day.

Bert is in the love seat between his granddaughter and her husband and their new baby, a girl if the bow around her head can be trusted. Laurie is surrounded by middle-aged men, possibly his sons, wearing earpieces and carrying pocket radios, listening to some kind of sport and announcing it for him. May is sitting with two women carrying rosary beads. Everyone is absorbed with their families, and they don't look up when Angus and I appear. There's a gentle hum of chatter, and I think of Anna. She won't like the noise. Then I realize she's not here.

'Where's Anna?'

'In her room, love,' says the woman pushing past, 'with Luke.'

The woman carries with her the yeast scent I caught earlier. *The cook.* I crane my neck as she whizzes away, trying to get a good look. She's short and thick and in a hurry – yet even from that quick glimpse, she radiates warmth. Then again, it's no surprise. What person who bakes cinnamon buns doesn't radiate warmth?

Angus has told me a little about how Anna and Luke have been these last few months. The confusion. The repetition. Now her memory is less than two minutes long. At least she has round-the-clock access to Luke, though. They've moved into Clara and Laurie's suite now. Instructions to separate them have been rescinded. They are allowed to live and move as they see fit.

I reach Clara and Laurie's suite – now Anna and Luke's suite – and peer inside. Peter, Jack, and a little boy around Clem's age are gathered near Anna and Luke. The boy is sitting on Anna's lap, chatting nonstop about baseball, about his friend Tom, about the dinosaur he wants for his birthday.

Peter glances up first and smiles. Then he looks at his daughter. 'Anna?' he says. 'You have a visitor.'

Jack offers a small smile of his own. 'Come on in, Eve.'

I remain in the doorway, inexplicably nervous. Angus steps forward, but I hold him back. 'There are too many people,' I whisper. 'She won't like it.'

'Hey, Eath,' Jack says. 'Why don't we go climb that tree in the garden?'

The little boy slides off Anna's lap. After kissing Anna's forehead, Jack guides his son out of the room by the shoulders. Peter follows close behind.

When they are gone, I enter. 'Hello,' I say.

Anna blinks up at me.

I scan her face for recognition, but I don't find it. 'I'm Eve. This is Angus.'

'Is it breakfast time?'

I have no idea if she recognizes me or associates me with cooking or what. In any case, it's two thirty in the afternoon, so breakfast isn't likely. 'Not yet,' I say. 'But I can get you a cinnamon bun, if you like.'

'No.' She looks at Luke and suddenly, inexplicably, she breaks into a smile. 'Would you like a cinnamon bun?'

He shakes his head, smiling back.

She's changed, even in the few months since I left. She looks older. Her face is more vacant and her shoulders have taken on a slight hunch. Still, there is a beauty to her. I think back to the day I met her, on the grass in the garden. *Help me,* she'd said. I hope, in some way, I did.

When Anna looks back at me, her expression is puzzled. I can almost hear her unspoken question. *When did you get here?* She cocks her head, perhaps searching for the information that her brain refuses to give her.

Instead of filling her in, reminding her of my name, I stay silent. Deep down, selfishly, I want the moment of recognition.

'Oh,' she says finally. 'Is it breakfast time?'

We stay for fifteen minutes. And when we say our good-byes, Anna barely notices.

'Are you sad?' Angus asks me in the foyer. His face is concerned. 'That she didn't remember you?'

'No,' I say. 'Why would I be sad? Anna and Luke got what they wanted – they'll be together till the end.' I take Angus's hand and lead him toward the door. 'If only everyone could be so lucky.'

50

Anna

S ix months ago . . .
   I think I'm in a garden. It's warm and bright and there's a pattern of light on the green spike-thingies at my feet. There is a man next to me. A young guy. He smiles a little, so I smile back. It makes me feel happy.

And just like that, a memory is coming at me. Sweeping through my mind and collapsing every part of my brain until there's nothing but a cloud of images. I'm as power-less to stop these visions as I am to, uh . . . what's the word, conjure? . . . them up. I'm in bed. This man and I lie tangled in each other. It's new, our relationship, maybe our first time together. He is smiling and I am happy.

'P-promise me we'll be together in the end,' he says. 'No switching a button, no ending it. Promise?'

I groan, but his face is determined. There's no arguing.

'Fine,' I say.

'Say . . . it.'

I roll my eyes. 'I promise. We'll be together in the end. Batshit crazy. And together. I promise.'

I swim out of the memory, and when I do, the man – Luke – is still smiling. *I remember*, I want to tell him. But for how long? If the memory starts in clouds, it finishes off a precipice, gone into blackness. This is what terrifies me.

Suddenly, a woman appears in front of me, planting a colorful thing on my lap. She smells of cream and cake. 'You dropped this,' she says.

I don't think I know this woman, but she has kind eyes. She's waiting for me to say something, but my mind is somewhere else. I need to tell someone something before the memory goes. Maybe this woman? Maybe she can help me keep my promise to Luke? But my thoughts come slowly, and before I can ask her, she is removing her hand from my lap.

I lunge forward and clasp on to it.

'Oh.' The woman pulls back, but I just hold her tighter. In a minute, the memory will be gone, and who knows when it will be back? It may never come back. 'I didn't mean to alarm you,' she says, 'I . . . I just didn't want you to lose your lovely scarf.'

'Please,' I say. 'Help me.'

The woman's eyes grow round. There's something about her. Do I know this woman? Was she once my friend? She looks like a friend.

'What did you say? Anna?'

Anna. She knows my name. I *must* know her. She will help me. I know she will.

The woman is waiting for a reply, but suddenly, I don't remember the question. It makes me feel nervous, and I look away from her, at the smiling man beside me. Immediately, I feel better.

The woman leaves, and I keep looking at the man. As long as I stick with him, I decide, things will be all right.

www.panmacmillan.com